"YOU WANT LONE MAN? HERE I AM!"

Sergeant MacGregor looked up to see an Indian with short black hair lifting a Winchester to his shoulder. The other Minnetaree braves moved aside, leaving him standing there alone.

"Put down your rifle," MacGregor said calmly. "I'm taking you back to Fort Walsh."

"Hah!" Lone Man laughed. "You not take me anywhere, redcoat!"

"If you kill me, another redcoat will take my place. If you kill him another will come. You canna kill us all."

"Empty words!" Lone Man shouted, squinting along the rifle barrel. "You die, redcoat!"

His finger curled around the trigger.

POWELL'S ARMY
BY TERENCE DUNCAN

THE SCARLET RIDERS

#7 DEAD OR ALIVE

IAN ANDERSON

ZEBRA BOOKS
KENSINGTON PUBLISHING CORP.

ZEBRA BOOKS

are published by

Kensington Publishing Corp.
475 Park Avenue South
New York, NY 10016

First printing: December, 1988

Printed in the United States of America

To Mary,
free as the wind.

CHAPTER 1

The four riders reined to the top of the rise and sat their saddles as they looked down on the small settlement a mile below.

"It don't look like much."

"It'll do."

Fort Turner was little more than a few ramshackle buildings sprawled along the south side of the Milk. Roughly halfway between the Missouri to the south and the Canadian border to the north, Fort Turner was a one-time trading post of the old American Fur Company. Now it serviced settlers and a few small ranchers strung out for forty or fifty miles on both sides of the river. Most of the ranchers raised horses and sold them to the army. The cavalry had been busy lately chasing the remnants of Sitting Bull's Sioux after the Indians' defeat of Colonel Custer down on the Little Big Horn on that fateful Sunday, the 25th of June, 1876, sixteen months earlier. Sitting Bull and six thousand Sioux had escaped across the border into Canadian territory, but the army were patrolling the border to stop any more from doing the same.

One of the riders, a man with a flat-topped black hat and a long white scar down the left side of his face that scraggly black beard failed to cover, spoke.

"We been lookin' long enough. Let's go."

They legged their horses down the slope toward the sprawling settlement below. Nothing further was said. There was no noise other than the snorting of a horse, the creak of saddle leather, the muffled *clib clob* of the horses' hoofs on the soft, loamlike soil. Above, the sky stretched pale blue. The day was Indian-summer warm, but the nights had a cool tang, a reminder that winter wasn't far away. Already it was the tail end of October.

As they rode closer, they sized up the settlement in closer detail. They noted in particular the depth of the river and the low bank on the north side. The river was little more than a stream, especially at this time of the year. As for the settlement, it was a main street with most of the buildings fronting the street and their backs to the river. The buildings were single-story, slapped-together frame or log shanties with sod roofs. The bar was of the latter variety, with a solitary log hitching rail in front, a pair of elk horns nailed just above the one-door entrance, and a carved sign reading simply *Saloon*. There was a lone horse standing hitched to the rail. There was nothing special about the horse, just an ordinary cowpuncher's horse with worn saddle and lariat. It carried no rifle scabbard, and the four riders' eyes swept on past it to the building alongside. It was frame, with a false front badly needing a coat of paint. It was the stage station, and it bore a sign which proclaimed: *U.S. Mail.* There was another log building with the words *General Store* painted on a board beside the door. On the opposite side of the street was a building that had once been a black-smith's shop but was boarded up — presumably for lack of business, the scar-faced rider guessed. But it was the bank that interested him most.

Inside the bank the manager had seen the approach of the four riders as they rode down the slope. They were spread out, in a single line, and there was something about them . . .

Through the glass door he watched the four ride right into the town. They rode along the street. They weren't talking. They just sat their saddles tight-lipped but looking everywhere. They weren't locals or ranchers from the district. They were drifters, a type frequently seen riding around the country after the war. He'd seen their types before. They were often dangerous, having little regard for life or property. As far as he was concerned, they were a menace and he didn't like seeing them in any town he was in.

There was no one else on the street, and only himself and his teller in the bank. The teller, a green eyeshade down over his brow, was busy adding up figures and he hadn't noticed the four horsemen riding along the dusty street outside.

Three of the men rode straight for the bank. As though hypnotized, he watched them approach.

They reined to in front of the bank and swung down from their saddles. A nasty feeling crept into the bank manager's gut.

He shook himself from his trance, snatched up a *Closed for Business* sign, and stepped around the end of the counter. He was on his way to lock the front door, but he was too late. He had waited too long. He was barely a quarter of the way to it when the first man pushed it open and stepped inside, immediately followed by the other two. The fourth man had passed from the manager's sight.

At the sound of the door, the teller put his finger on a column of figures on the paper he had been working on so he wouldn't lose his place and looked up.

Meeting the men as they came through the door, the bank manager gave a sickly grin.

"Morning, gents. Er . . . we're about to close for lunch. Now . . . if you wouldn't mind coming back after lunch . . . You could entertain yourselves in the saloon just down the street. It's open all day and half the night. My assistant and I will be back open for business right after lunch."

The three men did not stop. They kept walking, their booted feet heavy on the rough board floor.

"Our business won't take long," the leading man said.

9

His toneless dark eyes bore into the bank manager, stopping him cold in his tracks. A white scar slashed across the brown of his face, starting at his nose and running across his left cheek and down past his mouth to his jaw. His patchy black beard wouldn't grow over it. He was in his early forties, rangy, and stood just under six feet. Dust lay heavy on the brim of his black hat, and on the flat crown. He wore a chocolate-brown shirt, also coated with dust, and a black bandanna knotted around his neck. As he walked, big Mexican spurs clanked noisily behind him. The thing that particularly disturbed the bank manager was the sight of two guns in tied-down holsters.

Still holding the *Closed for Business* sign, the manager hurriedly backed up and moved around behind the counter where he had come from.

The second man was no more reassuring in appearance. He was younger, in his mid-thirties, thin and dark-haired, with a sallow complexion and hollow cheeks. Several days' black whisker growth stubbled his chin. He didn't look well. He wore his hat pushed back off his head, and his black hair was thinning on top. He wore a single gun at his waist, holstered on the left.

The third man differed in that he was an Indian or a halfbreed. He was tall and thin, wearing a stiff-brimmed black hat with a high crown that made him look taller still, yellow-checked shirt, and buckskin trousers, with beaded moccasins and leggings. He too wore a pistol on his hip.

Tiny beads of perspiration broke out on the manager's forehead. These men weren't customers, and they couldn't have any legitimate business with the bank. They looked as though they didn't have a cent between them, except for their gun belts, all with fresh cartridges stuffed into the bullet loops.

His finger still marked the figures where he had been calculating, the eyeshaded teller stared open-mouthed at the trio. There was an unspoken air of menace about them the likes of which he had never seen in his twenty-two years.

The next instant pistols appeared in the hands of each of the three. The scar-faced man, his dark eyes burning into the bank manager, spoke again. "You two jus' stand steady and keep your hands above the counter where I can see 'em."

His eyes moved from the bank manager's face to an iron safe against the far wall. The door was ajar. His voice snapped out like the crack of a whip. "Grab a couple of them canvas bank money bags, then step over to that safe and start fillin' 'em with all the money you got—bank notes, silver, gold. Everything! Now, get busy! And don't make no fool moves."

Frightened by the ominous tone of the gunman's voice, the young teller moved quickly to obey. Bending down to reach some canvas bags below the counter, his hand barely closed around them when there was a crashing explosion as the pistol in the Indian's hand bucked, a red jet of flame stabbing from the barrel. A bullet smashed into the teller's thin chest. His face contorted in pain as the punch of the bullet sent him flying backwards across a desk behind him.

"My god!" the bank manager cried, and he sprang over to help the teller. As he did so, the scar-faced man swung his gun hand and pulled the trigger. The Colt .44 crashed deafeningly and the bank manager spun around and fell over the teller's body.

"I told you not to make no fool move, goddamn you!" the scar-faced man screamed at the dying bank manager.

The sallow-complexioned man with the hollow cheeks took all this in in an instant. Although his features never changed expression, he shook his head almost imperceptibly. Holstering his gun, he vaulted over the counter and quickly examined the teller's body. The young man was dead. The gunman looked around behind the counter, saw the canvas bags the young teller had been reaching for, and stood up. He looked over at the scar-faced man.

" 'E was just reaching for the bags," he said in a French accent. He didn't say it, but his tone could have

11

suggested that there had been no need to kill the teller.

The scar-faced gunman looked back at him for a moment. "T' hell with him. Get the money and let's get outta here!"

The Frenchman grabbed up the bags, knelt down beside the safe, and started scooping bank notes and silver into one of the canvas bags.

The scar-faced man snapped an order to the Indian. "Lone, get outside there on the street an' help Ben cover us. Anyone moves out there, blast 'em!"

The Indian stared back at him. He opened his mouth to say something, thought better of it, then sidled out the front door onto the street.

The gunshots attracted attention. Two heads appeared at the saloon door, but the fourth man, gray-bearded, fired his rifle at them from his horse where he waited on guard at the corner of the bank building. The two heads disappeared instantly.

Just then a rifle barrel poked out through the window of the stage station. The rifle barked twice in rapid succession. The gray-haired man suddenly stiffened and his rifle dropped to the ground. He clawed out with a horny hand and grasped the pommel of his saddle to stop himself from falling.

Gunsmoke swirled as the Indian fired shots at the stage station. The rifle was hurriedly withdrawn as a hail of lead spattered against the walls.

Inside the bank the scar-faced man cursed at the sound of the shooting outside.

"Christ! Let's hurry it up and get outta here!"

Working quickly, he and the Frenchman swept bills and silver from the safe and stuffed them into the canvas bags.

Bullets were flying on the street when the two rushed out through the front door. His face wracked with pain, the gray-haired man was holding grimly onto the pommel of his saddle as his horse pranced restlessly around amid noise and bullets, while the Indian knelt on one knee firing his rifle at the man in the stage station.

"What happened, Ben?" the scar-faced gunman asked.

Grimacing, the gray-haired man said, "Some jasper down in the stage station opened up on me." He coughed heavily.

The scar-faced gunman glared down the street in the direction of the stage station. He thrust the canvas sacks into his saddlebags, pulled his rifle out of its scabbard, and raised it to his shoulder. Aiming at the stage station, he poured a withering hail of lead at the frame building.

Talking with an effort, but the gray-haired man called Ben managed to make his voice heard between shots. "He must've reckoned we was goin' to rob him."

The scar-faced man stuffed more shells into his Winchester. A light flickered across his eyes. Greed, perhaps. "Mebbe he's got somethin' in there we oughta look at. We didn't get much from the bank."

He lifted his rifle and was about to fire another burst into the stage station when the Frenchman's voice shouted behind him.

"Cess!"

There was a note of urgency in the Frenchman's voice and the scar-faced gunman whipped his head around. The Frenchman was pointing up toward the rise they had ridden down earlier. He followed the direction of the pointing arm and momentarily froze. Up there were a dozen horsemen. As the sound of shooting rolled up to them, they spurred their horses down the slope toward the collection of buildings.

"Come on!" the scar-faced man shouted. "Let's ride! *Pronto!*"

The three of them grabbed their horses, pulled themselves up into their saddles, and reined their horses around. The next instant they pounded out of town toward the river, splashed into the shallow water, and lunged to the other side. They spurred their horses furiously up the low bank and galloped off to the north.

CHAPTER 2

William James Edson and his eleven men thundered into Fort Turner. The four gunmen were already across the Milk and racing northwards.

Edson and his men reined to a stop in front of the bank, the frame building that jutted halfway into the middle of the street as though whoever had built it wanted it to dominate the other buildings.

Nothing stirred. There was no movement about any of the buildings. Probably everyone was afraid to venture out.

Edson legged his horse out in front of the others. He was a tall, lean man with a tanned, weathered face, a black mustache, and a square jaw. He stood in his stirrups so that he could be easily seen. "United States marshal," he shouted, pulling open his gray coat to reveal a gold badge pinned to his blue shirt.

A door opened in a frame building down the street, the one the gunman had been firing at. Edson read the words *U.S. Mail* painted on the false front above, alongside the name of the stage line. A balding man carrying a Winchester stepped out. A moment later a cowboy stepped out of the door of the saloon, and went over to his horse at the hitching rail and looked it over. Behind him appeared a man wearing an apron, presumably the bartender. Then someone stood in the doorway of the general store.

"What's been going on?" Edson called.

The man with the Winchester walked up the dusty street

toward him. "Bank robbery, Marshal," he said, pointing to the bank. "I reckon the stage station was next, but I held 'em off. I even got one of 'em, wounded him good, I reckon." He sounded pleased with himself as he huffed out his chest and grinned, patting the Winchester.

From beneath a low-crowned gray hat, keen blue eyes looked down at him. Bill Edson nodded approvingly. "Good," he said, then he reined his horse around so that he faced the bank.

"You inside there," he shouted, "Come on out. They're gone."

There was no answer.

Edson stared steadily at the bank, holding his reins in his left hand, his right hand closed in a half fist as it rested on his hip, just above his holstered Smith & Wesson .44. He sat his horse like a man accustomed to long hours in the saddle. There was an air of competence about him, and his men followed him with confidence. He was only thirty-seven, but his black hair was already graying at the sides and the temples.

"Better take a look," he said, and he swung down from his saddle and stepped up onto the boardwalk in front of the bank. Half the men of his posse climbed down from their saddles and followed him. He stepped inside, his men close on his heels. Reaching the counter, he peered over and saw the two bodies lying on the floor. He bounded around the counter and knelt down beside them. One, they younger of the two, was dead. The older man was alive—but only just.

"You hear me, mister?" Edson asked.

The bank manager's eyes flickered open and he nodded weakly.

"I'm a deputy United States marshal," Edson said. "What did they look like, the men who did this?"

The bank manager's mouth worked, but all that came from it was a stream of bright red blood. Edson reached into his coat pocket and pulled out a sheet of paper. He unfolded it. It was a poster, wearing thin along the creases from a lot of folding and unfolding. It bore a picture of a

15

man with a scar on the left side of his face that a dark beard did not hide. Underneath the picture was printed in heavy black lettering: *Wanted—Dead or Alive. Ceston Parker Oates, age forty-two. Five feet eleven inches tall, rangy build, brown eyes, dark brown hair, beard. Scar left side of face. Wanted for murder, bank robbery, armed robbery, stagecoach robbery. Reward five thousand dollars.*

Edson held the poster in front of the bank manager's eyes.

The bank manager stared at it, trying to focus his eyes, but he seemed to have trouble seeing. Behind Edson, the men of his posse crowded close, eager to hear what the bank manager had to say.

"Did one of them have a scar down the left side of his face?" Edson asked. "He tried to hide it by growing a beard, but his whiskers won't grow over it."

The bank manager's eyes lit up. He tried to struggle to a sitting position, but Edson put a restraining arm on him as he stared coughing, more blood bubbling out of his mouth.

"Don't move . . . just lay back there and take it easy."

The men hovering around behind Edson looked at one another. One shook his head.

"Was one of 'em an Indian?" Edson asked.

The bank manager nodded.

Edson's mouth tightened into a hard, straight line. He glanced momentarily at the open safe against the wall. "How much did they get away with?"

"Not . . . not much. Wasn't . . . much in the bank . . . two thousand . . . twenty-one hundred dollars . . . that's all. Some of it . . . in bills. Some in . . . silver. Bulky . . . heavy to carry . . ."

Edson stood up and looked around at the men behind him. "Is there a doctor in this place?"

The men behind him looked at one another and shrugged. "Wouldn't rightly expect so, Marshal."

"Ask the stage-line agent," Edson said.

"It's too late, Marshal," one of the posse said, kneeling down beside the bank manager. "Don't need no doctor now. The poor critter just kicked off."

Edson looked down at him. He sighed. "Well, I suppose it's just as well. He was pretty far gone. Just saved himself a lot of suffering."

He stepped outside onto the street again and looked beyond the buildings, to the undulating brown grassland stretching northward on the other side of the river. The stage-line agent, still holding his Winchester, stood beside him.

"Montana has become too hot for 'em," Edson said. "Looks like they're going to try and make for the Canadian border. How far would it be?"

"About fifty miles," the stage agent said.

"Anything between here and there?"

"Nothing but rolling prairie and coulees. Oh . . . there's some cavalry patrolling the border, looking for Sioux that took part in the Custer massacre down on the Little Big Horn last year."

Edson's hand went up to his black mustache. He ran a finger along one side of it, still staring off to the north. "Fifty miles, eh? That's a long ride on tired horses. If we could hire some fresh animals, we could maybe overhaul 'em before they can make it. We've been pushing 'em pretty hard. Their horses must be plumb near the end of their endurance."

The stage agent pointed his Winchester barrel off to the northeast. "Jake Hayden runs a good herd of horseflesh seven miles away. He'd hire or sell you some."

Edson grinned. "Thanks for the information. We'll ride on over and see him. With any sort of luck Oates and his gang will run into a cavalry patrol. If they do, maybe the cavalry will hold onto 'em long enough for us to get there."

Ceston Parker Oakes led his gang in a mad gallop away from the Milk. He repeatedly tossed glances back over his shoulder, expecting to see the posse come pounding up from the river bank behind. Each time he looked, instead of the posse, he saw Ben Zacks's pain-wracked face as the gray-bearded man hung desperately onto his saddle.

17

It had shaken Oates to see the posse riding down the slope toward them back at Fort Turner. He hadn't expected Edson to be so damn close.

He kept up the pace, spurring his horse cruelly. What little conscience he still possessed rankled him for the way he was treating his horse. Like all men whose lives and livelihood depended on horseflesh, he had an affection for his horse. But he spurred it regardless. He had far greater affection for his own hide.

Yet, without his horse, his own hide would be short-lived. And when he felt the horse start to blow—and when he still didn't see the posse coming behind them—he slowed down.

There was one consolation, Oates thought. The posse's horses must be giving out too.

Behind him the Frenchman rode close alongside Ben Zacks, ready to grab him if he fell. But Zacks clung on stubbornly. He was a tough old man, Ben Zacks.

The Frenchman had been on the verge of telling Oates they would have to slow down. He didn't want to get caught any more than did Oates, and although the price on his head was only three thousand dollars, two thousand less than that on Oates's head—at least it had been on the last *Wanted* poster he had seen—he had as much to lose as Oates or Lone Man. He too was wanted dead or alive. But the horses couldn't last at that pace.

The horses needed rest, and oats or grain feed, not just prairie grazing.

They slowed them down to a trot. But Oates kept looking back behind them. He still expected Edson and the posse to come thundering over the last hill.

When he wasn't looking back over his shoulder, Oates was studying the countryside. It was undulating, with little water and less timber. The only hiding places were coulees, and he didn't like coulees. You could get trapped in them too damn easy, especially if your enemies outnumbered you and knew the country. But he wasn't specifically looking for hiding places. He was looking for some remembered landmark, something to tell him how far they had to go.

But he saw nothing that he remembered.

"Prob'ly too far east," he muttered, the others not hearing him over the sounds of the horses. "It was more to the west when I was up this way in '72, toward the Bear Paws."

Oates glanced at the Indian. Lone Man had been this way before. He knew the country, but Oates was reluctant to ask him. He was the leader and he didn't want to weaken the appearance of his leadership by asking directions from his men, especially not from an Indian. They'd just keep riding north until they reached the Canadian border. They couldn't miss it. It was due north and it stretched all the way east and west.

"Cess!"

It was the Frenchman. Oates turned in his saddle. The Frenchman, riding alongside Ben Zacks, looked worried. And well he might, thought Oates, with a posse chasing hot on their heels.

But it was not the posse that was uppermost in the Frenchman's mind.

"We 'ave to stop," he said, inclining his head at the gray-haired man. "Ben, 'e needs patching up and rest."

Zacks grimaced. At forty-six, he was only three years older than Oates, but his hair and beard were completely gray and he looked older. Particularly now. All the color had drained from his face, and his skin was the shade of his beard. His shirt was all red on his right side, down below his ribs. He had lost a lot of blood.

Oates looked back over the way they had ridden for the umpteenth time. Still no sight of the posse. Maybe it wouldn't show for awhile. Edson must have been riding pretty hard to have almost caught up with them at Fort Turner. Maybe he and his posse were resting back at Fort Turner, taking the time for a good feed while they were at it. The thought of food made Oates's mouth water.

He nodded. "There's a rise up ahead. We'll stop when we get to it."

When they reached the rise, they reined to and dismounted. Oates loosened the cinches of his saddle while the Frenchman helped Ben Zacks from his horse. Lone

19

Man watched the rolling prairie behind them.

The Frenchman reached into his saddlebags and pulled out a couple of shirts. He ripped one apart, folded the pieces, and packed them into the wound under Zacks's shirt.

"Don't look too good, do it, Frenchy?" Zacks said painfully.

"I 'ave seen worse, Ben," the Frenchman replied. "But the bullet is deep. You need a doctor to get it out, and you need rest. As long as you ride, the movement of your 'orse pulls the flesh apart and makes you bleed more."

Oates stood anxiously scanning the prairie behind. Rest was out of the question as far as he was concerned. That posse wouldn't rest, or whatever the hell they were doing, forever. And the four of them still had a long way to go. They wouldn't reach the border by dark. Dark! Hell, the way they were going, they'd be lucky to make it by dark tomorrow night.

Zacks voiced what was in Cess Oates's mind. "We gotta keep goin'. Ain't no doctor around here, and there ain't no sense in restin'. If we keep on goin', at least I got a chance. If'n I stop to rest, thet posse'll get me for sure. Then I get my neck stretched. On top o' thet, I put you boys at risk. Nah . . . just bandage me up, Frenchy. I kin still ride."

They were back in their saddles within minutes and resumed their ride northward. Still the posse hadn't showed, and Oates was getting worried. After pressing him so hard for this far, with the Canadian border and the end of Edson's jurisdiction ahead of them, the posse wouldn't give up now. Not Bill Edson. Oates scanned the country all around as they rode. It was all rolling . . . you could see only as far as the next rise in all directions. It wouldn't be unlike Edson to come in at them from the side somehow. But he couldn't do that. Horses don't fly. There was only one way Edson could come after them and that was straight from behind.

Then, what the hell was holding him back?

Then the thought hit Oates. Christ! That was what Edson was doing! Changing horses. They were getting fresh horses from somewhere.

The four wanted men pushed on, urging their horses into a canter. The horses reluctantly broke into a canter, but it was a slow one, and pretty soon they had dropped down almost to a trot. Oates cursed. Yet, he knew it was useless to try to get more speed out of them. If he pushed them any harder, they'd give out. Then the four men would be at the mercy of the posse. They'd just have to do the best they could at a trot.

Two hours passed. Zacks hung onto his saddle, the Frenchman riding alongside him, still looking worried. That was the Frenchman's trouble . . . he was too damn soft. Still, Oates had to admit that Ben was a good man and a good companion, one of the few men Oates had met whom he felt he could trust.

It was late afternoon when they sighted the posse. Coming over a hill in the distance. Oates cursed.

The posse was a couple of miles behind, but they were covering ground fast. They had made up the time they'd lost in getting the fresh horses.

"How far before we reach the Canadian line, Lone?" Oates asked, no longer concerned over the appearance of leadership. It was more important that he knew how far they had to go than to worry about being the boss. If the posse caught up with them, it wouldn't matter a damn who was the boss. They'd all hang.

"A day's ride," the Indian said.

A day's ride. That could be thirty, forty miles. Too damn far. They'd never make it. If they could keep ahead of the posse until nightfall, maybe they could lose them in one of the coulees. In the dark it might be easier, especially with someone like Lone. He could show them the way.

Ben Zacks provided their salvation. He pointed off to their right front, to the northeast.

"Head for thet pile o' rocks over there. I'll hole up among 'em. When the posse comes within range o' my rifle, I'll open up on 'em. Might hold 'em back a little while. Give you boys a chance to get away."

Oates jumped at the chance. That might do it. If they

could keep riding until dark, they could lose themselves in a coulee. Even Bill Edson couldn't see in the dark.

But the Frenchman objected. "No, Ben. You can not do that. That is suicide."

Zacks managed a smile. "I've had it, Frenchy. I ain't goin' to make it. I know thet. Comes to all of us sooner or later. I reckon I've been lucky I didn't collect it afore this. At least I'll go with my boots on. Never did fancy the idea of dyin' in bed. I'll go givin' thet posse somethin' to think of, somethin' to remember Ben Zacks by. Now, do like I say. Ride over toward them rocks. The lay o' the land sort of goes thet way, anyhow. You kin cut down into thet dip an' up the other side. Soon as the posse follows an' gits down in the dip, I'll open up on 'em. They won't be expectin' it. I'll catch 'em right by surprise. Might be able to shoot thet Edson feller clean out o' his saddle."

It was a good plan, Oates reckoned. They veered their horses so they would pass by just to the left of the rocks. They rode toward them gradually, following the undulating lay of the land, without making it appear too obvious.

They urged their horses into a canter, riding down over the lip of the rolling prairie, down the slope into the shallow dip and up the other side. Moments later they were up on top of the next rise, in plain view of the posse behind. The rocks were just a few yards to their right. Already the posse had gained on them further. Then they rode on over the rise and down the other side.

The moment they were out of sight, Ben Zacks wheeled his horse, made a wide U turn, and came up behind the rocks, reining in. The Frenchman rode alongside. With difficulty, Zacks lifted his leg up over the saddle. Then he slid down from his horse onto the ground. He stood there, holding onto his saddle for support.

"Hand me m' rifle, Frenchy."

The Frenchman slid Zacks's rifle out of its scabbard and handed it to him.

"Now . . . 'ppreciate it if you'd reach into m' saddlebag an' hand me m' chawin' t'baccy."

When he had his rifle and a plug of tobacco, Zacks

staggered toward the rocks. The Frenchman jumped down from his horse and helped him. Zacks clambered among the rocks, settling down into a cleft where he could lie prone yet at the same time fire effectively down into the posse from cover.

"Now quit fussin' over me an' git movin'. You need ever' minute you kin muster. Take m' horse. Might come in handy. No use leavin' it here for them would-be lawmen."

Oates and Lone Man sat their saddles a few yards down from the rocks. Oates fidgeted impatiently. "Come on, Frenchy, for Christ's sake!" he urged.

Zacks looked up into the Frenchman's hollow-cheeked face. "Good luck, Frenchy."

The Frenchman patted him on the shoulder. "You too, *mon ami.*"

Bending low, the Frenchman ran toward his horse and leaped up into the saddle. With a backward glance he rode off, towing Zacks's horse.

For a moment Ben Zacks watched them ride away, then turned to look between the rocks at the oncoming posse. He stuck the plug of tobacco between his teeth, gave it a twist, and bit off a piece. Then, chewing away, he slid forward his rifle and lay alongside it, watching the approaching horsemen, ready to open up on them the moment they reached the bottom of the dip.

CHAPTER 3

The moment they crested the hill and saw Fort Walsh standing on the valley floor below, Sergeant Colin Campbell MacGregor stiffened his back as he sat his military saddle. It was an unconscious gesture, typical of the big Scot, as though he was back on formation with B Troop on the parade ground below.

Bright scarlet tunic throwing a blaze of vivid color against the autumn-browned hills, Sergeant MacGregor reined his horse to a stop and waited for the wagon following behind to draw alongside.

"Be careful with that wagon, Bennett," Sergeant Mac-Gregor warned the red-coated constable sitting on the wagon seat, the leather traces in his hands. "The trail is a bit tricky up here. We dinna want to jolt our patient too much. We want him fit to return to duty as soon as possible."

"Don't worry about me, Mac," said a voice from the back of the wagon, where a dark-haired man with steel-blue eyes lay on an improvised bed. "I've lived through worse than this."

Sergeant MacGregor grinned, his teeth white against the deep tan of his face and the black of his mustache. "Aye, I know that, Cav, but Surgeon Kittson will have my hide if I deliver you to the post hospital in worse shape than you were when he was down at Pine Butte to fix

24

your wound."

They resumed their journey along the trail, down the pine-dotted hills to the broad valley floor. Afternoon sunlight danced off the sparkling headwaters of Battle Creek, giving an air of Indian-summer warmth. Some two hundred yards beyond the fort's north palisade sprawled a settlement of sorts—log cabins, lean-tos, canvas tents, and frame structures. They contained the trading posts, saloons, billiard parlors, and dance hall that had magically mushroomed within the protective presence of the log fort the North West Mounted Police had built in the Cypress Hills two and a half years before. Farther along the valley stood a dozen or so tepees, where a visiting band of Indians had pitched camp and decided to stay, secure in the knowledge that they would not be attacked by more aggressive, more powerful tribes.

Sergeant MacGregor rode through the east gates of Fort Walsh, the twelve-foot-high log palisade towering above. Constable Bennett drove the wagon alongside him. A carbine-carrying sentry, in scarlet tunic and white helmet with a brightly burnished brass spike on top, stood guard beside the open gates. The sentry's uniform and accoutrements were immaculate, but Sergeant MacGregor eyed him critically nonetheless.

Directly ahead, almost in the center of the enclosure, stood a log guardroom, and in front of it a tall whitewashed flagpole, from which the Union Jack waved in the light afternoon breeze. Lined along the parade ground were eight field pieces—four seven-pounders, two nine-pounders, and two brass mortars.

"Take Sergeant Cavannagh to the post hospital," Sergeant MacGregor said to Constable Bennett. "I'll be over for a few words after I've reported to Major Walsh."

Sergeant MacGregor wheeled his horse to the right and headed toward the commanding officer's quarters. Sitting to attention, he rode along the edge of the parade ground, his back ramrod straight, left hand lightly holding his reins, right arm pressed rigidly against his side. Despite the fact that he had been on the trail for five days since leaving Pine Butte outpost, a hundred miles to the east, Sergeant MacGregor looked fit to take part in a general parade. There was barely a wrinkle in his form-fitting scarlet tunic, the wide yellow stripes down the sides of his dark blue riding breeches were free of travel stains, his shiny leather riding boots and belt were polished to perfection, and his spurs and brass buttons were burnished to brilliance. Even in a headquarters post like Fort Walsh, where strict discipline and smart turnouts were as sacred as the Ten Commandments, Sergeant Mac-Gregor's appearance in uniform caused heads to turn. And MacGregor enjoyed it, for he was a soldier.

Just turned forty, Sergeant MacGregor had been a member of the North West Mounted Police for four years, since the Force's inception in the fall of 1873. He was an *original,* having made the long march west across the plains from Fort Garry in Manitoba to the foothills of the Rocky Mountains, where Colonel Macleod had established law and order among warring Indian tribes and driven Montana whiskey runners back across the line. MacGregor had then accompanied Major Walsh and B Troop to the Cypress Hills in the spring of 1875. They had cut down spruce and jack pine from the surrounding hills, and built Fort Walsh with their bare hands.

MacGregor reined to in front of a log building north of the east gates. Swinging down from his saddle, he handed his reins to an orderly who stepped out of the building. Sergeant Major Francis met him at the door.

"Back from Pine Butte so soon, Sergeant MacGregor?"

MacGregor drew himself to attention. He and the sergeant major spoke the same language. They were both old soldiers. Sergeant Major Francis wore the ribbons of Turkish and Crimean medals on his scarlet tunic. He had ridden with the famous Light Brigade during its immortal charge into Russian guns at Balaklava nearly a quarter of a century earlier.

"Aye, sir. Acting under Major Walsh's orders, I've brought Sergeant Cavannagh in to the post hospital to recuperate from a knife wound he got in a fight with a

Sioux."

Sergeant Major Francis nodded. "I'll see if the major's free." He turned back into the building, Sergeant MacGregor following. He stopped at an inner door, knocked, and waited until a voice from within told him to enter. He opened the door and stepped in.

"Sergeant MacGregor reporting in from Pine Butte, sir."

"Have him come in, Sar-Major."

The sergeant major turned to MacGregor and nodded. Sergeant MacGregor marched into the office, slammed to a halt with a clash of spurs two paces in front of Major Walsh's desk, and saluted.

Major Walsh was four years younger than MacGregor. Already he had established an international reputation on the frontier for raw courage and colorful language. He had a full head of bushy brown hair, intense brown eyes, and a wide moustache. An embroidered crown adorned the gold-laced collars of his scarlet tunic.

"At ease, Sergeant . . . stand easy. Good trip? How is Sergeant Cavannagh bearing up?"

"We took five days to do the hundred miles, sir. Surgeon Kittson gave orders that he did nae want the wound in Sergeant Cavannagh's back breaking open, so we took the trip easy. In compliance with your orders sir, Constable Bennett brought his full kit with him for transfer to medical duties at the post hospital under Surgeon Kittson. As for Sergeant Cavannagh, he's in good spirits, but Surgeon Kittson can give you a better report on his medical condition that I can, sir."

Major Walsh nodded. His face was tanned from exposure to sun and wind, but his forehead was pale where it had been shaded by the brim of his helmet. The Sioux called him White Forehead.

"I'll be discussing that with Surgeon Kittson after he's had an opportunity to examine Sergeant Cavannagh. In the meantime, you will remain at Pine Butte in charge until Sergeant Cavannagh is fit to return to duty. You'll want to spend the night here and start out on the ride back first thing tomorrow morning, I presume?"

"If it's all the same to you, sir, I think I should be starting back immediately. Now that Constable LeBlanc has been transferred to Wood Mountain, there's only Constable Jenkins and the scout Prefontaine left at the outpost. Jenkins is a good man in a tight situation, sir, but he's nae the most responsible mon I've met in the Force, and I dinna like leaving the two of them unsupervised, sir."

Major Walsh's hand strayed up to stroke his moustache. He knew Constable Jenkins well enough to understand what Sergeant MacGregor meant. He nodded his agreement, then went on to speak of matters that were more prominent in his mind.

"You will be aware, Sergeant, that Sitting Bull and the other Sioux chiefs who took refuge in Canadian territory following the Custer battle rejected the Terry Commission's amnesty offer."

"Aye, sir." Everyone in Fort Walsh knew it. Brigadier General Alfred H. Terry of the United States Army, acting under special instructions from Washington, had visited Fort Walsh a short time before, where he met with Sitting Bull and the other Sioux chiefs and offered them an amnesty if they would surrender their weapons, return to their own country, and live on reservations Washington allotted them.

"It's unfortunate. It leaves us with a potentially explosive situation on our hands. We have close to six thousand of the most warlike Indians on the North American plains within a hundred and fifty miles of this post. There are one hundred of us here, with a handful more scattered at a few small outposts throughout this part of the North West Territories. I've had talks with Sitting Bull and some of the other Sioux chiefs, and they have promised to obey our laws and live at peace. But there is no denying that our own Indians resent the Sioux intrusion, especially in light of the rapid depletion of the buffalo herds. If our tribes combined, they would be more than a match for the Sioux. It would take only one incident to

28

spark things off. Another thing we have to worry about is the danger of the Sioux making raids down into their own country, using Canadian territory as a base. All it needs is a few hotheads among the younger braves. That concerns me more than anything else.

"Our government would like to see the last of the Sioux, but official policy is to let them stay as long as they abide by our laws and keep the peace. For the moment, the American government has given up efforts to persuade the Sioux to return to their own country. However, there have been attempts by well-meaning—if misguided—individuals to try to talk them into going back. The Right Reverend Father Marty of the Benedictine Order, for one. He went to Sitting Bull's camp with an American army scout and an interpreter. The Sioux immediately took them prisoner. They were highly suspicious and thought they were spies or some such. After a series of broken promises and breached treaties, the Sioux have lost faith in the American government. They suspect retaliatory action will be taken against them over the Custer battle if they go back. They don't trust the American government, and they see all American whites as their enemies. Fortunately, we were able to secure the release of Father Marty and the other two unharmed."

Major Walsh sat back in his chair, his right arm resting on his desk, his fingers drumming a staccato on the top. "Father Genin tried the same thing. He was somewhat critical of us, suggesting that we haven't tried hard enough to persuade the Sioux to return. He even accused us of *petting* Sitting Bull." His fingers drummed harder. "*Petting!*" He almost spat the word. "That's the last goddamned thing we've done. This whole Sitting Bull issue has drawn very wide coverage in the American press, and in the press in this country for that matter. It's bound to draw even wider coverage now that the Terry Commission has failed. And I say that with all respect to General Terry. He was given an impossible mission. The next thing that's likely to happen is some overzealous journalist is going to wander into Sitting Bull's camp and try to get his life story, or a firsthand Sioux account of the Custer battle. A journalistic coup. That would be the last straw as far as I'm concerned. We have more to do with our time than go riding into the Sioux camps rescuing every meddling white who doesn't have the brains to realize the danger they're putting themselves in."

Major Walsh sat forward on his chair, leaning both forearms on his desk as he looked up hard at Sergeant MacGregor. "I'm not allowing any more whites into those Sioux camps, Sergeant, not while they're on our side of the border. That means *everyone!* Clergymen, journalists, traders—the whole damned lot! There's that trader Gregory, over near War Bonnet's camp. I'm not impressed with him, and I know Sergeant Cavannagh wasn't. I don't want him going anywhere near the Sioux. If they want to trade with him, they can damn well go over to his trading post. But I don't want him going into their camps. I've heard he used to peddle whiskey to Indians down in Montana. So far we've had no reason to suspect him of doing the same since he's been in Canadian territory, but God help him if he does and we catch him."

Pushing his chair back, Major Walsh stood up behind his desk, an indication that the interview was over. Sergeant MacGregor returned to attention.

"We must watch the Sioux situation very closely, Sergeant. Keep your eyes and ears open. Send me a detailed report of anything out of the ordinary that arises. Take whatever action you deem appropriate. Any questions?"

"None, sir."

"Very well. Carry on."

Sergeant MacGregor swept his right arm up from his side in salute, his stiffly extended fingers held in front of his right eyebrow and immediately below the blue and yellow pillbox cap sitting at a jaunty angle on his head.

"Verra guid, sir!"

He snapped his arm down by his side again, made a drill-book about-face, and marched smartly out of the major's office.

Sergeant MacGregor rode his horse along the trail that would take him back to Pine Butte. The weather continued warm, Indian summer at its finest, although most of the trees, other than the spruce and pine, had lost their leaves and the hills had that bare look of late autumn.

It was already dusk, and MacGregor started looking for a place to camp for the night. He had passed two suitable sites within the past hour, sites with jack pine to provide protection against any sudden storms that had a habit of unpredictably blowing up, or with a nearby lake or stream with water to boil a cup of tea and deadfall timber to fuel a campfire. But he was anxious to get back to Pine Butte, anxious to make the return trip in half the time it had taken to complete the Fort Walsh journey. Freed of the encumbrance of the wagon and the need to attend to Sergeant Cavannagh, he was confident he would make it.

He was about to pull in to a grove of pine when he spotted a thin column of smoke spiraling lazily upwards from a stand of spruce about a mile or so to the southeast. Curious, he headed his horse toward it. The Montana border was only twenty miles away and the Mounted Police made it their business to know who was traveling around the country. Could be whiskey runners, although there was little habitation in this part of the Cypress Hills, and therefore little outlet for a whiskey runner's business. There were no permanent camps of Indians. The closest were the Sioux, but the nearest Sioux were still fifty miles farther east.

MacGregor's horse covered the distance at a cautious trot. Buttoned in a holster on his waist he carried a .450-caliber six-shot Adams revolver. From a saddle bucket behind his right leg protruded the butt of a .577-caliber Snider-Enfield carbine. The Snider was single-shot. Most of the inhabitants of the West, including many of the Indians, carried repeating rifles. But the Snider had a range of a thousand yards, against a Spencer's six hundred, or a Winchester's four hundred.

Dusk was falling quickly, and there was a haze about the landscape. As he got closer, MacGregor could see a team of horses and a high-topped wagon. The wagon was large enough to haul whiskey. But the next thing he saw were two tents.

"Hmmm. I've seen a few whiskey runners in my time, but nae a one who pitched a tent on a trip."

He was soon only thirty yards from the fire. He could see only two people, sitting on stools around the campfire. After another ten yards one of his horse's iron shoes rang loudly on a stone. Two people stood up quickly and stared into the purple shadows toward him.

To MacGregor's astonishment, one was a woman.

He could see her plainly, illuminated by the light of the fire. She was in her late twenties, he guessed, with a freckled face and high cheekbones. She had a rather wide mouth, a high forehead, and wavy auburn hair swept up in a loose knot on top of her head. She wore no makeup, but she was attractive in a schoolma'am sort of way.

The other was an older man—tall and thin, wearing a long black frock coat, a travel-grimed white shirt with a black string tie, a black vest, and black trousers. His face was long and ruddy, and his hair dark brown, straight and very thin on top. A black hat lay on the ground beside his feet. His age MacGregor estimated to be close to sixty.

Apprehension was written on their faces until he reined his horse to within a few feet of their campfire. Relief swept the apprehension away when they saw the wide yellow stripes down the legs of his dark blue breeches and the bright scarlet tunic with its shiny brass buttons.

MacGregor was pleased to find they weren't apparent lawbreakers, just bona fide travelers. He decided to camp alongside them and enjoy an hour or two of cordial conversation.

"Good evening, ma'am," he said, raising a white-gauntleted hand to his pillbox in an informal salute, his mark of respect for the presence of a woman. "Sir," he added, nodding to the man.

The man eyed the crown and three gold chevrons on MacGregor's tunic sleeve. "Good evening, Sergeant."

"I noticed your campfire smoke frae a mile back," MacGregor said, inclining his head back toward the trail. "If you hae nae objection, I'll camp alongside you. Companionship is a wee bit scarce oot here in this part of the country."

The man smiled. "We'd be delighted, Sergeant. Do get down from your horse and join us for some supper. I'm afraid it's only beans and bread, but we have sufficient, and we've plenty of coffee."

"There's nae any need for me to eat your food, sir. I hae my own patrol rations. But I would enjoy a cup of coffee. I can smell it. It's tantalizing my tastes."

MacGregor swung down from his saddle.

The tall man in the black frock coat extended his hand. "Allow me to introduce us. I'm the Reverend Theodore Hatcher, and this is my daughter, Sarah."

MacGregor shook the man's hand and introduced himself. He gave the man a quick, appraising look. A reverend gentleman, indeed. The woman wore no rings, so she was obviously a spinster daughter. Certainly they weren't the type of travelers he expected to run across out in such a lonely stretch of wild country.

When they were seated eating supper around the campfire, the Reverend Hatcher and his daughter perched on their stools on one side, MacGregor sitting on a rock on the other, they talked.

"This can be verra dangerous country for two unarmed people to be traveling around, Reverend, especially a man and a woman. For generations these Cypress Hills hae been a battle ground for warring Indian tribes frae both sides of the international boundary. Although we—the Mounted Police—hae established law and order in the North West Territories, it can still be dangerous."

The Reverend Theodore Hatcher smiled benignly. "We have no fear for our own personal safety, Sergeant. The Lord will protect us."

Sergeant MacGregor didn't smile back. He looked

33

doubtful. Glancing across the fire, he caught the woman's eyes on him. As they sat, he caught her eyes on him often, and he colored under his tan. A strapping six-footer in the already famous uniform, MacGregor was a handsome man in a rugged way.

"Where are y' frae, Reverend?"

The Reverend Hatcher frowned. *"Fray,* Sergeant?"

MacGregor laughed. "Agh! It's m' accent, Reverend. I'm frae Scotland. Where are y' frae?"

Reverend Hatcher laughed, merriment sparkling in his blue eyes. "Baltimore, originally. But Sarah and I have been traveling through the West for the last four years, spreading the Gospel. Most recently we've been among the mining camps around Helena, and at Fort Benton. Sarah helps me in all my work."

"And what brings you up to the North West Territories?"

"To spread the Lord's word among the heathen savages who so barbarically massacred the gallant General Custer and his poor comrades of the famous Seventh Cavalry," Reverend Hatcher said, his voice shaking with righteous indignation, "and then fled like cowards across the international boundary into your country."

Christ Almighty! MacGregor almost choked on his food. He coughed and spluttered.

Sarah Hatcher leaned forward, concern on her face. "Is something wrong, Sergeant? Did you swallow some food the wrong way?"

MacGregor washed the food down with a mouthful of coffee. The conversation he'd had with Major Walsh the other day flooded through his mind. "Nae, ma'am," he said, shaking his head. "I'm all right."

The brief interruption over, the Reverend Hatcher continued what he had been saying, but in a more moderate tone. "Sarah and I will show the pagan Sioux the way to salvation if they will repent for their sins and promise to live peacefully evermore."

They resumed eating. MacGregor eyed the couple across the fire. He especially eyed the reverend gentle man. The reverend seemed blissfully ignorant of the extreme danger in which he was placing himself and his daughter. Even being out on the northern plains this late in the season was dangerous enough. True, the weather was pleasant at the moment, but any day now it would turn cold and snow would sweep down out of the north, or across from the Rocky Mountains far to the west, and cover the trails. Blizzards had been known to sweep the country as early as September. It was almost the end of October.

"Perhaps you could give us directions to Sitting Bull's camp, Sergeant," Reverend Hatcher said.

Draining his cup, MacGregor nodded. "Aye, Reverend, I could give y' directions to Sitting Bull's camp. But, the fact is, y' canna go there, or to any of the Sioux camps."

The Reverend Hatcher's eyes widened in surprise. "I don't understand, Sergeant. Why not?"

"Because it's too dangerous. We've already had some gentlemen of the Church visiting Sitting Bull and trying to talk him into returning to his own country. The Sioux damn near . . ." His face reddening, MacGregor looked quickly at Sarah Hatcher. "Begging your pardon, miss, Reverend. I'm forgetting m' language. I'm nae used to being in the company of a lady or a reverend gentleman. Er . . . that is, the Sioux nearly burned them at the stake."

The Reverend Hatcher's eyes locked onto MacGregor. "But we have no wish to talk Sitting Bull or any of the Sioux into returning to the United States. All we want to do is spread the Lord's word and save their souls."

MacGregor shook his head. "The Sioux will nae thank you for it, Reverend. You'd be wasting your time. The Indians have their own gods, which seem to serve them well enough."

Sarah Hatcher's face took on a shocked expression. "Are you not a God-fearing man, Sergeant?"

MacGregor looked across the fire at her. "Aye, I'm a God-fearing mon, Miss Hatcher. But I've been a soldier most of my life, and I've soldiered in a lot of different places throughout the British Empire. I've seen heathens, and I've seen people more enlightened than us whom we regard as heathens. I've seen well-meaning missionaries go into their lands to try to convert them. Those people hae their own beliefs and their own ways of life. Frae what I've seen, most of them were better off without our interference. When it comes right down to it, we all worship pretty much the same god . . . a Supreme Being, an Almighty. We just have different names for him."

There was silence from the other side of the campfire, broken only by the crackling of the fire. Both Sarah Hatcher's and her father's faces looked like frozen masks.

Sergeant MacGregor pulled out his pipe and started filling the bowl with tobacco. "The simple fact of the matter is that Major Walsh, commanding the Mounted Police in the Cypress Hills, has given orders that no whites are to venture into any of the Sioux camps. That includes missionaries."

"Does your Major Walsh have the constituted authority to make such a dictatorial order?" the Reverend Hatcher asked icily.

MacGregor locked his eyes onto those of the reverend gentleman. "I'd say, Reverend, that if Major Walsh issues an order, he has the authority to do so. And he knows what he's talking about."

"Would he change his mind if I could convince him that we're not trying to talk the Sioux into returning to the United States?"

Striking a match, MacGregor held it over the bowl of his pipe and drew on it. He talked between puffs, looking across the bowl as he did so. "That's nae the issue that concerns him, Reverend. He has nae objection to the Sioux returning to their homeland. Indeed, if they did, it would be a weight off his mind. What he is concerned about is the danger you and anyone like you might be in while wandering near those Sioux camps. The Sioux hae no liking for whites. There are hotheads among the younger warriors. There's nae knowing how they might react. You could find yourself standing tied to a stake in

36

front of a great flaming fire."

Reverend Hatcher sighed. "The Lord sent Sarah and me from Fort Benton up to this desolate country to spread His word and save souls."

Puffing his pipe, MacGregor said, "Under the circumstances, I'd think the Lord would understand if you did nae continue. Anyway, I'm afraid y' nae hae any choice in the matter. By all means, ride to Fort Walsh and discuss it wi' the major. But I'm sure he will nae change his mind. Personally, I think you'd be better off driving straight back to Fort Benton before the winter snows fall. It's getting verra close to winter, and this is nae the sort of country you want to get caught out in during bad weather."

They broke camp the next morning. Sergeant MacGregor helped Reverend Hatcher and his daughter fold their tents and harness their horses. Once they were sitting on the seat of their wagon, Reverend Hatcher holding the traces in his hands, MacGregor stood looking up at them.

"If you want to go to Fort Walsh, just follow that trail up there," he said, pointing. "It'll take you all the way. There's a good trail from there to Fort Benton. It will take you five days. There are travelers on it . . . freighters, mail carriers, and the like. There's chance of help if you run into any problems."

The Reverend Hatcher stared stonily down at MacGregor from the height of his wagon seat. "Thank you, Sergeant. You've been most kind."

The reverend gentleman's manner was decidedly cool, MacGregor thought. The previous evening he had been the very essence of cordiality until he had been told he couldn't go into any of the Sioux camps. His daughter, Sarah, continued to eye MacGregor furtively, but each time he caught her looking, she quickly looked away. It wasn't that she was flirting with him—heaven forbid, MacGregor thought. She simply seemed curious. Maybe she had never seen a redcoat before, he speculated. Anyway, he had more important matters to think about. Such as getting back to Pine Butte before Freddie Jenkins and the *metis* scout, Prefontaine, got into some sort of trouble.

MacGregor raised his hand to his cap. "My pleasure, Reverend, Miss Hatcher. Hae a safe trip."

He stood watching them drive away, watching the wagon lumber up to the trail and turn west toward Fort Walsh and Fort Benton.

MacGregor swung up onto his saddle, reined his horse around, and headed in the opposite direction, east toward Pine Butte.

CHAPTER 4

Deputy United States Marshal Edson was pleased with the horses he had obtained from the Hayden ranch. They were good stock, in good condition and strong. He was particularly pleased with the gelding beneath him. It was a sturdy, fleet-footed animal, a light bay, so light that it looked like a palomino, except that its mane and tail were dark.

He was well aware that his jurisdiction ended at the Canadian border. However, on fresh horses he was confident he could overtake Oates and his gang long before they got that far. He was confident he would overtake them before dark. He *had* to overtake them before dark. Otherwise they might be able to slip away in the darkness. Especially with that Indian riding with them. The Indian knew the country. But Oates had a wounded man, and that would probably slow him down. From the stage agent's description, the wounded man sounded like Ben Zacks.

The posse rode at a good clip, but Edson was careful not to push the new horses too hard. They had to be run in, allowed to get used to the weight of the saddles and riders on their backs.

After the first few miles, they cut Oates's trail. A couple of hours later they caught sight of them in the distance, about two miles away.

Edson's confidence soared. There was now no doubt in his mind that he'd have Oates before nightfall. The long chase was nearing its end, a chase that had started down in Witchìta, Kansas, six months ago. A grin spread across Edson's face. With every length his horse took, he was that much closer to taking Oates.

He leaned forward over his horse's back, as though willing the animal to greater speed. The light bay pulled ahead of the other horses. They pounded over the rolling prairie. Edson's grin widened. They were narrowing the gap. The distance between the posse and Oates's gang lessened to a mile and a half.

Edson dropped a hand to the Smith & Wesson .44 holstered on his hip. He eased the gun in its holster, making sure it was ready for instant use. He would give Oates a chance to surrender. He'd give him more chance than he deserved, a better chance than Oates had given the bank manager back at Fort Turner. And his other victims as well. But if Oates would not surrender, Edson would have no compunction in blasting him and his gang away. They were wanted men, wanted whichever way they could be taken—dead or alive.

There they were little more than a mile ahead, cutting down into a dip. Leaning further along his horse's neck, he saw them a moment later as they rode up the other side out of the dip.

Ben Zacks watched them draw closer, watched along the barrel of his Winchester. He watched the leader of the posse, the tall man on the light-colored horse. His eyes squinted against the light of the late afternoon sun. Was that Edson? It looked like it could be him. Zacks grinned. Edson would be the first to go.

Zacks sighted along his rifle barrel, the barrel resting between the rocks. He was getting tired. He'd lost more blood, the blood seeping through the rough dressing and bandage the Frenchman had tied around him. But he could still sight a rifle, he could still pull a trigger. He'd go, but he'd take as many of the posse with him as he could. They would remember Ben Zacks, by cracky. Men would talk about him throughout Montana, and maybe Dakota as well, and Wyoming and Nebraska, and maybe even as far down as back home in Kansas.

His finger curled around the trigger. The posse was riding down into the dip, the lead rider on the creamy horse, the others bunched up behind him.

There they were . . . dropping down into the bottom of the dip now. Zacks studied the tall fella, the one in the gray coat and the black mustache, the one on the creamy horse. Just then the wind whipped open the leader's gray coat. Zacks saw the flash of a gold badge on his shirt. *Edson!* It was him, by cracky!

Zacks squeezed the trigger. The rifle bucked against his shoulder. The gray-coated man tumbled off the creamy horse. Zacks managed a grin, pain-racked but full of satisfaction. Quickly he levered another round into the chamber, aimed . . . and fired again. He had to work fast, he had to get as many of them as he could while they were bunched up down there in the bottom of the dip.

Zacks's rifle cracked a third time and another of the posse fell from his horse.

Shouts and curses rose from the dip. Men and horses scattered, scrambling over one another to get out of there. Zacks fired again. He saw the big creamy horse racing away riderless up out of the dip.

Ben Zacks started to laugh. Then he coughed, coughing up blood. His face contorted in pain as he hunched up coughing. But then the coughing fit passed and his face went calm as he stretched his body back into the prone firing position.

Bill Edson hit the ground cursing. He had ridden right into it, like a damn fool greenhorn. Shots cracked out from the rocks up on top of the rise. He should have had the trail experience to have spotted those rocks as a likely

41

place for an ambush. He had seen them up on top of the rise, but they hadn't registered significantly in his mind. It *should* have registered when the gang rode by them, close enough to scramble into the rocks and open fire from cover.

Momentarily winded but his head clear, Edson rolled over onto his stomach and lifted his head to look around. Two more shots had sounded after the one that had knocked him from his saddle. Two of his men had come off their horses, and he himself was wounded. He had a burning feeling high up on the right side of his chest, along the rib cage. It hurt, but not a hell of a lot.

"Scatter!" he heard one of his posse shout. He heard a lot of other shouts as well, curses mostly. The pounding of hoofs and the frightened whinnying of horses rang in his ears. Dust swirled up all around him. Then there was a deafening burst of gunfire, the men in his posse shooting back with rifles and revolvers as they whirled their horses around and around.

Edson scrambled to his feet. He had to get the hell out of there!

He looked around for his horse, but he couldn't see it amid all the confusion. The next thing, he felt a strong hand tighten around his left arm. Almost at the same time another hand caught him around his right arm. It hurt his chest along the rib cage, but he knew the wound he had was little more than a graze. An instant later he felt himself being lifted up and his feet cleared the ground. It was then that he realized two of his men had picked him up, one on each side, and were galloping with him back up the slope, up out of the dip.

Throughout the wild dash, which lasted no longer than a minute, Bill Edson expected a bullet from the rifleman in the rocks to smash into his back, or to knock one of his rescuers off his horse, and himself to be caught under flying hoofs. But that didn't happen. Ground blurred quickly by beneath him. He seemed to be bouncing up and down with the movement of men and horses, to be swaying dangerously from side to side. But the next thing he knew he was back on the ground, prairie grass beneath the high heels of his spurred boots. He was safe—*they* were safe, on the other side of the slope they had galloped down moments before.

Taking their rifles, his men threw themselves down on the ground just below the top of the slope. Carefully they pushed their rifle barrels over the top and peered along their sights.

"Seems like there's just one of 'em holed up in them rocks, Marshal," one of his men said, pointing to the rocks on the far side of the dip.

"You all right, Bill?" another asked.

"Yeah," Edson nodded. "I'm all right. Anyone else hit?"

"Lew West and Dan Patrick are hit. They're still down there in the bottom of that dip. They don't seem to be movin' none."

Edson dropped to his stomach and crawled to the edge of the slope to look down into the dip below. Rifles barked in his ears as the posse opened up at the rocks on top of the rise opposite. There was no answering fire from the rocks. Edson stuck his head over the lip of the slope and peered down into the bottom of the dip. He could see the still bodies of two of his men down there. A saddled horse, its reins hanging down over its head, stood near one of the bodies, not knowing what to do. Edson couldn't see his own light bay.

"Goddamn it!" he cursed again. Lew West and Dan Patrick down there dead or badly wounded because of him. Because he had been too eager to catch up with Oates and his gang before dark, too damn blind to recognize the potential for ambush from those rocks over there.

"Goddamn you, Oates!" Edson muttered, his brows drawing tight together in an angry frown as he stared across at the rocks. "That's two more you'll pay for."

The rifle fire continued for two or three minutes, then eased off. Their hats jammed low over their heads, the posse peered across at the rocks.

43

"Looks like we could've got him, Marshal. He ain't shootin' back."

"Who's goin' to go over there and take a look?" asked one of the men, lifting a hand to push his hat back off his head.

"If anyone goes," Bill Edson said, his voice ringing out above the others, asserting his leadership, "it'll be me. I got you boys into this. If I'd been a bit more wide awake—"

Something whipped through the air, sending one of the posse's hats flying, followed by the crack of a rifle from among the rocks on the far rise. Edson saw the puff of smoke come from the rocks a split second before he heard the shot.

"Get your head down," he shouted. "He's still shooting."

The men flattened themselves against the earth. Three more shots sounded from the rocks.

Edson cocked an ear and listened. "Still sounds like only one rifle over there," he remarked to the man next to him. "Must be Zacks. He's wounded, so they left him behind to hold us up while the others make a dash for the Canadian border."

There was an added urgency now. Edson turned his head and looked at the sun. It was a long way over to the west. There was another hour of daylight. No more. With every passing minute, Oates and the other two would be getting farther away. He had to get after them, goddamn it! But as long as Zacks was holed up in those rocks, they couldn't get down into that dip and cross.

He scanned the surrounding countryside. The posse could mount up and detour around the rocks, keeping out of the range of Zacks's rifle. They could go on after the other three and come back and pick up Zacks later. Wounded, Zacks wouldn't get far. But if they did that, Edson reckoned, he would have to leave the bodies of West and Patrick down in the dip. He didn't want to do that. He didn't want to leave them for the prairie wolves. Besides, one of them might still be alive.

44

While the posse returned Zacks's fire, Edson contemplated the alternative course. That was to split the posse, leaving four men to try to take Zacks. Two of them could stay where they were while the other two could detour around and come at the rocks from behind, forcing Zacks to fire on two sides, front and back. While they were doing that, he could take the remainder of the posse—five men—on after Oates and the other two.

That would leave six of them to apprehend Oates, the Frenchman, and Lone Man. Two to one. Apprehend them or shoot it out. Take 'em—dead or alive!

He thought about the two alternatives for a moment before rejecting the second one. He needed the full posse, or what was left of it—ten men, himself included. With the Indian to guide him, Oates had a chance of getting away in the dark. Edson doubted that he'd be able to overtake them before nightfall now, even with fresh horses. He would need the posse to spread out and search for them come first light.

He tapped the shoulder of the man next to him. "Bob, you and Tom and one of the others keep up a fire on those rocks. I'll take the rest of the boys and mount up. We'll ride off to the east, swing around out of range of Zacks's rifle and come in behind him. That'll force him to fire frontwise and backwards. We'll have a better chance of picking him off that way. As soon as we've got rid of him, we'll resume the chase after Oates and the other two."

The sun came up in a burst of pink in the big sky over northern Montana. Oates, Lone Man, and the Frenchman pushed their tired horses relentlessly northward. All around them the country was much the same as the day before. They might just as well have been back near Fort Turner, apart from a butte here, a different-shaped hill there, and a long coulee coming up ahead of them to the northwest. But they had been riding nonstop since galloping out of Fort Turner the previous high noon. They were tired and hungry, and so were their horses. They needed rest, but they didn't dare stop.

Oates still kept looking back over his shoulder, expecting to see the grim specter of the posse tenaciously pursuing them. The Canadian border was somewhere up ahead, but the horses felt like they would give out anytime now.

They had heard the rifle shots late yesterday afternoon, when Zacks opened up on the posse. The shooting had lasted longer than Oates had expected. It had lasted until dark. It had filled him with a grudging respect for Ben. Oates hadn't thought the "old man" had it in him. They had always used him as a lookout or for a backup rather than to stage the actual holdups. Zacks had lacked flair, the aggressive instinct of the holdup man.

As he legged his horse on, Oates turned in his saddle and looked back over his shoulder again. He couldn't help it. He couldn't resist the urge.

Was that dust back there? Christ! It looked like it.

How many were left in the posse? How many had Zacks been able to knock off? Four? Maybe five? Hardly likely any more. That could mean there might only be eight coming after them.

"Lone?" Oates snapped, his voice raw and edgy.

The Indian looked over at Oates.

Oates pointed behind him. "Is that dust I see comin' up behind us? It looks like it, but my eyes are damn tired. Mebbe I'm seein' things."

Without slowing his horse, Lone Man turned his head and scrutinized the rolling prairie behind them.

"Well, is it?" Oates demanded impatiently.

The Indian nodded, but didn't speak.

"How far behind is it?"

"Five, six mile."

"Goddamn it! It must be Edson." Oates glared hotly at the Indian. "How far are we from that goddamn border?"

"Not far."

"If we can see that posse's dust, they can see our'n,"

46

Oates said anxiously.

The Indian raised an arm and pointed to the coulee half a mile ahead. "We go down there. No see dust."

Lone Man had led them down into a coulee the previous evening. That was how they had eluded the posse in the dark. At sunup, the posse had had to lose time trying to pick up their trail again. But it looked like Edson and his men had found it, if that dust cloud was any indication.

They reached the entrance to the coulee. Lone Man glanced inquiringly at Oates. Oates nodded and the Indian rode his horse down into it, Oates and the Frenchman following.

The coulee ran deeper as they rode along it. It was like a long ravine, with a narrow bottom about ten feet wide and towering sides that rose steeply up to the prairie above. In places thick dry brush covered the bottom and ran partway up the sides, and the horses had to pick their way around it. But it afforded them some cover.

Once they got through the dry brush, they pushed the tired horses along at a trot, occasionally forcing them into a slow canter for short distances in their urge to escape the pursuing posse. Oates kept craning his neck to peer up at the blue sky above the coulee sides, half expecting to see heads peering down at them.

They rode single file, no one speaking. There were no sounds other than the movement of the horses, the creak of saddle leather, and the occasional jingle of a spur rowel or the click of a bit.

They had been riding for an hour when the morning stillness was shattered by sudden laughter.

It was Lone Man, riding in the lead. He sat back on his horse, his body shaking with laughter.

The sudden laughter startled Oates. "What's the matter with you, you goddamn fool?" he shouted at Lone Man irritably. "Shut your goddamn mouth! You want that posse to hear you?"

But Lone Man continued laughing, pointing to a stunted, lopsided pine tree growing out of the side of the coulee halfway up.

Oates stared up at it. "What the hell's so goddamn funny about that?"

"It mark medicine line," Lone Man said. "We crossed medicine line. This white woman's country."

"You sure?"

"Me sure. Hunt wapiti down here many time. We crossed medicine line. In white woman's country now."

CHAPTER 5

"Looks like they went down along that coulee, Marshal," one of the riders said, pointing at the mouth of the coulee.

Bill Edson sat the saddle of his light bay, looking down into the coulee. Pete Cato was one of the best trackers in the country. He had the eyes of an Indian, which was natural enough, seeing as how his mother was a full-blooded Crow. If he said Oates and the other two had gone down into the coulee, that was good enough for Bill Edson. It figured. That'd be where Lone Man would take them.

Standing in his stirrups, Edson peered at the rolling prairie ahead. Almost without a doubt, they would continue along the coulee and come out the other end. How far did the coulee run? From his stirrups, it looked like several miles.

There were nine of them in the posse now. He'd left one man behind to bury Zacks and the bodies of Lew West and Dan Patrick while the rest of them pushed on. They had lost time trying to pick up the outlaws' trail once the sun came up, but once they had found it, they'd ridden on with all speed.

Edson sat back down in his saddle. "Bob," he said to one of the posse, "you and a couple of the others stay here and watch, just on the off chance those polecats decide to double back and come out again. I'll push on with the others along the top of the coulee and try and overtake 'em. Maybe we can get to the other end before they come out. We'll make better time ridin' along the top than they can make down below."

"Providin' thet coulee don't branch off, splittin' into two coulees a little further along," Bob said.

Edson nodded. "We'll have to take that chance. If we hear your guns, we'll come back a'gallopin'."

A moment later they rode on, cantering along the edge of the coulee, following it northwest. Edson had found his horse wandering around the prairie a short distance from the rock pile where Ben Zacks had holed up. He was glad to be back on the big light bay. He could feel the power beneath him as he sat the rocking-saddle.

As they rode, they reined their horses over to the edge of the coulee two or three times and peered down into the recesses below. But the sides were too steep and there were outjuttings here and there, preventing them from seeing all the way to the bottom.

Some distance off to the north stretched a long green rise, extending west as far as the eye could see. An unsettling feeling began to stir within Edson at the sight of it. Although he had never been in that part of the country before, he knew there were forested hills on the Canada side of the line. They were close to the Canadian border, close to the end of his jurisdiction. But how close?

The answer became all too apparent two miles farther on . . . a small stone cairn standing on the grassed prairie a short distance ahead.

When he reached the cairn he drew rein and sat staring grim-faced down at it. Wordlessly he read the inscribed words facing him. *U.S. Territory.*

He legged his horse a few feet beyond the cairn, reined the light bay around, and read the words on the north side. *British Possession.*

They had reached the Canada line.

So had Oates and his gang. The coulee continued on

past it, continued on northwest.

They all reined their horses around the cairn as they sat staring down, reading the words or simply looking at it.

"Well, what now, Marshal?" someone asked.

Bill Edson didn't answer right away. Instead he reached into his coat pocket and pulled out the makings. Sitting slump-shouldered in his saddle, he rolled a cigarette.

No one else spoke. A silence spread across the six men, a gloom, a sense of deflation, a feeling of failure.

Edson stuck his cigarette between his lips, leaned over and struck a match on the heel of his boot, then cupped a hand around it as he thrust the end of the cigarette into the dancing flame. Clouds of blue smoke rose around him and were quickly whipped away by the prairie wind.

Using knee and rein, Edson turned his horse around until his narrowed blue eyes were staring across into Canada.

At last he spoke.

"You boys go on back home. I'll give you all chits. You can turn 'em in to the United States Marshal's office at Helena and draw what's due you."

Silence followed his words for a minute or two, until someone said, "You don't sound like you're a'comin' with us, Bill. What're you plannin' on doin'?"

Still staring off into Canada, Edson said, "I'm going on after Oates."

"Alone?"

Edson nodded. "That's right."

A chorus of protests followed.

"You cain't do thet."

"We're goin' with you, Bill."

"Yeah, even if you don't pay us, we're still goin' with you. We ain't lettin' you face Oates and them other two alone."

Bill Edson reined his horse around to face them. Their loyalty touched him and he felt a lump in his throat. "I appreciate your offers, fellers. I really do. You've all followed me through a lot of hard riding these last weeks and I hate to see us split up. The thing is, I can't take a posse of armed men across the border into a friendly country. It's against government policy. Washington would have my guts."

"But, you goin' alone? That's plumb crazy, Marshal. One man agin them three!"

Edson grinned. "I don't figger on doing it alone. I'll call in at the nearest Mounted Police outpost and see if they'll lend me two or three men."

Lone Man led them up out of the coulee where it ended in a long tongue of heavy timber. The timber was so heavy that it cut out most of the sunlight for the last half mile and Oates reckoned it could almost have been getting on to nightfall, except that he knew damn well it was still the middle of the day.

Lone Man was grinning as he legged his horse through the thick stands of jack pine. He was pleased with himself. They had beaten the posse. *He* had beaten the posse. No one would find them in this thick timber.

They let their horses pick their way through the trees, reining them around deadfall here and there. They could afford to relax, they could afford to let the horses plod along slowly.

Oates thought they could be lost, except that the Indian led the way through the trees without hesitation. He seemed to know where he was going.

Riding behind the other two, the Frenchman felt relief at having evaded the posse, at having found sanctuary in Canadian territory. But for how long?

After they had been riding through the timber for what seemed a long time, they emerged into a little glade with a lake in the center and pine trees all around it. Above the spear tops of the pines, they could see forested hills rising in the distance off to the northwest.

They made camp beside the lake, unsaddling their horses and hobbling them in the long grass. But they kept their rifles handy.

They slept the sleep of exhausted men, taking it in

turns to guard their camp. But they were so tired that even the one on guard slept, unable to stay awake.

Toward evening they dug a pit in the ground among the pines and lined it with stones. Then they tied the tops of the trees together overhead to diffuse any smoke that might be visible to curious eyes in the gathering dusk and built a fire. Sunken into the ground, its flickering flames were not visible beyond a few feet. Famished, they sat around it, their mouths watering as they fried the last of a slab of salted pork and boiled water to make rice and coffee.

It wasn't until they had finished eating and sat around the fire drinking coffee and smoking that they began discussing what they would do now that they had escaped into Canadian territory.

"Do you think it was such a good idea coming up to this country, Cess?" the Frenchman asked. "I 'ave 'eard there is a force of redcoats on this side of the border—mounted gendarmes. Perhaps the American government will ask them to look for us."

Oates said, "Them redcoats have got their hands full just makin' sure Sitting Bull's Sioux don't go back on the warpath now that they're up on this side of the line. They won't have time to come lookin' for us."

"You come with me to my people's camp," Lone Man said. "We stay there for winter."

Staring into the fire, Oates was silent for a moment as he considered what the Indian had said. Finally he shook his head. "No. I don't think that's such a good idea. I reckon we ought to split up. Three of us together just could draw a bit o' notice. We split up, we got a better chance . . . just in case the government does ask the redcoats to keep an eye out for us, like Frenchy says. No point temptin' trouble."

"Then, where will we go?"

"I reckon I'll ride north a bit, then west . . . to the Cypress Hills. There's good huntin' there. I can lay in a supply of meat before winter sets in, and there's a tradin' post I know of where I can get flour, coffee, and tobacco and such, and ride out until spring. At least, that tradin' post used to be there five years ago."

Oates looked across the fire at the Indian. "Lone, you can go stay with your people, like you said." Then he looked at the Frenchman. "As for you, Frenchy, the best thing you can do is ride east. There's some half-breed settlements over near a place called Wood Mountain. They're buffalo hunters . . . half-French, half-Indian." He looked back at the Indian. "Ain't that right, Lone?"

Lone Man nodded, his tall black hat bobbing with the movement. "The *metis*. You can ride north with me a little. I point out Wood Mountain . . . show you way. You find place with them. You speak their talk."

A long, low log building stood on grassland just beyond a stand of timber. A wisp of smoke curled lazily upwards from a stone chimney. Sitting straight-backed on his saddle, the lone scarlet rider trotted his horse toward it.

His face was long, lantern-jawed, and as hard as a slab of rock, with alert gray eyes that were just as hard. His nose had been broken at least twice. He was a lean six-footer, in his early thirties. In tight-fitting scarlet tunic and small, round blue and yellow pillbox cap tilted forward over his right eyebrow, Constable Freddie "Cockney" Jenkins looked like a soldier.

He reined to in front of the cabin and swung down from his saddle. Above the door was nailed a sign with painted words reading *Trading Post*. Freddie pushed open the door and sauntered inside, his spurs jingling on his polished boots as he moved.

Inside was a low-ceilinged room with a counter running along the far side and stocked shelves lining the wall. Behind the counter an open door showed a room with the furnishings of a living room. Drawn by the sound of Freddie's footsteps, a wiry, baldheaded man stepped through the door and stood behind the counter. He scowled the instant he saw Freddie's uniform, glaring at him with undisguised hostility.

"What d' you want? The last time you were here, you stole damn near half my stock, including my horses and wagon."

Freddie glared back at him with the same sort of look. "I'm not 'ere on a bleedin' social visit," he replied, belligerence rising in his voice. "And I didn't steal anything. I requisitioned that stuff in the name of the Queen. It was for a bleedin' 'umanitarian cause, for some Indians that ad been cut up in a fight. There was women and children among them."

Freddie's nasal accent left no doubt as to his London origin, hence his nickname "Cockney," although Ed Gregory probably wouldn't have recognized the difference.

"Goddamn Indians," Ed Gregory growled.

"Anyway, you got paid fair and square for it, so what are you bellyachin' for? And speakin' of Indians, that's why I'm 'ere." Pulling off a white gauntlet, Freddie unbuttoned one of the brass buttons on his scarlet tunic, reached inside, and pulled out a folded sheet of paper. He unfolded it and handed it to the trader.

Ed Gregory looked at it. "What's this?"

"A notice from Sergeant MacGregor. Major Walsh has issued an order that says all white traders, missionaries, and everyone else other than an Indian is prohibited from enterin' any Sioux camp for any reason at all." Freddie grinned. "That means you."

Ed Gregory's scowl deepened. "He ain't got no right to do that."

"Just try disobeyin' his order, cock, and you'll bleedin' well see what right 'e's got."

"That's suppressin' free trade!"

Freddie turned to go. His hand on the door, he looked back over his shoulder at the trader. "You can trade with em all you like as long as you don't go into their camps."

With that, Freddie stepped out of the cabin, mounted up, and headed back toward Pine Butte.

He had ridden only three miles when a rifle shot cracked out from somewhere behind him. He reined to and twisted in his saddle, looking behind him.

Riding toward him at a canter was a man on a light bay horse. The man was waving an arm as he rode. He was riding from the south, from the direction of Montana. He was about half a mile away. Freddie waited for him.

"Howdy," drawled the rider, a tall man with a wide black mustache and direct blue eyes looking at him from beneath a wide-brimmed, low-crowned gray hat. "Saw your red coat from a way off. Sure stands out bright. You a soldier, or one of those new mounted police I've heard tell about?"

Freddie eyed him curiously. "North West Mounted Police, but if there's any soldierin' to be done, we do it. Isn't anyone else."

William James Edson grinned. "Then you're just the man I'm looking for. I'm a deputy United States marshal." He pulled open his gray coat to reveal the gold badge on his shirt. "I've just come up to your country looking for three wanted men from down below the border. I'd sure appreciate any help you boys can give me to round 'em up."

"You'll 'ave to talk to Sar'nt MacGregor about that. He's in charge of the detachment at Pine Butte."

"Where would I find him?"

Freddie inclined his head in the direction he had been riding. "Up north a bit, about seven miles. You can ride with me. I'm goin' back there now."

"Obliged."

Bill Edson couldn't take his eyes off Freddie's scarlet tunic, vivid against the brown grass of the rolling hills and the pines across the river. He had never seen anything as bright, anything as brilliantly ablaze. And the small round pillbox cap, dark blue with a yellow band around it, perched at a rakish angle over his right eyebrow and held on his head by a thin patent leather strap around the point of his chin. Aware of the tall man's attention, Freddie started fidgeting with his reins as he rode. When he heard the tall man chuckle, Freddie snapped his head

56

sideways and glared.

"What's so bleedin' funny?"

Smiling, Bill Edson raised a hand, palm outward, "No offense meant, but that little cap, it don't cover much of your head. It wouldn't shade your eyes from the sun none, and it wouldn't keep rain off your head."

Freddie grunted. "We got white 'elmets for the sun, and as for rain it don't do much of that around 'ere."

As they rode, Freddie pointed to a tall butte rising out of the rolling hills to the north. "That's Pine Butte. See them pines up on top? That's 'ow it got its name. The outpost is just this side of it."

Bill Edson had seen the butte from a long way back. You couldn't miss it. It towered above everything else for miles around and must have been four hundred feet high, but otherwise he hadn't paid it any particular attention.

A few miles later they rode over a rise and saw, half a mile away, the foot of the butte. A hundred yards from it stood three log buildings. The Union Jack floated above them from the top of a flagpole. A short distance to the east flowed a wide but shallow river with low banks that allowed for easy fording.

"There's the outpost," Freddie said as they rode down toward the log buildings.

He led them to the larger of the three buildings. "That's the barracks and the sar'nt's office. The other two is the stables and the store shed."

Hands on hips, Sergeant MacGregor stood framed in the doorway as they reined to in front of the building. He gave Edson a quick, appraising look.

"This 'ere is an American marshal, Sar'nt," Freddie said as he slid his Snider-Enfield carbine from the saddle bucket behind his right leg and swung down from his saddle.

MacGregor stepped out of the building and extended his hand to Edson as the American dismounted. "I'm Sergeant MacGregor. I'm in charge here."

Edson took the sergeant's hand and they shook. "Bill Edson, Sergeant. Deputy United States marshal. I've got warrants for the arrest of three United States criminals who've just crossed over into your country. I'd sure appreciate your help in rounding them up."

"Well, if you'd like to unsaddle your horse and give it a wee bit of a rest, you're welcome to use our stables. We have extra stalls and we can spare some feed. Then we can sit doon and talk about it."

Fifteen minutes later Edson was seated at a table that Sergeant MacGregor used as a desk. On the table he laid his credentials as a deputy United States marshal, together with warrants for the arrests of Ceston Parker Oates, Lone Man, and Henri Foucade, and *Wanted* posters showing pictures of what the three men looked like.

"These posters are a year old," Edson was saying to an attentive Sergeant MacGregor, who sat on the other side of the table puffing away at his pipe. "It says here that Oates is forty-two. Well, he's forty-three now, but I don't reckon he's changed much since that picture and that description was put down there. That's a good likeness of him, from what I hear. I've never been that close to him, but I've been following him for six months now. That scar down the side of his face, it don't go away. Beard won't grow over it.

"Oates is the most dangerous of the three. Wears two guns, Colt forty-fours. There's a five-thousand-dollar reward for him, dead or alive. Charges of murder, robbery. He's seen lots of violence and it don't bother him none. Fact is, he thrives on it. Comes from Kansas. Fought with the Kansas irregulars, the Red Legs, during the war along the Kansas-Missouri border and the War Between the States. That's where he learned his trade.

"The other two aren't much improvement. Lone Man— full name's Lonesome Young Man, I believe—he's an Indian from one of your tribes. He's thirty-three, thirty-four, looks like an Indian but dresses like a breed. He's also wanted for murder and bank robbery. Price on his head of three thousand dollars—dead or alive. Cold-blooded killer. Likes shootin' people down, particularly bank tellers. Even been known to laugh while doin' it.

"The third one is Henri Foucade, a Frenchman, age thirty-four. Reward of three thousand dollars—dead or alive. Same kind of offenses as the other two. Don't know much about him. Hasn't done as much killing, and he usually does it in self-defense. But he's been implicated with the other two, taken part in the same holdups, so as far as the law's concerned he's just as guilty."

Sergeant MacGregor struck another match and held it to his pipe. The pungent aroma of his pipe tobacco filled the room. "And you've reason," he said between puffs, "to believe the three of them hae crossed the border into the North West Territories?"

Edson nodded. "They've been heading north for a long time. Posse and me tracked 'em into a coulee. It ran across the line. International law being what it is, I had to leave the posse behind. When I got to the other end of the coulee, I found it came out into thick timber and I lost Oates and the other two. They're up here, all right. I reckon they plan on holing up in your territory for the winter."

Sergeant MacGregor took the pipe from his mouth. "I'll be glad to do whatever we can to round up those three outlaws. Hae you any idea where they might 'hole up,' as you put it?"

Edson nodded again. "Lone Man is a Minnetaree, a tribe somewheres north in your country. I reckon the three of them will head up to the Minnetaree camp. They'd likely see that as a safe place to be."

Segeant MacGregor looked up at the door to the next room and shouted. "Freddie!"

Spurs jingling, Freddie sauntered in from the barrack room. "Sar'nt?"

"Do you know any Minnetarees in the area, Freddie?"

Freddie nodded. "There's Walkin' Thunder's lot, camped about two days' ride to the north." He walked over to a map of the North West Territories on the log wall behind Sergeant MacGregor, peered at it for a moment, then jabbed a forefinger at it. "About there. It's

59

pretty flat up there except for a bleedin' long ridge. They used to be camped just over the ridge and down by a river . . . there it is, you can see it on the map . . . the Ghost River. It's a good spot for an Indian camp, so they're probably still there."

Sergeant MacGregor turned his head to look at the map. Then he looked up at Freddie. "You know this Walking Thunder, Freddie? Would his camp be a likely place for a Minnetaree and two American criminals to hide oot for the winter?"

"Yeah, it'd be a likely place. I reckon Walkin' Thunder would accommodate 'em."

Edson said, "If you can spare me a couple of your men for a week, I'll go up there and round those three up, then haul them off back across the line into Montana before they can make any trouble for you up here."

"I can nae spare you a couple of men, Mister Edson. There's just the two of us—Freddie and me—here, and a *metis* scout."

Edson looked surprised. "Just the two of you? I sort of thought you'd have at least ten men."

MacGregor laughed. "There were five men here. I'm just here temporarily, relieving Sergeant Cavannagh, the regular NCO in charge. The other three constables who used to be here were transferred elsewhere, and there's only Freddie and the scout left. But Constable Jenkins and I will give you whatever help we can. We'll go with you to Walking Thunder's camp and make the arrests if the three wanted men are there. But I canna let y' take them back to Montana with you. Constable Jenkins and I will hae to escort them to Fort Walsh, where they'll be held in the Mounted Police guardroom for proper legal proceedings."

Edson frowned. "I'd sort of figured on taking them straight back to Montana with me, Sergeant, and saving on a whole heap of fuss and bother."

Sergeant MacGregor shook his head. "I'm afraid we canna do that, Mister Edson. You'll hae to make legal application through the courts up here in the Territories.

It's called extradition, I believe."

"How long will that take?"

MacGregor shrugged. "I dinna rightly know. Could be several months, communication facilities being what they are out here. I think Washington has to get in touch with Ottawa, then Ottawa—has to appoint legal counsel and notify Fort Walsh. Then there has to be the proper legal hearing, like a court of law. It's a wee bit involved, I hae to admit, but it's the law and we hae to abide by it."

Bill Edson's mouth went into a tight line beneath his wide black mustache.

"Anyway," MacGregor continued, placing both hands on the table as he was about to rise, "we'll hae ourselve a bite to eat, then Freddie and I will saddle up and ride with you to Walking Thunder's camp. If those three wanted men are there, we'll take them into custody."

MacGregor had just finished speaking when the sound of galloping hoofs drew his eyes to the door. He remained on his chair, waiting as the sound grew louder. Freddie and Bill Edson also turned their heads toward the door.

Presently a black-bearded man wearing buckskin, Indian moccasins, and a battered, floppy-brimmed hat clattered up to the building. Jumping down from his cayuse, he rushed in through the front door. Around his waist he wore a Mounted Police gun belt.

"Hey, *mon* Sergeant," the *metis* exclaimed breathlessly. "Beeg trouble over at War Bonnet's camp. The Sioux, t'ey catch a preacher an' 'is daughter in t'eir camp. Sioux t'ink t'ey spying on t'em for American army. Sioux holding t'em prisoner. Younger braves, t'ey wan' kill t'em."

Sergeant MacGregor jumped up from the table with such force that his chair toppled backwards. "Did you say a preacher *and* his daughter? A missionary?"

The *metis* nodded his head excitedly. *"Oui! Oui, mon* Sergeant."

His face dark with rage, the big Scot smashed his fist down on the table. Papers bounced and flew everywhere. *"By God!* The fool! The bluidy, ignorant fool! He assured me he was going back to Fort Benton, damn him!"

Edson glanced at Freddie, unspoken questions in his eyes.

Freddie leaned forward and whispered. "That's Prefontaine, our scout."

MacGregor reached for his pillbox and gun belt hanging from a peg on the wall. Buckling the belt around his waist, he snapped an order at Freddie. "Grab your carbine and saddle up, Freddie."

He glanced at the American lawman. "Constable Jenkins and I hae to ride over to that Sioux camp immediately. Stay here while we're gone. We should be back sometime tomorrow. Feel free to stretch oot on one of the bunks in the barrack room next door. Help yourself to anything y' fancy to eat. When we get back, we'll ride north to Walking Thunder's camp and look for those three wanted men."

The next moment, carbine in his hand, Sergeant MacGregor ran out the door after Freddie Jenkins toward the stables.

CHAPTER 6

Deputy U.S. Marshal Bill Edson stood in the doorway of the log building watching the two Mounted Policemen and their *metis* scout ride away from the outpost. They splashed across the river and rode over broken prairie on the far side. He watched until their scarlet tunics were no more than two bright red dabs in the distance.

He turned inside and strolled thoughtfully across the floor to Sergeant MacGregor's table. Sitting on one corner, a leg hanging over the edge, spurred boot swinging backwards and forwards, he reached into his coat pocket and pulled out tobacco and papers. As he built a smoke, he let his mind toss around the conversation he had had with Sergeant MacGregor. It left him disturbed.

He had intended getting the Mounted Police to help him round up Oates, Lone Man, and the Frenchman, expecting them to escort him and his three prisoners back to the border. From there he would have taken them, securely manacled, to the closest lawman's office and, with a couple of sheriff's deputies to ride shotgun, on to a territorial or federal prison. He hadn't counted on the Mounted Police wanting to hold his prisoners while he applied for extradition. That seemed like a hell of a lot of bother and expense, and a waste of time, when he should be able to simply haul them back across the line into Montana. He hadn't counted on returning empty-handed.

Striking a match, he lit his cigarette and dropped the match into an ashtray beside MacGregor's still-warm pipe. He sat on the corner of the table a moment longer, drawing on his cigarette. Presently he stood and stepped over to the map on the log wall and peered at it. As he did so, he floated Constable Jenkins's words through his thoughts, looking for the spot on the map the constable had pointed to. The Ghost River, he had said . . . there it was. Edson put his finger on the spot on the map, then drew an imaginary line back down between the Cypress Hills on the left—the west—and Wood Mountain on the right—the east. He drew the imaginary line down until he came to a flagged pin stuck into the map. Beside the flagged pin were the words *Pine Butte*.

Bill Edson took another draw on his cigarette as he studied the map a moment longer. No, he hadn't counted on going back home empty-handed.

The Sioux camp stretched out on the prairie no more than half a mile in front of Sergeant MacGregor, Constable Jenkins, and Scout Prefontaine as they trotted their horses across the high-grassed ground. A sea of tanned buffalo-hide tepees, with dozens of thin columns of smoke rising into the fading blue of the late afternoon sky. The two red-coated Mounted Policemen sat their saddles with the same stiff-backed military bearing and outward imperturbability that characterized everything they did. To them it mattered not in the slightest that in this camp were several hundred *Ogalala* Sioux warriors, the dreaded Tigers of the Plains, battle-flushed victors of the Custer battle on the Little Big Horn, the most warlike Indians on the northern plains. It mattered not in the slightest to these two redcoats because, in the white Queen's country, theirs was a God-given right.

Yet it mattered to Jules Prefontaine, their half-French, half-Cree *metis* scout. A mere mortal all too familiar with the unbridled ferocity of the Sioux, he was unprotected by the mystique of the fabled scarlet tunic, by the discipline of the small but already famous corps of Scarlet Riders that imbued officers and men with steadiness and the rigid belief that duty well done, whatever the hardships and danger, was of the highest order of virtue. Theirs was an almost fanatical belief, something akin to an Eastern religion that promised its followers everlasting life in the Hereafter. Sergeant MacGregor and Constable Jenkins showed absolutely no fear as they rode into this camp of fierce, white-hating savages, but Jules Prefontaine shook until his teeth chattered.

Jules had never made any pretense of being a brave man, and he had been nowhere near the Sioux camp when he learned of the capture of the white preacher and his daughter. It had been a Sioux maiden, Morning Child, daughter of the great Sioux fighting chief War Bonnet, who had told him about them. Taught English by a white priest who had lived among the Sioux years before, Morning Child understood the ways and motivation of white missionaries. She had become concerned over their fate if hotheaded young braves had their way, and she had been on her way to the Mounted Police outpost at Pine Butte when she saw the *metis* scout out on the prairie hunting meat for the detachment, and told him what had happened.

From his earliest days growing up among the *metis* buffalo hunters of the plains, long before he hired on as a scout with the Mounted Police, Jules had seen at first hand the result of Sioux attacks on white and *metis* settlements. He had seen the hapless victims of Sioux scalpings, the quivering crimson messes left by those sharp, broad-bladed knives. He knew what it was like to be under attack by a Sioux war party. Yet, regardless of the number of times he had encountered the Sioux, he had never lost his fear of them.

Looking to their front as they jogged up and down on their saddles, Sergeant MacGregor and Freddie Jenkins saw the tepees grow larger as they rode closer. They were less than a quarter of a mile from the camp when dozens of mounted warriors suddenly appeared between the tepees, blocking access to the camp. They were big men, the *Ogalala* warriors, each one holding a rifle. They sat motionless, watching the two approaching redcoats and the buckskin-clad *metis*.

Jules started muttering a prayer.

"Stop nattering, Jules, for Christ's sake," Sergeant MacGregor said without turning his head. "If you had nae wanted to come on this little ride, you shouldna told me about the preacher and his daughter."

Jules fell silent.

"Prefontaine's scared shitless, ain't 'e, Sar'nt," Freddie, riding at MacGregor's left, cracked out of the side of his mouth.

Still looking straight ahead, MacGregor replied, "He may be scared, but he's nae a shirker."

MacGregor turned to say something to Jules, riding beside him on his right, when he spotted something off to the far right of the line of tepees. A high-topped wagon and two canvas tents. Abruptly he wheeled his horse and legged it into a canter toward them. Freddie and Jules followed.

Without any change of expression on their faces, the mounted warriors watched them cantering off to their front.

When they reached the two tents, MacGregor reined to and swung down from his saddle. Handing his reins to Freddie, he sauntered across the grass and stepped into the first tent. The inside looked as though a cyclone had struck. Suitcases and boxes had been torn open, and clothing, bibles, books, and everything else strewn all over the grass floor. In the second tent it was the same, except that the clothing belonged to a woman, with a woman's personal toiletries as well as sketching pad and several pencils lying in the grass.

From the tents MacGregor walked over to the wagon. The team of horses wasn't there. Probably among the camp's horse herd, MacGregor guessed. He peered into the wagon. The interior was the same as inside the two tents. There was more clothing, a case of bibles, books, a

66

volume of verse, some pictures, and food, all scattered around.

Taking his reins from Freddie, MacGregor swung himself back up onto his saddle and reined his horse around. The next instant the three of them were riding back toward the Sioux camp, some seventy yards away.

Warriors gathered at the edge of the camp, moving their ponies out in front of the outer row of tepees. Straight-backed, MacGregor rode directly toward them, his head high, eyes looking straight ahead. Freddie rode beside him. Jules legged his short-stepping cayuse along behind them.

When the two redcoats were no more than five yards away, the warriors pulled their ponies aside and made way. MacGregor rode through them as if they weren't there. He guided his horse toward the center of the camp, remembering where the big ceremonial lodge stood. He had been in War Bonnet's camp twice before, once with Major Walsh and once with Sergeant Cavannagh. He remembered that War Bonnet's tepee stood beside the ceremonial lodge.

Indian women and children stood in front of tepees watching the two redcoats and the *metis* ride by. The outward calmness that characterized the two redcoats was contrasted by the manner of the plainly nervous mixed-blood riding behind them, whose head constantly turned from side to side, restless black eyes darting everywhere. But the two redcoats, although looking straight ahead, missed little. They had both been in enough Indian camps to recognize the undercurrent of excitement, of disturbed unease, running through the Sioux camp. The atmosphere was distinctly different from the last time MacGregor had been there. The camp grew noisy as they trotted their horses among the tepees . . . babbling voices, shouts, yapping dogs, and rifle shots as bullets whistled upwards into the sky. MacGregor couldn't tell whether the shouts were jeers, but he didn't worry about them enough to ask Jules for a translation. He had a duty to carry out, and he intended carrying it out regardless of the mood of the Sioux.

MacGregor could see the conical top of the big ceremonial lodge standing above the tops of the other tepees, and he rode toward it.

A moment later they reached the center of the camp. The sight that met MacGregor's eyes caused him to raise an eyebrow, but no other expression crossed his face. There must have been two hundred Sioux warriors massed in front of him, most standing but two dozen or more sitting on horseback. They were all armed, the majority carrying rifles but a few holding tassled war lances. Stony-faced, they were bunched rank upon rank in front of the ceremonial lodge and on either side of War Bonnet's tepee.

MacGregor reined to a stop before a tall, broad-shouldered warrior dressed in richly beaded buckskin. The warrior wore a single eagle feather in graying black hair and he gazed up at MacGregor through glittering black eyes set in classic Sioux features . . . oval face, high cheekbones, prominent Roman nose. His face was lined, but it had an ageless quality, making it difficult to determine how old he was, though MacGregor estimated him to be in his early fifties.

MacGregor had no trouble remembering War Bonnet. Aware that he was facing one of the most notable war chiefs in the Sioux nation, he held the steady gaze. But as he realized what those glittering black eyes had seen in a lifetime of fighting and savagery, even Colin Campbell MacGregor—who had been in some pretty bloody battles in the far-flung corners of the British Empire—felt a slight shudder tremble through his body.

MacGregor raised his right hand, palm outward.

"Ho, War Bonnet."

War Bonnet returned the greeting. He spoke in English, as MacGregor had expected, his voice deep and rich.

"What brings the *Shagalasha* to the camp of the *Dacotah?*"

So, we're playing games, are we? MacGregor thought. *It should be bluidy obvious why we're here.* Pointing with

68

a thumb flick over his right shoulder in the direction of the high-topped wagon and the two tents, he said, "The white man and the woman who belong to the wagon . . . where are they?"

War Bonnet's jaw tightened. "My braves caught them spying on us."

"Spying—agh! They're missionaries. The mon is a white-collar—a preacher. The woman is his daughter. She helps him in his work. Why would they be spying on you?"

"So they can return to the land where they came from and tell the Americans how many warriors we have, how many horses, how many guns."

"Agh! They'd nae hae any reason to do that.

War Bonnet said something in Siouan to a pock-faced warrior standing nearby. Wearing a blue U.S. Cavalry jacket with gold captain's bars on the shoulders, the warrior turned and disappeared among the assembled Indians. As he watched from his saddle, MacGregor's attention was drawn to the jacket. *The murderous bastard probably killed the officer who had worn it down on the Little Big Horn and stripped it frae his body.*

A moment later the warrior returned with several sheets of paper. At a nod from War Bonnet, the warrior handed them up to MacGregor. The sergeant looked down at them. They were black and white sketches, each sketch occupying a full sheet of paper. It was the same sketching paper he had seen in Sarah Hatcher's tent. One sketch showed the Sioux camp as one would see it approaching from the west, the direction MacGregor, Freddie, and Jules had approached from. Another showed the tribe's horse herd grazing on the far side of the camp. A third showed the geographical layout of the camp, identifying a stand of jack pine that screened the camp to the west and the stream from where they obtained their water. Yet another showed four warriors holding different types of rifles; two looked like military weapons, probably U.S. Army Springfields captured on the Custer battleground down on the Little Big Horn. The sketches were very good. MacGregor peered at the signature in the bottom right hand corner—Sarah H.

Leaning forward over his horse's neck, MacGregor handed the sketches back. The pock-faced warrior in the cavalry officer's jacket passed them to War Bonnet.

"They're verra guid sketches," MacGregor said, "but what hae they to do with spying?"

War Bonnet held up the sketches angrily. "Word pictures tell the Americans how many tepees we have. From them the Americans can tell how many warriors we have, what sort of guns we have. Word pictures show the Americans our strengths and our weaknesses."

"Why would the Americans want to know that?"

"It will help them prepare to fight us. They want us to return to our homeland so they can punish us for what we did to Yellow Hair Custer, even though we were only defending ourselves and our homes. Because we have refused to go back, the Americans are angry. They will continue to try and trick us with false promises to lure us back. They might cross into this land and attack us. We do not know. But *this* we do know: We allowed the white man and the woman among us. We made them welcome. They stayed among us for two days. We allowed them among our lodges. Then they repaid us with *this!*"

Fire danced in War Bonnet's eyes as he held the sketches up high with one hand and slapped them violently with the back of his other hand. Then he threw them disgustedly onto the ground in front of him. Suddenly a nearby warrior uttered a fierce whoop, raised his arm, and threw a lance at the ground. The point tore into the paper sketches, pegging them onto the grassy ground. The lance shaft quivered, its string of feathers dancing like paper cutouts.

"Aiiiiyiiiii!"

Warriors took up a refrain of blood-curdling yells, shaking rifles and lances. Shots cracked out and bullets whistled into the air. Freddie's horse started prancing nervously. Freddie tightened his rein and knee pressure but didn't move his body, didn't relax his military-straight posture, didn't take his eyes from his front.

War Bonnet held up his hands and looked around at his warriors. Gradually the noise subsided. He looked back at MacGregor.

"The white man and the woman have betrayed us. Now we wonder what we will do with them. Some of my braves want to burn out their eyes so they will not see any more here, and to cut out their tongues so they will not go back to the Americans and tell them what they saw."

MacGregor stiffened. "That's damned savagery!"

"White eyes have been savage with us, killing our women and children."

Damn the Reverend Hatcher! This is what happens for disobeying Major Walsh's order.

Leaning forward on his saddle, MacGregor stared unblinkingly into War Bonnet's black eyes. "You allow that to happen, War Bonnet, and you'll hae the entire British Empire making war on you."

The Sioux chief stood proud and straight, staring back at MacGregor. MacGregor did not avert his eyes. War Bonnet's face showed no change of expression, only the eyes gave any hint of the emotions running through him. His tribesmen standing around him had not understood the *Shagalasha*'s words, but they had caught the steel in his voice. Muttering broke out among them. MacGregor had given War Bonnet something to think about. The Sioux had found refuge in Canada, and provided they lived at peace and did not break the white Queen's laws, they were safe, regardless of whatever efforts Washington made to induce them to return. War Bonnet knew that.

MacGregor decided to follow it up.

"Take me to the two white people, War Bonnet."

War Bonnet stared back at MacGregor a moment longer, then nodded. MacGregor swung down from his saddle and handed his reins to Freddie. With a meaningful glance at Jules, MacGregor grabbed the shaft of the lance that pegged the paper sketches to the ground and gave it a sharp pull. Tossing the lance aside, he bent down and picked up the sketches, then turned and followed War Bonnet through the ranks of Sioux warriors. War Bonnet led him to a tepee, where two strapping braves stood guard outside the entrance. At War Bonnet's approach, they stepped aside. Stooping forward, War Bonnet entered the tepee, MacGregor behind him.

Inside sat the Reverend Theodore Hatcher and his daughter, Sarah. They appeared unharmed, although their faces were drawn. Sarah's eyes flashed with recognition, then relief, at the sight of MacGregor's red tunic. The big Scot glared at Reverend Hatcher. The preacher's face took on a sheepish expression under MacGregor's cold, angry stare.

MacGregor held up the sketches for Sarah to see. "What was the purpose of these?"

Sarah's eyes went from MacGregor's face to the sketches in his hand, then back to his face. "I . . . I like to sketch," she said, her voice cracking with emotion. "I . . . I sketch frequently. There was no *purpose* in it . . . no purpose at all. The Indians . . . the camp . . . I thought they were interesting subjects . . . so I sketched them."

"You're aware that the Sioux think you were spying on them?"

"Yes, *he* told us," Sarah replied, taking her eyes off MacGregor to look up at War Bonnet for an instant. "But that's preposterous."

MacGregor nodded. "Aye, you know that and I know it, but we hae to convince the Sioux. If you'd both stayed away from here, like I told you—or if you'd gone back to Fort Benton like you and your father led me to believe you were, none of this would've happened."

MacGregor turned to War Bonnet. "The lady draws these pictures because she likes to draw. She and her father are nae American spies." He held the sketches up in front of War Bonnet's eyes and pointed at them. "Look, you can see that this picture shows only a few tepees . . . twenty or so. You hae hundreds. The same wi' your horses. This picture shows just a small herd. I've seen your herd. You hae more than a thousand head.

72

And the rifles—the Americans know how many rifles you hae. They know that from the Little Big Horn, and they know how many Springfields they lost, how many you took from the dead soldiers. How could any of what's in these pictures be of any value to the Americans?"

War Bonnet looked at the sketches. "Perhaps there are secret messages in the word pictures. Perhaps each lodge shown means ten or twenty real lodges. Perhaps each horse in the picture means thirty or forty of our horses. The Americans sent General Miles's chief scout to Sitting Bull's camp with a white-collar priest. They tried to talk Sitting Bull into going back to the White Father's land. Bear Coat Miles's chief scout would have told the blue-coats everything he saw in Sitting Bull's camp."

MacGregor looked the Sioux chief right in the eye. "War Bonnet, if I was an American, I'd be just as happy to see you and your tribe stay on this side of the line. If I was an American, I'd be breathing with relief, and I'd say good riddance to you after the trouble you've caused down there. Why would they want you back? These people"—he pointed a finger at the Reverend Hatcher and Sarah—"I met them on the trail in the Cypress Hills six days ago. They were on their way here to your camp to try to make you Christians, to tell you about their God, nae to spy on you. I told them not to come. White Forehead over at Fort Walsh has given an order than no whites are allowed to enter any Sioux camp without permission from the Mounted Police. This mon and his daughter disobeyed me. They disobeyed White Forehead by coming here. He will be verra angry. He'll want to punish them himself, for disobeying his order."

War Bonnet's dark eyes danced. "You mean White Forehead would punish them for coming here?"

Sergeant MacGregor nodded. "Aye, he would. He'll nae burn oot their eyes nor cut oot their tongues, but he'll give them a mighty good roasting. He's got a temper, White Forehead. He'll send 'em packing back to their own country."

"My braves want to punish them."

"Your braves are nae going to hae the chance, War Bonnet. If there's any punishing to be done, it'll be done by White Forehead. That's the law in the White Mother's land."

"I might have trouble convincing my warriors to release them."

MacGregor stood eyeball-to-eyeball with the Sioux chief. "You're a great chief, War Bonnet. Sergeant Cavannagh—you call him Stripe Arm—has told me all about you. Do you mean to tell me that what he said aboot how great you are was nae true? That you hae no control over your warriors? Agh! I find that verra hard to believe."

War Bonnet lifted his head high, as befitting the nobility of his position and reputation. Fire danced in his eyes. "I will call a council. We will talk. You will be given an answer after the next sun rises. The white-collar and the woman will remain here until then. They will not be harmed. You and the other redcoat and the mixed-blood who ride with you are welcome to share our food and our lodges."

MacGregor nodded. "Aye. That will be good."

He knew what the answer would be.

CHAPTER 7

Sergeant MacGregor rode alongside the high-topped wagon as they made their way toward Pine Butte outpost. Reverend Hatcher sat on the wagon seat with the team's leather traces in his gloved hands. His daughter sat beside him. Freddie rode a short distance behind the wagon. Jules rode fifty yards out in front.

There had been very little conversation since they left War Bonnet's camp shortly after breakfast. Reverend Hatcher and his daughter had passed a few words between themselves, but that was all, except for Sergeant MacGregor giving a few brief instructions when they started out. He was still angry with the apparently unrepentant missionary, and his anger included the missionary's seemingly unrepentant daughter as well. As for the Reverend Hatcher, he still resented what he considered to be Mounted Police attempts to prevent him and Sarah from carrying out the Lord's will.

They were approaching the log buildings of the outpost when the Reverend gentleman leaned forward on his seat and addressed himself to Sergeant MacGregor. "What happens now, Sergeant?"

MacGregor turned his head to look at him. The sergeant's eyes were still angry. "After a brief stop here, you're going on to Fort Walsh—under escort!"

"Under escort? Are we under some form of arrest?"

"You can call it what you like, but Fort Walsh is where you're going—and this time I'm making sure you

75

get there."

"I resent this high-handed treatment—" Reverend Hatcher started to bluster, but MacGregor cut him off.

"I should think that you'd be only too happy to be leaving this part of the country after what almost happened to you. And if y' dinna care aboot your own life, y' should at least hae a little regard for the life of your daughter."

Sarah Hatcher spoke up quickly in defense of her father. "We were never in any real danger. The Lord would have protected us."

MacGregor flicked his eyes to her. "You may be right, miss. It seems he sent the Mounted Police to do the job."

She gave him a strange look but said nothing in reply. MacGregor turned his head back to the front.

Reverend Hatcher said, "The Lord has called upon us to spread his word among the heathen savages. You are hindering us in our work. I intend complaining to my government about this high-handed treatment by your force."

MacGregor snapped his head sideways again and looked at him in disgust. "Do y' nae hae any sense of shame at all? Any sense of gratitude?"

MacGregor looked to his front once more. Putting Reverend Hatcher from his mind for the moment, he turned his thoughts to other matters. They had almost reached the outpost. He was surprised that the American law officer, Edson, wasn't standing in the doorway to watch them ride up. Edson should have been pleased to see them back. Their return meant he could now get on with his own business of seeing the three wanted American criminals brought to justice. Perhaps the deputy U.S. marshal was a late riser and was still in bed. *But hell!* MacGregor thought, looking up at the blue sky. *It's bluidy high on noon.* He wouldn't be sleeping. Edson didn't strike MacGregor as a late riser.

They reined to in front of the flagpole. MacGregor

swung down from his saddle and stepped over to the wagon to help Sarah Hatcher down, but she ignored his presence, waiting for her father to get down, then climbed down on his side. With a shrug of his shoulders, MacGregor sauntered around the wagon and went to the front door of the log building. It was closed. Unlatching it, he pushed it open and stepped inside.

"Mister Edson?"

There was no answer. MacGregor walked across the room that he used as an office and on into the barrack room beyond. There was no sign of the American law officer. The beds—palliasses laid on trestles and covered with sheets and blankets—hadn't been disturbed. He bounded back to the front door and shouted to Jules, who was over by the stables.

"Hae a look in there and tell me if there's a light bay horse inside."

After a moment Jules shouted back. "T'ere is no 'orse in 'ere at all, *mon* Sergeant."

Grunting, MacGregor turned back inside his office. He was followed a moment later by Reverend Hatcher and Sarah. Freddie stepped in behind them and stood looking over their heads.

"That's odd," MacGregor said, looking around the room. "He's gone. No note, no message, or anything. I wonder where he went."

"I'll tell you where 'e's gone," Freddie said from the doorway. " 'E's gone to Walkin' Thunder's camp after them three outlaws 'e's been chasin'."

MacGregor's brows drew together in a sharp frown. "But he dinna know the way."

" 'E can read a map," Freddie said, nodding his head at the map on the wall. " 'E got this far."

MacGregor stepped over to the map and stood looking at it. He started rubbing his jaw, the friction of his fingers against his dark whisker stubble making a rasping sound.

" 'E should've waited for us. That Walkin' Thunder's a

right nasty piece of work. 'E'd make Sittin' Bull look like a fairy godmother."

MacGregor turned back from the map. "Tell Jules nae to unsaddle the horses, Freddie. We're leaving for Walking Thunder's camp immediately."

A broad grin spread across Freddie's lantern-jawed face. "Right, Sar'nt. Maybe this time we'll see some action."

Freddie was about to step out the door and shout to Jules when MacGregor's next words stopped him. "There's nae going to be any action where you're going, Freddie. You'll be escorting these two people"—MacGregor inclined his head toward Reverend Hatcher and Sarah—"to Fort Walsh."

Freddie's jaw dropped. *What!* Me escort a bleedin' preacher and 'is spinster daughter to Fort Walsh! Christ! Come on, Sar'nt, 'ave a bleedin' 'eart!"

Reverend Hatcher and Sarah stood with mouth agape, shocked by Freddie's outburst.

MacGregor said, "I'll like to hae you along with me on this patrol, Freddie. Frae the sound of this Walking Thunder, I might be able to use you, but I need someone to escort these people to Fort Walsh."

"Send Prefontaine," Freddie said, almost as though he were issuing an order. " 'E don't like excitement."

MacGregor shook his head. "I canna do that. I want a regular member. You'll hae to make a report to Major Walsh. Besides, I might need Jules to interpret."

"Father and I are quite capable of traveling to Fort Walsh without an escort," Sarah Hatcher said, tilting her chin up and regarding MacGregor coldly.

MacGregor cast her and her father a look that was equally as cold. "I'm afraid I'm nae impressed with your honesty of purpose, which dinna say much for two people who are supposed to be religious."

Reverend Hatcher and his daughter both started talking at the same time, protesting at MacGregor's stinging indictment. He silenced them with the sudden loud smacking of his open hand hitting the top of his table.

"Enough! You're going to Fort Walsh under escort, and that's final. And Constable Jenkins, you're escorting them!"

MacGregor glared angrily at the three of them. No one said another word. Freddie stepped out of the building to tell Jules not to unsaddle the horses, as Sergeant MacGregor had ordered.

William James Edson sat his saddle easy, letting the light bay make its own way toward the long ridge ahead.

That must be the ridge Jenkins had mentioned, Edson reckoned. The river he had called the Ghost would be on the other side, and just short of it the Minnetaree camp.

As the light bay carried him closer to the ridge, Edson wondered about the best way of handling what he had to do. Should he just ride down into the Minnetaree camp and ask the chief to be kind enough to hand over Lone Man, Oates, and the Frenchman? That mightn't work so good. Why should the chief hand over one of his own tribesmen to a perfect stranger—a white man at that? He mightn't care much about Oates and the Frenchman, but Lone Man . . . his own tribesman?

Edson shook his head as he thought about it. Uh-uh. Better to have a look-see first.

His blue eyes scanning the ridge, he legged the light bay into a canter. When he didn't see any sign of movement, he kept on going until he was just a few yards short of the ridge top, when he pulled the horse down to a walk and finally a stop. He swung down from his saddle and removed his hat. Then he bellied down into the grass and slid forward until just the top of his head and his eyes were above the ridge.

He saw the camp right away. Screened by a grove of leafless cottonwoods, it stood a short distance from the river. The riverbed was wide but there wasn't much water flowing along it. Beyond, the prairie stretched flat into the infinite distance.

The camp numbered about sixty tepees, spread in a loose arrangement. Horses grazed on a flat between the camp and the river. Edson made a rough count of the horses. Close to a hundred. That gave him an approximate idea of the number of braves in the camp . . . between eighty and ninety. There was activity down in the camp . . . children playing a game with a ball, women carrying bundles of firewood and buffalo hides among the tepees, braves and old men sitting in front of tepees smoking and talking. Over on the side of the camp closet to the river, two braves were mock-fighting while several more watched. Near the horse herd a young brave galloped a wiry cayuse backwards and forwards.

Edson couldn't see any white men down there. He looked for Lone Man's distinctive, high-crowned black hat, but he might have discarded it now that he was back home with his own people.

Edson decided the distance was too far for him to see what he wanted. He needed to get closer. He had to get down there. The cottonwoods were bare of leaf but there was some underbrush among them. If he could get down into it . . . The slope from the top of the ridge down to the cottonwoods was bare. He'd have to go down it at night. Once down there, he'd have to remain all day, and he wondered whether the underbrush would be thick enough to hide him that long.

There was another problem. What would he do with his horse while he was down there? He couldn't leave it hobbled on the slope in plain view. He turned his attention to the riverbank . . . maybe there was a cutback or something like that reasonably close.

As he studied the river, his horse snorted and stamped a hoof. He turned his head to see what had drawn the horse's attention. Instantly he froze.

A dozen yards behind him three dusky-faced Indians sat on their ponies. Each one held a Winchester pointed at him.

For several seconds no one moved and no sounds passed other than the prairie wind. Edson had been in tight spots before, but there were damn few things more discomforting than staring into that small, round black hole at the end of a gun barrel pointing at you.

Finally one of the Indians made a sharp upward movement with his rifle barrel. Taking it as a signal that he should get up, Edson rolled over real slow, keeping his hands where the three Indians could see them easily. He picked up his hat and put it back on his head, then clambered to his feet and stood with hands raised.

The Indian who had signaled grunted something to one of the others. A brave slid down from his pony and slunk toward Edson with pointed rifle, advancing until the barrel was pressed hard into the white man's chest. His dark, beady eyes never leaving Edson's face, the brave reached under Edson's coat and lifted the Smith & Wesson .44 out of its holster. Then he stepped back, shoving the revolver into his waist band. Next he took the reins of Edson's horse, returned to his pony, and pulled himself back up onto it.

The Indian who had signaled rattled out a torrent of words that Edson couldn't understand.

He managed a sick grin, saying, "If you boys would just lower those rifles a piece, maybe we can talk and I'll tell you why I'm here."

The Indian flung off another string of words at him.

"Sorry, fellers. I don't speak your lingo." He inclined his head down toward the camp below. "You fellers from that camp down there? If you'd take me to your chief . . . Maybe there's someone down there who speaks English."

The Indian made another gesture with the rifle, pointing the barrel in the direction of the camp.

"I guess you want me to go down there. How about letting me ride my horse?" He pointed to the light bay.

The Indian waved his rifle barrel again and shouted. It was a sharp, impatient shout and Edson got the message. He turned around and started walking down the slope to the Indian camp below. They tied a long rope around his neck, the end of it in the hand of the Indian who had done the shouting. The brave rode out in front, the other two following, one towing Edson's horse.

The sudden appearance of a white man with his hands above his head, escorted by three armed braves, aroused excitement in the camp. Braves, old men, women, and children stared as the mounted warriors took Edson along a path that countless moccasined feet and unshod hoofs had beaten between the tepees.

They stopped before one tepee made of the finest tanned buffalo hides and covered by intricately painted symbols in red, green, yellow, black, and blue. The entrance flap was pulled open and smoke spiraled upwards from the vent at the top where the poles joined together. The leading brave slipped from his pony and stepped over to the entrance. Stooping forward, he disappeared inside. He reappeared a moment later and motioned with a jerk of his head to the two braves behind Edson. They slid off their ponies, Edson felt a rifle barrel prod him sharply in the back, and he was half pushed, half pulled through the opening into the tepee.

Smoke hung thick inside the lodge as half a dozen warriors sat around a fire smoking pipes. The air was heavy from the heat of the fire on a day when the sun's unseasonable warmth already raised the temperature inside the buffalo-hide tepee. The heat was almost overpowering and Edson wondered how they could stand it. It seemed to suck the breath from his body.

Then his attention was taken by a massive warrior sitting prominently in the small circle. Even sitting crosslegged on a buffalo robe spread on the ground, he was massive. Unusually light eyes glowered up at Edson from a broad, flat face with high-balled cheekbones and a slash for a mouth. The warrior listened to what the brave holding the rope had to say.

This must be the chief, Edson reckoned. There seemed little doubt about it. The brooding, stormy look on his face . . . When he finally spoke to the brave holding the rope, his voice rumbled like thunder from the depths of his chest as words rolled from his slash of a mouth. Thunder . . . Walking Thunder . . . that's what Jenkins had said his name was.

The brave holding the rope said something else, after which Walking Thunder sat back on his buttocks, holding his pipe in one hand, his other hand clasping one of the folded knees in front of him. All the while the strangely colored eyes stared up unblinkingly at the white man.

Hands still raised shoulder high, Edson stood looking back at him. "I've been holding my hands up for a long time, Chief. You boys have got my guns. I'm not here to cause you any trouble. How's about me lowering my hands?"

Walking Thunder made no response as he sat on his buffalo robe staring up at him. Edson might not have even said anything at all for all the attention his words seemed to have gained.

Edson looked around at the other faces of the Indians in the circle, all looking up at him. Those with their backs to him sat with heads turned around so they could see him.

Slowly he lowered his hands. "I'm a deputy United States marshal . . . from the country on the other side of the line." He moved his left hand to his gray coat and pulled aside the coat to reveal the badge pinned to his shirt. Instantly there was a flurry of movement from the three standing braves as they whipped up their rifles.

"Hold it, fellers," Edson said quickly. "It's just a badge. It don't bite and it don't shoot bullets."

One of the braves reached across to Edson's shirt. With a sharp jerk he tore off the badge, tossing it to Walking Thunder. It landed on the buffalo robe in front of the Minnetaree chief. His hand closing around it,

Walking Thunder held the badge up in front of his eyes and studied it.

"I'm up in your country looking for three bad men," Edson continued, looking at each of the faces staring up at him from the circle. No expressions showed on any of them. They did not seem to comprehend what he was saying. *Hell! Doesn't anyone here speak any English?* He kept on talking. He had to do something, and talking was the only thing he could think of. But as he talked, his mind raced, trying to come up with something that he could use to get out of the mess he'd gotten himself into.

"These three bad men . . . two are white but the third one, he's an Indian. He belongs to your tribe, and I reckon him and the two white men could be in your camp right now. Would've got here just a couple of days ago. Names Lone Man.

"Now . . . I've got something in my pocket to show you . . . so long as you don't think I'm going for a gun." Very slowly, he pulled his coat open once more to show the inside pocket, then, just as slowly, he reached a hand inside the pocket. The Winchesters pointed at him, the muzzles only inches from his body. Slowly he withdrew the *Wanted* circulars he had shown Sergeant MacGregor back at Pine Butte. Opening them, he held them in front of Walking Thunder.

The Minnetaree chief frowned as he scrutinized the three pictures of Lone Man, Oates, and the Frenchman. Suddenly he barked an order as he raised an arm and jabbed a pointed finger at one of the braves with the rifles. The brave left the tepee.

Walking Thunder continued to glower up at Edson. Tiny beads of perspiration burst out on Edson's forehead. It was damned hot and stuffy in the tepee. Or maybe he was scared. *Hell, no,* he told himself. It was the heat. But Walking Thunder left him feeling uneasy. There was something about the Minnetaree chief that he didn't like, something that wasn't quite right. Those eyes . . .

Moments later there was shouting from the lodge entrance. Edson looked around as two rifle-carrying braves pushed an unarmed brave in through the entrance ahead of them. Even without the tall black hat, Edson had no trouble recognizing Lone Man's sullen features, the short black hair tumbling down over his forehead.

A grin spread across Edson's face. Now, that was more like it. He took back what he had been thinking about Walking Thunder. Maybe the Minnetaree chief wasn't such a bad fellow after all.

He looked back at Walking Thunder. "That's right agreeable of you, Chief. I'll take him off your hands before he causes you some headaches. As for his two white friends, I'll be glad to take them as well. They *will* cause you trouble, believe me. Now, if you'll just tell your braves to hand me back my gun and my horse—"

Edson's words were cut short by Walking Thunder uttering a mighty bellow that echoed around the inside of the tepee like a cannon shot. The Minnetaree chief jumped to his feet. Bill Edson was tall—six-one-and-a half—but Walking Thunder dwarfed him. In that moment Edson understood why Walking Thunder was chief of the Minnetaree band—he was too damn big for any other contenders for the job to argue with.

Suddenly Walking Thunder lashed out with a fist, striking Edson high up on the chest. The blow sent him reeling backwards. Two braves immediately grabbed him from behind.

The lodge exploded into noise and activity. Shouting broke out and Edson felt himself thrown to the ground. He flung up a fist; it smashed into a nose. A moccasined foot slammed against the side of his neck, another hit him in the head, a third kicked him in the ribs. Broad, dusky faces bore down on him. A pair of hands grasped him around his throat. He struck up with his fists at the buckskin-covered bodies on top of him. The hands around his throat tightened and he felt his life being choked out of him. Fighting to break the grip, he looked up into a pair of smoldering black eyes. It was then that he realized the hands around his throat belonged to Lone Man.

Using arms and legs, Edson fought like mad. Desperation lent him strength. He got the heel of a hand under Lone Man's jaw, splayed his fingers until they spread up across his face, the tips of his fingers stretching up for the fugitive's eyes. At the same time he managed to double his knee up in front of him. Simultaneously he pushed back with his hand under Lone Man's chin, fingers gouging at his black eyes, while he rammed his knee into the Indian's crotch. Lone Man yelled agonizingly.

Edson flung Lone Man to one side. He was halfway to his feet when a mighty blow from a knee caught him in the side of his face and sent him flying backwards. He landed jarringly on his back. The next instant the rawhide rope tightened around his neck and he was dragged backwards. The rope burned his neck as it took hold. In a moment he was dragged out of the tepee. He felt himself sliding on his back quickly along the ground. He heard pounding hoofs . . . shouting . . . laughter. The sky whirled by above, blue with white flecks of cloud . . . tepee tops . . . He was jolted along on his back at increasing speed, bouncing sideways onto his shoulder, bouncing back onto his back again. *Christ!* They were dragging him behind a cantering horse! Indians stood alongside the track laughing, gesturing, pointing. He reached up with both hands, grasping the rope before it choked him to death.

"You red-skinned sons of bitches!" Edson swore, until something hit him on the head and he lost consciousness.

CHAPTER 8

The trail wandered higher and higher among folds of jack-pine-dotted hills, sometimes edging along precipitous rocky cliffs that looked down into dark, forested ravines.

Snatches of memory returned as Ceston Parker Oakes legged his gray mare along what had been wagon wheel ruts. The trail was barely visible, and if he hadn't known it was there he likely wouldn't have even noticed it. It hadn't been used in five years, probably not since '72 when his whiskey wagons made it. Occasional flashes of light bounced back from down in the ravine below, where the sun's rays caught the waters of a stream. He was reminded of the good fishing down there, and of the bountiful game that allowed a man to live heartily during the long months of isolation . . . elk, antelope, bear—and farther back along the grassed slopes of the hills were buffalo. Oates grinned pleasurably. With a good supply of bullets, he would do it again—at least for the winter, until the heat had cooled down below the border and he could decide what to do and where to go come spring.

He crossed another hill before he saw, over on a knoll off to his left, a solitary lobstick pine. He grinned again, grinned with the memory of it. He had marked that pine himself, back when he was new to this part of the country, so he could find his way in again. The cabin would be over the next hill.

It would probably need some work. Five successive winters of snow had likely caved the roof in, although he and his partner had built it plenty strong, strong enough to stop Indians trying to break in to steal their trade whiskey. The walls should be all right . . . they'd built them to double thickness to withstand attack, not only from Indians but from rival whiskey-trading outfits.

He would need supplies and gear—maybe a tarpaulin, depending on what shape the roof was in, an axe, saw, hammer, some nails, a chisel, rope, maybe a keg of black powder, bacon, flour, beans, coffee, tobacco, some cold-weather clothes, and a few other things. For a moment he wished he had taken the spare horse, Ben Zacks's horse. He could have used it as a pack horse in the months ahead, but he had let the Frenchman keep it. No matter. He could fashion an Indian travois to haul the stuff. Might have to make two trips. There was a trading post over by a crescent-shaped lake about ten, twelve miles off, down on the southern slopes of the range of hills—*if* it was still there. If not, he'd have to look for another one. That could present a problem. The mild weather couldn't last much longer, he thought, looking anxiously up at the sky. *Snow has to come soon, any day now.*

It was close to sundown when he crested the last hill and looked down on the hollow below. He found the cabin almost immediately, by sighting a column of smoke drifting above the green, spear-topped pines, which he traced to the chimney of his cabin.

Cess Oates reined his gray mare to a quick stop.

Some son of a bitch is living in it, goddamn him!

Oates sat his saddle staring down at the cabin, half-hidden among the pines on the slope of the far hill facing him. *Who? And how many?* He couldn't see any horses around, but there was a lean-to stable at the back, which he couldn't see from where he sat. There weren't many who knew about that cabin, and he doubted any of them were still alive. Certainly not his partner. He'd been killed in a saloon gunfight down Benton way in '73.

Studying the cabin, Oates concluded there was only one way to find out who had taken up residence, and that was to ride down there. First, though, he pulled out both his Colt .44's and checked the loads and the actions. Satisfied, he slipped them back into their holsters. Then he slid out his Winchester from its saddle scabbard and checked it. Only then did he leg the gray down the slope toward the hollow and the log cabin among the pines on the slope beyond.

He had reached the hollow and had started up the far slope when he heard a man's off-key singing from inside the cabin. His mouth drawn into a thin, tight line across his dark-bearded face, he legged the gray on. He could smell the smoke, and thought he detected the odor of cooking food. His stomach growled. He hadn't eaten for a day.

He had almost reached the cabin when a good-sized black and white dog with pointy ears and lots of shaggy hair came bounding out the door, barking viciously. Instantly the singing stopped, and a moment later a burly, red-bearded man, his woolen trousers held up by suspenders over a green-checkered shirt, appeared in the doorway.

The dog slid to a stop below Oates's boots, looking up with sharp, pointed teeth showing ominously against the black hair. The gray mare snorted and wide-eyed the snarling dog, stepping off sideways to distance itself from the threatening beast. Oates only barely resisted the urge to draw his gun and shoot the damn dog.

"Shut up, Blackie," the red-bearded man shouted at the dog. "Lay down and stop that racket." He squinted up at Oates and nodded. "Howdy. Don't mind Blackie none. We don't see many strangers out here. Hardly none at all. Fact is, you're the first."

Oates sat his saddle, eyeing the cabin. It looked in pretty good shape. Maybe this man had fixed it up. That was good. It saved him the trouble.

"You been here long?" Oates asked. There was resentment in his voice.

The red-bearded man didn't seem to notice the resentment. He grinned, a wide, partly toothless grin. "Since spring. Name's Harper, Casper Harper . . . from down Ioway. Just rustlin' up some supper. Can put on some extra, make it enough for two. You look as though you could stand a good feed. Climb down off your horse and come on in."

The dog continued barking.

"Don't mind him none. Bark's worse'n his bite."

From the safety of the gray mare's back, Oates glared down at the dog with a jaundiced eye. Despite assurances, it still looked damn mean. It had that biting look in its eye.

"There's a place out back where you can put your horse."

Right, old man, Oates thought. You're damned right there is.

Reluctantly he stepped down from his saddle. The dog flew around to the side of the horse where Oates dismounted and snapped at his spurred boots. The dog's hair was standing straight up.

"Scat, goddamn you!" Oates shouted, cringing.

"Blackie!" shouted the man, ambling after the dog, grabbing it, and picking it up. "That's enough of that barkin'. I don't know what's got into you."

While Casper Harper carried the dog into the cabin, admonishing it all the while, Oates stabled his horse in the lean-to at the back. The lean-to had a new roof, and the log poles of the corral fence were new. There were two horses inside the lean-to. One was a saddle horse, the other a pack. So this Casper feller lives here alone, Oates reflected. Good. That makes it easier.

After he had finished, Oates stepped inside the cabin. Harper was busy at the old wood stove Oates and his late partner had brought in on their wagon years before. The dog was sitting on all fours beneath a table. As soon as Oates entered, it rose and started growling. It would have made a lunge for him if Harper hadn't silenced it with a shout.

Forcing his attention from the dog, Oates glanced quickly around the cabin. There were glass windows, two of them, where he had used heavy boards with loopholes for rifle barrels. Harper must have hauled the glass in. The double-logged walls were unchanged, and so was the hard-packed earth floor, the only difference being a bearskin scatter rug. His eyes lifted to the roof. Nothing new had been added. Still looked solid. It had stood up under the winter snows after all.

Casper Harper served up elk steaks, with wild onion stew and bread, with steaming black coffee to wash it down. Oates devoured his plateful, ignoring the growling dog under the table. The dog sounded as it wanted to dine on Kansas outlaw, either *filet mignon* or *a la carte*.

"How'd you find this place?" Oates asked, wiping gravy from his beard with the back of his hand. "You come across it by accident?"

Wiping onion stew around his plate with a piece of bread, Harper shook his head. "Feller I met at Fort Walsh told me about it. Old whiskey trader . . . name of Dick Hardstone. He was in these Cypress Hills afore some Indian massacre back in '73 or thereabouts, the one that brought the Mounted Police out into this part of the country. He knowed I was lookin' for a place to hunt an' trap. There used to be an old wagon track up here from the southeast. It's growed over now. I come in from the west, the way Dick told me. Took me a piece to find the place. Couple fellers built it, old Dick told me, the year or so afore the massacre. Built it for t' trade whiskey. Built it real solid, they did. I didn't have t' do much to it. Even had a stove. The place hadn't been lived in since they left it."

He looked at Oates. "How's about you? You headin' for Fort Walsh? You're a small piece off'n the reg'lar trail."

Oates took a mouthful of coffee. "I cut up from the south. Got lost a bit. Yeah, I'm headin' for Fort Walsh."

"It's one and a half, two days' ride west, dependin' on the condition of your horse. You're welcome to put up here for the night. Come mornin', I can point you off in the right direction."

"Obliged," Oates nodded, looking at Harper over the top of his tin cup.

Oates waited until Harper was clearing the table before he shot him. He killed him with one shot, a bullet straight through the heart. Oates was standing by the door when he did it, where he could see the dog under the table. He shot the dog before it could do anything. He killed it with pleasure, shot it twice, both bullets in the head.

CHAPTER 9

Walking Thunder handed the gold badge to Lone Man. They were alone in Walking Thunder's lodge, sitting cross-legged on buffalo robes.

"The white man who followed you here wore this. What does it mean?"

Lone Man looked at the badge and read the wording: *Deputy United States Marshal.* "It tells people he is a law officer."

"What is a law officer?" Walking Thunder did not like admitting ignorance of anything, but his curiosity overwhelmed him.

Lone Man thought about his answer. Walking Thunder and his band had had little exposure to whites other than traders of the Hudson's Bay Company and an occasional priest. Walking Thunder knew little about the white man's law. Not like Lone Man, who had traveled extensively in the western states and territories during his career as an outlaw. He knew all about law officers. "He punishes people who break white eyes' law."

His eyes on the badge as Lone Man passed it back to him, Walking Thunder nodded slowly. "I have heard about laws. It is said there are laws in this country now. There are redcoats here. They came into the country after you left. They say they enforce the Big White Woman's laws."

A strange light entered Walking Thunder's pale, brooding eyes, a burning light, like a smoldering fire, a fire of hate. "The redcoats say that they are so many that they cover the prairie like the buffalo once covered it. I do not know whether they speak the truth, for I have seen only four of them." He held up the four fingers on his right hand.

"The first time, one rode into our camp near Medicine Lodge Coulee. He was alone, except for a stinking Cree mixed-blood." Walking Thunder hated Crees, the Minnetarees' hereditary enemies. He hated whites almost as much. It had been white traders who first gave guns to the Crees, enabling the Crees to kill many Minnetarees. "It was that same redcoat who told us there were many more like him. It was he who told us that the redcoats enforce the Big White Woman's laws.

"That redcoat, when he was angry he had eyes the color of a new gun barrel. The next time I saw him, he rode into this camp with three others. They rode as if they were invincible, as though they were the Great Spirit. We had caught Crees killing buffalo on our hunting grounds. The Crees should have stayed where they belonged, north along the River of Many Turns. We took their kill and told them to go back where they belonged. They were lucky we did not kill them. We should have. They went running, their tails between their legs like the dogs they were. But they told the redcoats. Then the four redcoats came. They made us give back the meat and skins."

Lone Man's eyes widened, but only momentarily, before he checked himself and masked his face with an expression of impassiveness. But he was thinking. Only *four* redcoats! Who were these redcoats that only four of them could ride into an Indian camp and make Indians do things that were contrary to their nature, contrary to everything they had ever been brought up to believe? Walking Thunder had seventy warriors. He should have killed the four redcoats. Hah! Imagine four bluecoats riding into a Sioux or Cheyenne camp down on the other side of the medicine line! Their scalps would have been hanging from the chief's lodge pole very quickly. However, Lone Man was cunning enough not to say anything like that to Walking Thunder.

Lone Man was something of a hero in the camp. He had been gone five years. He had ridden across much of the country below the medicine line. He had seen many things and he had defied the white man. But Walking Thunder was the most dominant member of the band. He had lived among white traders at Fort Ellice for three summers as a boy, and had learned much from them. The people of the tribe thought of him as wise. Lone Man knew better. He and Walking Thunder had been boys together, although Walking Thunder was two years older, but Lone Man knew Walking Thunder well enough. Walking Thunder was a bully, and maybe he was a bit mad. Because of his size, he forced his will on the rest of the band. None of the older men, the ones who would be chief and councillors, dared stand up to him.

Lone Man was not awed by Walking Thunder's knowledge. He knew more about the world beyond than Walking Thunder, the world that would overtake the Indians all over the country on both sides of the medicine line. That was partly the reason Lone Man had ridden the white man's trails. Yet he knew better than to contradict Walking Thunder, or argue with him, or demean him in any way. Lone Man felt superior to Walking Thunder as long as he had a gun at hand, but man to man he stood no chance against him. Walking Thunder had strength and a temper to match. He was very vain, and no one made a fool of him, or belittled him in any way, except at their extreme peril! Lone Man needed sanctuary. He had to live among these, his own people, at least for the coming long snow. If he looked too big, if the rest of the band regarded him as too much of a hero, Walking Thunder might feel his own standing threatened. Lone Man knew he had to patronize him, and to be careful not to antagonize him.

From Walking Thunder's manner, Lone Man guessed the four redcoats had backed him down. Lone Man was curious to learn more about them, if only for his own protection. However, he deemed it best not to ask questions. Judging by the burning look in Walking Thunder's eyes, he hated redcoats as much as he hated Crees. Anyway, Oates had said the redcoats wouldn't have time to come looking for them; they had their hands full keeping Sitting Bull and the Sioux at peace.

"Will more white men from below the medicine line come after you?" Walking Thunder asked.

"No. I know only of this one," Lone Man said, pointing at the badge in Walking Thunder's hand.

"How did he know where to find you?"

"I do not know. He might have caught Oates, one of the white eyes I rode with. He knew."

"Where did Oates go?"

"Somewhere into the Thunder Breeding Hills."

"What are we going to do with the white man?" Lone Man asked after awhile.

Walking Thunder sat on his buffalo robe, stoop-shoulders, his strangely light eyes staring broodingly through the tepee opening. "Kill him," he replied simply, without breaking his stare.

"How?"

"There are many ways. We could stake him out on the prairie and leave him for the wolves. They will become hungry soon, as soon as the long snows fall. Or we could tie his arms, cover his eyes so he can not see, then take him somewhere far out in the middle of the prairie and leave him, letting him wander around until he dies from hunger or falls down into a coulee or freezes to death. Or we could tie him up and throw him into the

River of Many Turns. Maybe his stinking carcass would float down to a Cree camp and poison some of them."

Walking Thunder broke out into loud, almost maniacal laughter.

Sergeant Colin Campbell MacGregor and Scout Jules Prefontaine rode steadily northward. MacGregor's scarlet tunic contrasted vividly with the dun-colored prairie, his brass buttons glittered, his belt and boots gleamed in the sunlight.

Jules pointed to the distant ridge. "Walking Thunder's camp, she just on other side of t'at ridge, *mon* Sergeant."

MacGregor nodded. He was aware the Minnetarees would know he was coming long before he arrived at their camp. They would see his scarlet tunic from a long way off. There were some members of the Mounted Police who argued that red coats were too bright, too visible, and should be replaced by uniforms of brown or some neutral color that would blend into the countryside. He hoped the Powers That Be would never listen to them. He liked the scarlet, he believed implicitly in its moral power. It carried an air of authority among the Indians, who were fascinated by bright colors. He had been in enough Indian camps to know the effect of the scarlet tunic. It had magic, as the Blackfoot said. It enabled the Mounted Police, with only three hundred men, to maintain law and order over more than a quarter of a million square miles of savage, inhospitable country inhabited by some thirty thousand warlike Indians, countless half-breeds, and an ever-increasing number of whites.

As they drew closer to the ridge, MacGregor expected to see mounted warriors outlined against the prairie sky. Yet he saw nothing. All the same, he knew his approach hadn't passed unnoticed.

The weather was still unseasonably warm, though it was already November. Great billowing puffballs of fleecy white clouds floated across the wide blue sky, carried by the prevailing winds from the Pacific coast and across the majestic, snow-crowned Rockies far to the west.

As they rode, MacGregor heard a distant honking noise above. Lifting his eyes from the ridge for a moment, he watched a long V formation sailing southward across the sky. He had been seeing them for two days now, geese on their way to warmer climes in the south. A sure sign that winter was not far away. Farther west, around the Fort Macleod country, warm spells were common, even in the middle of winter, but the weather wasn't so benevolent east and north of the Cypress Hills.

MacGregor turned his attention back to where he was. They had almost reached the ridge. He and Jules had made good time since leaving Pine Butte the day before yesterday. He estimated they had probably cut by a few hours the lead Edson had had on them because they knew where they were going, whereas the American had been riding through unfamiliar country and had to find his way.

They crested the ridge and without pausing rode on down the other side. Wide-open prairie stretched endlessly before them. The Ghost River meandered lazily across the flat landscape, as though trying to find a way out of its prairie prison. The Indian camp lay down on their right and MacGregor reined his horse toward it.

In the camp braves bunched in small groups beside their tepees or at the edge of the camp, eyes turned up to the ridge. MacGregor's scarlet tunic blazed brightly against the dun color of the autumn-browned grass forming a backdrop behind him as he and Jules rode down the slope.

Sergeant MacGregor rode into the Minnetaree camp the same way he'd ridden into the Sioux camp three days earlier—as though he owned it. Dusky faces turned up at him as he rode among the tepees. Sullen black eyes stared up at his bright red tunic, at the sunlight glinting on the polished brass cartridges in his belt. He could see the hostility in the eyes. He saw something else. There were only braves, and they all carried rifles. There were no women or children. That meant only one thing—the Indians were ready for trouble.

"Where is Walking Thunder's lodge?" MacGregor asked his scout.

Jules's voice trembled. "It . . . It prob'ly in middle of camp."

MacGregor cursed silently. He wished he had Freddie alongside him instead of Jules. He should have sent Jules to Fort Walsh with the preacher and his daughter. "Take me to it."

The braves crowded around the redcoat and his *metis* scout, but MacGregor ignored them as he pushed his horse through. Jules legged his short-stepping cayuse to keep up. Shouting broke out as braves followed on foot.

Jules found Walking Thunder's tepee. Indians pressing in behind him, MacGregor reined to and sat his saddle looking at it. The entrance flap was tied shut. Cocking an eyebrow, MacGregor glanced at Jules. The *metis* shrugged, his black-bearded face pale and drawn under the floppy brim of his hat.

"It looks like Walking Thunder does nae want to talk to us, Jules," MacGregor said in a loud, slow voice. "Maybe he is nae longer the chief of this band. If he isn't, we dinna need to talk to him. Let's find a squaw to talk to instead."

MacGregor was reining his horse away when the entrance flap of Walking Thunder's tepee was suddenly thrown open and a giant figure stepped out. He wore buckskin trousers and moccasins but was naked from the waist up. Over his left arm he carried a folded red and black Hudson's Bay blanket. Light eyes glowered up at

MacGregor from beneath a wide forehead and brooding brows.

MacGregor reined his horse back and stared down at the massive Indian. He didn't need to be told that this was Walking Thunder. The name fitted.

Walking Thunder shouted in his own tongue. Moments later a brave ran up leading a big horse. Walking Thunder snatched the rawhide reins from him. Turning his back on MacGregor, the Minnetaree chief heaved himself up onto the horse's back. The horse was bigger than the average Indian pony, but Walking Thunder dwarfed it. His moccasins almost touched the ground on either side of it. Taking his time, he slid the blanket from his arm, shook it out, and tossed it over his bare shoulder. Only then did he pull the horse around to face MacGregor. Arrogance written all over his face, he thrust out his jaw and sat glaring belligerently back at the redcoat.

You egotistical son of a bitch, MacGregor thought as he held the Minnetaree chief's hate-filled eyes. Low muttering reached MacGregor's ears, reminding him that Walking Thunder's braves crowded in behind him and his horse.

Walking Thunder held up a big arm. The muttering ceased and there was complete silence. He lowered his arm and addressed MacGregor in slow but recognizable English. "I am Chief Walking Thunder, Lord of the Plains and the Thunder Breeding Hills. I speak for all the Northern Minnetarees."

Walking Thunder said no more, waiting for MacGregor to speak. His eyes were fastened on MacGregor. He ignored Jules completely, as though the *metis* was not there.

MacGregor said, "I am looking for a white man, an American from below the medicine line. He said he was coming here to find three bad men who broke the law in his country. Two of the men he seeks are white. The

100

third is an Indian."

"Why should he seek them here?"

"Because one of them is a Northern Minnetaree. His name is Lone Man."

"He has not come here. No white men come to my camp."

"Is Walking Thunder sure of that?"

Walking Thunder sucked in a great draught of air. His words rolled out from his mouth like thunder. "Does redcoat say Walking Thunder speak *lie?*"

MacGregor gazed calmly back at him. "I am asking if the white American came here."

Walking Thunder shook his head. "He did not come here."

"Has Lone Man come here, with the two bad white men from below the medicine line?"

Walking Thunder shook his head again, more emphatically this time. He shook it as though he liked shaking it. "None of my people have been away. None leave Walking Thunder's camp. They are all happy here. No one wants to leave. None have left, none have come back."

The two of them sat their horses facing one another, eyes locked. Muttering started up behind MacGregor again, and his horse stood tossing its head, unaccustomed to the closeness of Indians. MacGregor felt something behind him, felt his horse half-kick out with a hind leg, and he realized one of the milling braves must have jabbed it with something, probably a knife or a rifle butt. He went to look behind but caught himself before he had turned his head more than a fraction. By the time he looked back at Walking Thunder an instant later, the Minnetaree chief was staring fixedly beyond him, as though dismissing the redcoat from his mind in the same way he had ignored Jules.

There seemed little to be gained from remaining in the camp. It was possible, MacGregor reasoned, that Edson had gotten lost somewhere along the way and missed the Minnetaree camp, although he and Jules had come across one of Edson's overnight campsites on the way. However, it was also possible the American law officer had found some other lead and gone off in a different direction.

"Verra well, Walking Thunder," MacGregor said. "We will leave."

Walking Thunder did not reply. He did not remove his eyes from whatever real or imaginary object beyond MacGregor he was staring at so fixedly.

MacGregor reined his horse around. With Jules stirrup to stirrup alongside him, he was about to ride out of the Minnetaree camp when an outbreak of noise suddenly erupted. Jeers rang in his ears, mixed with mocking laughter. Clenched fists or rifle barrels waved in front of him. Here and there sunlight flashed off a knife blade or a tomahawk.

MacGregor's horse began prancing nervously, tossing its head and snorting as yelling braves closed in on them. Tightening his reins, MacGregor pressed spurs to his horse's flanks and the animal jumped forward, its shoulder knocking a brave reeling back among his tribesmen. Momentarily the Indians broke aside. MacGregor rode through them, Jules cantering his short-legged cayuse along behind to keep up.

A moment later they trotted their horses out of the camp, a running, jeering, yelling mob of braves following, shouting abuse and insults. Breaking into a canter, the horses quickly outdistanced them. The tepees dropped behind, becoming smaller. The noise grew dim.

"Whew," said Jules, pushing his hat back off his head and wiping the back of a hairy hand across his brow. "Me, I damn glad to be out of t'at camp. Walking Thunder, he is ver' bad Indian."

"We'll ride back to Edson's last campsite and try to pick up his trail," MacGregor said. "He must hae found

102

something and branched off somewhere."

They were about to ride up the slope toward the top of the ridge when MacGregor glanced casually in the direction of the Ghost River. Grazing alongside its banks was the band's horse herd. Among the ponies, conspicuous by its size, stood a cream-colored horse. It was no Indian pony.

MacGregor stiffened in his saddle. "Wait a minute, Jules!"

He reined his horse over toward the herd. As he cantered closer to it, he saw that the cream horse was a light bay.

"I'll be damned—!"

Abruptly MacGregor wheeled his horse around and rode back toward the Minnetaree camp. Shaking his head in resignation, Jules cantered his cayuse along behind the big sergeant.

The Indians watched MacGregor ride back. They watched in silence, confused by the redcoat's unexpected return.

MacGregor rode into the camp at a fast trot. Indians scattered out of his way. He didn't stop until he was back in front of Walking Thunder's tepee. Walking Thunder was nowhere in sight. The flap over the entrance was drawn tight again.

His face dark with anger, MacGregor swung down from his saddle, tossed his reins to Jules, and in great long strides, stormed across the flattened grass until he was in front of the entrance.

"Nice try, Walking Thunder," MacGregor shouted. "But you forgot one thing—the American's horse. Where is he, goddamn it?"

There was only silence from Walking Thunder's lodge.

MacGregor pounded a fist on the buffalo-hide wall of the tepee. The tepee shook. "Come oot of there, damn you!"

There was still no response.

"Come oot, Walking Thunder, or I'll come in after you." MacGregor turned and shouted at Jules. "Throw me your knife, Jules."

Jules sat his saddle, holding MacGregor's reins. Pulling a knife from his belt, he tossed it to MacGregor. MacGregor caught it and turned back to the tepee. Braves crowded around twenty yards away and watched in silence. An air of expectancy hung heavily.

"I'm coming in, Walking Thunder," MacGregor shouted, gripping the knife.

He was about to thrust the knife into the buffalo hide to cut away an opening when the entrance flap was throw open and a plainly agitated Walking Thunder stepped out.

The massive Minnetaree chief drew himself to his full height and stood glowering at MacGregor no more than six feet away.

"You say Walking Thunder speaks *lies?*" Walking Thunder demanded, thumping a big fist against his bare chest.

Standing on feet planted firmly eighteen inches apart, MacGregor pointed his right shoulder at the Minnetaree chief and locked dark eyes onto him. "The American's horse is with your ponies, Walking Thunder. The American is somewhere in your camp. Or you've killed him. If you have, you'll *hang!*"

Walking Thunder's Adam's apple bobbed. Hate contorted his face. His hand closed around the handle of a knife at his belt, but he made no other move.

"Where is he, Walking Thunder?" MacGregor snapped.

"He is not here."

"Then *where* is he?"

"I do not know."

"You're a *liar!*"

"No one may call Walking Thunder *liar!*" the Minnetaree chief growled.

104

MacGregor took a stab at Walking Thunder's vanity. "If you're not a liar, you're not the *real* chief here, because you dinna know what's going on, or is it the fugitive, Lone Man, who is the *real* chief now? He's a big mon. He's ridden the white man's trail and defied his laws."

Walking Thunder let out a mighty roar. Suddenly he threw himself at MacGregor. But MacGregor had been expecting it. He had seen it coming, seen it in Walking Thunder's eyes. He threw a right fist straight from his shoulder. It caught Walking Thunder high on the cheek. Immediately Walking Thunder's body hit MacGregor, but at the same time MacGregor turned his shoulder, swiveled a hip, and bent both knees. His movement deflected Walking Thunder's charge. A roar of approval went up from the watching Indians. It all happened so fast they thought their chief's momentum had caught the redcoat, but then they saw Walking Thunder sailing past the redcoat and landing heavily on the ground. Their roar instantly subsided and became deathly silence as the huge Minnetaree chief lay shaken on the grass in front of his tepee.

MacGregor turned to face Walking Thunder as the Indian slowly began to pick himself up. Shock and indignation covered the broad, dusky face. Walking Thunder couldn't believe what had happened. Worse, it had happened in front of his band.

Bellowing like an enraged bull, Walking Thunder charged MacGregor a second time. MacGregor neatly sidestepped and aimed a fast one-two chopping jab at Walking Thunder's ear as he hurtled by. This time Walking Thunder stopped short and swung around like a mountain lion, advancing on MacGregor in a low, crouching movement, massive shoulders hunched, arms spread wide like a giant crab. MacGregor met him with short, sharp jabs to the face, stepping back out of reach each time. Each time MacGregor's fists hit his face with a resounding and distinctive smacking sound, Walking Thunder snarled like a giant cat, shook his head, but continued advancing. Jules watched apprehensively as he sat his saddle and held Sergeant MacGregor's reins.

MacGregor was a big man, six-one and a well-muscled one hundred and ninety pounds. Besides having been in barroom brawls as a young soldier from Bombay to London and from Edinburgh to Capetown, he had fought his way into and out of a dozen bloody battles in India, Africa, and Egypt with lance, sword, rifle, and bayonet. He had learned speed, skill, and hardness. Walking Thunder, on the other hand, towered above MacGregor by several inches and outweighed him by more than sixty pounds. But Walking Thunder ruled his band by bullying. He had fought Cree war parties, but because of his size, seldom had an adversary stood up to him. He was not used to defeat or defiance, and he had trouble coping with it now. He possessed greater brute strength than MacGregor, but he didn't have the Scot's fighting skill or experience.

Whenever Walking Thunder made a lunge to grab MacGregor, the sergeant struck him a sharp left or right to the face, then quickly stepped back. When a groggy Walking Thunder kept lunging forward, shaking his head each time MacGregor struck him, the redcoat unexpectedly changed his tactics and stepped forward to rain several fast, stinging blows to the face. Blood spurting from his nose, Walking Thunder staggered backwards and fell.

Wild elation shook Jules. He had known Walking Thunder's reputation as a minor but nonetheless dangerous troublemaker for years. He had seen his friend, Sergeant Cavannagh, back down Walking Thunder twice, the first time by threats, the second time with a gun in his hand, but MacGregor was beating him with his fists. Confidence washed over the *metis*. Maybe they would get out of the Minnetaree camp with their hides unscathed yet.

MacGregor stood looking down at the sprawled Minnetaree chief. "What happened to the American, Walking Thunder?"

Walking Thunder glared up at the redcoat. He began to shake with rage. Wiping blood from his face, he got to his feet and fronted MacGregor. He dropped into a half crouch, spread his arms, and waited for his opportunity. Standing on feet spread comfortably apart, MacGregor half turned, presenting his right shoulder to the giant Indian. He raised his fists, holding them ready. Blood was smeared across his pipe-clayed white gauntlets.

This time Walking Thunder did not rush forward. He crouched warily. His face, full of hate and anger, the strangely light eyes carrying an almost glazed look, was frighteningly hideous. The eyes seemed to convey a single message—destroy the redcoat!

MacGregor waited for him.

Walking Thunder made no move, other than his giant chest lifting and falling, lifting and falling as he breathed air into his lungs. A stream of blood trickled from his nose down to his mouth, forming a small lake on his lips, some of it overflowing and running on down his chin.

MacGregor had faced some ugly adversaries during his soldiering days, and a few since he had been in the Mounted Police, but there was something disturbing about the Minnetaree chief. MacGregor wasn't quite sure what it was; he thought the eyes. They looked as though the man behind them was a wee bit mad—which made him a very dangerous opponent.

In the deathly silence that hung over the camp, Jules heard the sudden rattle of a Winchester lever from somewhere behind him. Whipping his head around, he was in time to see among the watching Minnetarees a brave lifting a rifle to his shoulder, aiming the barrel at

107

MacGregor's red coat. Jules reacted immediately. It happened so fast he didn't realize it—one instant he was watching the brave lifting the rifle to his shoulder, the next he held a revolver in his hand pointed at the brave.

Jules shouted. The brave hesitated, turning his head in the direction of the shout. He found himself staring into the small black hole of Jules's Enfield. Slowly the brave lowered his rifle. From his saddle, Jules kept his revolver pointed at him, in case the brave changed his mind.

Hearing Jules shout, recognizing the scout's voice, MacGregor turned his head from Walking Thunder. In that instant the Minnetaree chief seized his opportunity. He lunged at MacGregor. MacGregor caught the sudden movement in his peripheral vision. He snapped his head back and tried to step aside. He was too late. Walking Thunder closed with him, throwing his huge arms around him.

Excited shouting rose from the watching braves as the fight took a turn in Walking Thunder's favor. Jules felt his spirits sag as he tried to keep his gun on the brave and watch the fight at the same time.

MacGregor fought to free an arm to fight his way clear, but Walking Thunder's embrace pinned his arms to his sides.

Walking Thunder drove his jaw down on MacGregor's head, forcing it back, trying to break his neck. Walking Thunder squeezed. MacGregor attempted to expand his chest and shoulders, tried to force upwards and outwards with his arms in an effort to break clear of the Indian's life-crushing hold. But his efforts failed. Walking Thunder was too strong, his embrace too tight.

His neck hurting, the life being squeezed out of him, MacGregor next felt the bony knuckles of a closed fist pressed against his back, then kneaded into his spine. He gritted his teeth against the excruciating pain.

In desperation MacGregor lifted a foot, twisted his leg, then raked his steel spur hard against Walking Thunder's shin. The giant's grip weakened momentarily. Mac-Gregor repeated the tactic, but this time driving the spur in a sharp backward kick against Walking Thunder's shin, then raking the spur up and down the bone. Walking Thunder grunted but stifled a howl of pain. In retaliation he lifted MacGregor clean off his feet as though he were a rag doll, then flung his body violently onto the ground. MacGregor's blue and yellow pillbox went rolling off his head.

There were more shouts of approval from the watching Minnetaree braves.

MacGregor hit the ground with jarring force. Walking Thunder swung a leg to aim a vicious kick at MacGregor's head, but like lightning the sergeant swiveled on his back, got one foot behind the leg Walking Thunder was standing on, at the same time placing the other foot on his shin, then simultaneously pressed with the foot on Walking Thunder's shin and pulled with the one behind his leg, knocking the Minnetaree chief's supporting leg from underneath him. Walking Thunder hit the ground with a loud thud. This time there was no sound from the watching Minnetaree braves.

They both rebounded back up onto their feet. Walking Thunder aimed a kick at MacGregor's face. MacGregor ducked his head sideways, grabbed Walking Thunder's ankle, and jerked him off balance. Walking Thunder landed heavily on his back.

MacGregor stood over him.

"Y' dinna look bluidy much like the Lord of the Prairie and the Thunder Breeding Hills noo. Y' could hae saved yourself frae being made to look like a bluidy fool in front of your tribe by telling me what happened to the American."

Walking Thunder rolled back onto his feet.

MacGregor stood waiting for him.

"What happened to the American?"

Walking Thunder's hand reached for the knife at his

waist. Sunlight flashed off steel as the Minnetaree chief held the knife blade-first in his right hand. Dropping to a half crouch, he moved in on MacGregor.

MacGregor stepped back quickly, hand dropping to the Enfield holstered at his hip. Before Walking Thunder could reach him, MacGregor had him covered. Walking Thunder came to a sudden stop.

"You'll be telling me what happened to the American, Walking Thunder, or I'll slap handcuffs on you and take you to Fort Walsh to be locked up."

Walking Thunder shook his head. "No white man come here."

"You're lying!"

"You shoot me, redcoat, you never leave camp alive."

MacGregor laughed grimly. "If I dinna shoot you, I'll nae leave it alive if you hae your way. But I will shoot you if you dinna drop that knife."

Walking Thunder stood half crouched, knife held ready. Four feet separated him from MacGregor. The muzzle of MacGregor's Enfield was large and intimidating. The Minnetaree chief's eyes moved from the gun, held rock-steady in MacGregor's hand, to MacGregor's stern face. Walking Thunder saw no fear in that face. Only strength and determination.

All of a sudden, resignation seemed to wash over Walking Thunder. He straightened up from his aggressive, crouching stance. His shoulders sagged submissively. He glanced at the knife in his hand, then tossed it onto flattened grass a dozen feet away.

MacGregor looked at him for a moment. Then he nodded in agreement with Walking Thunder's unexpected change of heart, his seeming acceptance of the authority of the scarlet tunic. "Now you're being sensible," MacGregor said. He thrust the Enfield back into its holster, glancing down at the holster for an instant as he buttoned the flap. "Tell me where—"

MacGregor saw it coming. A blur of movement. He

110

ducked, but Walking Thunder's fist caught him a glancing blow on the side of the head. The unexpected blow almost snapped his head off and sent him reeling. But when Walking Thunder went to follow up his momentary advantage by attempting to grapple with the redcoat, MacGregor spun around and threw him with a rolling hip lock. Walking Thunder hit the grass heavily but vaulted back onto his feet.

They faced each other once more. Again Walking Thunder dropped into his crouching stance, circling MacGregor warily. He knew that if he could get his hand on the redcoat, he could destroy him.

Facing him, MacGregor recognized the same thing. His only chance was to keep out of the reach of those huge grappling arms. Yet he decided to give the Minnetaree chief a lesson. Walking Thunder had been a bad influence on the Northern Minnetarees for too long. MacGregor intended smashing his power over the band.

Walking Thunder didn't give him long to wait. Tiring of circling, the giant Minnetaree suddenly rushed at MacGregor. MacGregor met him with a hard, straight right, thrown from the shoulder. It smashed Walking Thunder full on the mouth, cracking a tooth and splitting his lips. MacGregor followed it with a driving left, catching him jarringly under the breast bone. Walking Thunder coughed and an expression of stunned surprise registered on his face. But he kept on coming. He swung his arms to wrap them around his enemy, and his left arm caught MacGregor around the neck, threatening to draw the redcoat into his embrace. MacGregor threw his head forward and down and slipped it out from under the Indian's arm. At the same time he grabbed Walking Thunder's wrist and twisted it up around behind his back. Holding it there with one hand, MacGregor reached up for one of Walking Thunder's braids, gripped it, and yanked the Minnetaree chief's head back. Walking Thunder let out a howl. MacGregor ran him straight

111

toward his tepee, gave him a mighty heave, and sent him careening face-first into the buffalo-skin lodge. The tepee shook from the impact, but the buffalo-hide wall bounced him back. MacGregor caught him on the rebound, cracking him over the left eye with a straight right, and crunching his nose a second time with a swinging left. Walking Thunder's knees buckled under him and he slumped to the ground.

MacGregor stepped back and stood, fists raised, waiting for him to get up again.

Walking Thunder got up more slowly this time. But he advanced on MacGregor once more, flailing with his giant arms, desperate to grapple with the redcoat. Moving on the balls of his feet, MacGregor met him with hard fists to the face and body. Blood ran freely down Walking Thunder's face, from his twice-bloodied nose, from split lips, and from a cut above his left eye. The giant Indian's face was beginning to swell. There was no noise from the watching Minnetaree braves, only dead silence.

Walking Thunder did not rush forward. Instead, he stood opposite MacGregor, sucking in great gulping draughts of air. MacGregor took advantage of the momentary lull to breathe deeply, but his breathing was controlled and regular. It increased his confidence and built his staying power.

Then Walking Thunder made his next move. MacGregor had seen it in his eyes. He knew it was coming, but he didn't know what it would be. He saw Walking Thunder tense, then the giant Minnetaree chief was transformed into a mass of flying buckskin as he suddenly threw out both moccasined feet at MacGregor.

If they had hit, they might have struck MacGregor with such force that they could have broken his neck. There was not only the hardness of Walking Thunder's big feet, there was also the weight and strength of his gigantic legs, body, and arms as two hundred and sixty

112

pounds of muscle and bone hurtled at MacGregor.

Because MacGregor had read Walking Thunder's eyes and had time to react, only Walking Thunder's left heel caught him, and it got him high on the left shoulder. It jolted him but he was able to roll his body with it, and he only went down on one knee as Walking Thunder's bulk sailed past him.

They were both back on their feet in an instant. Walking Thunder wasted no time, anxious to come to grips with the redcoat. He moved in quickly. Again MacGregor saw something in the pale eyes, a cunning, but he didn't know exactly what.

As Walking Thunder tried to grapple with him again, MacGregor threw out left and right jabs. They struck Walking Thunder in the face, making his head bob with each blow. They struck him on the shoulders and one caught him in the stomach. Yet they did not stop the Minnetaree chief. He continued advancing, his arms held ready to lock around MacGregor. MacGregor knew he couldn't afford to let them grab him. He continued raining blows at Walking Thunder.

Walking Thunder made his move. He snatched at one of MacGregor's fast-moving arms. With a great bellow of triumph, he pulled MacGregor into his embrace, wrapped both arms around his neck, and yanked MacGregor's head hard against his chest. Then he squeezed, trying to crush MacGregor's head.

MacGregor felt his head about to explode. He couldn't breathe. Walking Thunder's hold was blocking the flow of blood to his brain.

MacGregor tried to twist free, but Walking Thunder held him too tightly. He drove his fists into Walking Thunder's body, but Walking Thunder's grip didn't weaken. In desperation, MacGregor threw up his legs, intending the sudden displacement of weight to jerk Walking Thunder off balance so that he could pull him back with him, land on his back, and toss Walking

113

Thunder over his head. It didn't work like that. However, it was just as effective. One of MacGregor's upward-flung knees drove squarely into Walking Thunder's oversized testicles, ramming them right up into him.

Walking Thunder bellowed mightily, not in triumph but in pain. The crushing grip around MacGregor's head was released.

MacGregor stepped back quickly, beyond Walking Thunder's reach. The big Minnetaree chief doubled up, his blood-smeared face grimacing with pain.

The fight had gone on long enough. For the success of his plan to break Walking Thunder's influence over the Northern Minnetarees, MacGregor had to finish him off quickly. He couldn't afford to get caught in his embrace again.

MacGregor moved in to take advantage of Walking Thunder's preoccupation with his testicles. The Scot drove a right straight from the shoulder, connecting with Walking Thunder's chin. Walking Thunder dropped to the ground.

MacGregor waited for him to get up. Walking Thunder took his time, glaring up at the redcoat through hate-filled eyes. He wasn't beaten yet. He still wanted to destroy MacGregor.

As soon as the Minnetaree chief was back on his feet, MacGregor waded in with battering blows to his face and body. Each time he hit, he had to move quickly back out of his opponent's reach. Walking Thunder flung his arms about wildly, trying to grab MacGregor or trying to stun him with a lucky swing. MacGregor watched his opportunities and jabbed punches whenever he could get in under Walking Thunder's arms. His blows rocked Walking Thunder but they did not put him down. The massive warrior not only had size and strength, he had endurance as well.

MacGregor wanted to end the fight. It was lasting too long. But he could not get in close enough to land the really punishing punches that would knock his opponent down for good. He could not get close enough without running the risk of falling into the Minnetaree chief's grappling embrace.

MacGregor decided to match cunning with cunning. He stepped back, lowering his fists a fraction. Walking Thunder moved toward him, arms still swinging, reaching out to grapple. MacGregor feinted a slow left that came nowhere close to the warrior. It lacked force and speed. Walking Thunder kept advancing. MacGregor took another step back, keeping out of reach of those powerful, grappling arms. He feinted another slow, lackluster left.

It looked like MacGregor was getting tired. A new awareness shone in Walking Thunder's eyes. The beginning of a grin appeared on his face. He lunged forward, but MacGregor stumbled back just beyond reach.

Walking Thunder advanced again. MacGregor threw another punch but it fell short. Sure the redcoat's endurance was giving out, Walking Thunder grinned cruelly and advanced once more.

When Walking Thunder stopped swinging his arms and presented an opening, MacGregor moved clumsily and threw a left that connected with Walking Thunder's right cheek. Walking Thunder barely felt it. Now he *knew* the redcoat was tiring.

Walking Thunder moved forward once more, confident, eager to close. MacGregor fell back, still keeping out of the Minnetaree chief's reach. He kept falling back, moving around in a wide circle in front of Walking Thunder's tepee.

Uttering a triumphant whoop, Walking Thunder sprang at MacGregor, raising his big hands above him to bring them crashing down on the redcoat.

It was the opportunity MacGregor had been waiting for. Overly confident, eager to demolish the redcoat, Walking Thunder had momentarily left himself open.

MacGregor stepped in. Leaning forward, he drove a hard right that shot up and smashed Walking Thunder on the left side of his neck. Part of MacGregor's fist caught Walking Thunder under the jawbone. Walking Thunder's head rocked back. MacGregor followed up with a roundhouse left that slammed in under his ribs. Pain and sheer surprise appeared on the Minnetaree chief's face.

MacGregor advanced with more hard-driving right and left blows to Walking Thunder's face and body. Each blow forced him to stagger back a step. He dropped to a knee, and MacGregor followed up with more blows.

Walking Thunder tried to get back up onto his feet, but MacGregor kept hammering him. The Minnetaree chief held up an arm in front of him to try to ward off the blows, but MacGregor knocked his arm out of the way.

MacGregor stepped back just long enough to let Walking Thunder stagger back onto his feet, but the instant the Minnetaree chief was up, MacGregor let him have the hardest right from his shoulder that he could drive. His fist thudded full into Walking Thunder's face. Blood spurted, teeth flew. Walking Thunder went sailing backwards, then landed heavily on his back.

He did not get up.

He lay where he fell, face a bloody mess. Only his eyes moved, staring up at the sky.

MacGregor looked down at him for a moment. Then he stepped over beside Walking Thunder's tepee, reached down, and picked up his pillbox. After dusting it off, he put it back on his head, adjusting the thin leather strap around his chin. Next he dusted grass and dirt off his uniform, pulled his red tunic down at the back, and straightened his gun belt. Only when he was satisfied that he presented a regimental appearance did he turn to face the onlooking Minnetaree tribesman. Bunched together in the space around their chief's tepee, they stared

116

back at the redcoat in silence. Their faces were expressionless, except that there was no longer hostility in their eyes, nor sullenness. If anything, they seemed to stare at MacGregor in awed respect.

Glancing at Jules, MacGregor said, "Tell them that the White Mother's law spreads all over the North West, over all the plains and the hills, the rivers and the forests and the mountains far away. Everyone who lives in this land must live peacefully and obey the White Mother's laws. Tell them that the redcoats are her servants and soldiers. We make sure that her laws are obeyed."

From his saddle, Jules interpreted what MacGregor said, using a mixture of the Minnetaree's own dialect and sign talk, the commonly understood language of the plains tribes. As soon as Jules had finished, MacGregor continued.

"Walking Thunder has nae led you wisely. He has defied the White Mother's laws. Whoever disobeys her laws is liable to be punished. There is a large yellow-looking horse among your ponies. It belongs to a white mon, an American frae below the medicine line. He came to your camp looking for three bad men who broke laws in the American's country and crossed the medicine line into the White Mother's country. One of the three bad men is an Indian, one of your own people. His name is Lone Man. I want to know what happened to the American. Where is he? I also want Lone Man and the other two bad men who crossed the medicine line."

Jules resumed translating MacGregor's words. He was barely finished when there was a shout from behind the assembled Minnetaree braves. An Indian with short black hair tumbling down across his brow lifted a Winchester and pointed it at MacGregor. The other Indians moved aside quickly, leaving him standing there alone.

"You want Lone Man? Here I am! Now what, redcoat?"

117

MacGregor looked calmly at him. "Put down your rifle, Lone Man. I'm taking you to Fort Walsh to be locked up until a court decides what to do with you."

Lone Man laughed. "Hah!" He curled his lip contemptuously. "You not take me anywhere, redcoat. You not leave this camp alive."

"If you kill me, another redcoat will take my place. If you kill him, yet another will come, until one of them takes you. You canna kill them all. The redcoats are invincible. They are the White Mother's law."

"Hah! Empty words. I kill you now, how will other redcoats know?"

"The redcoats will know. They always know."

"Hah! You die, redcoat!" Lone Man took aim, squinting along the barrel. His finger curled around the trigger.

Lone Man did not pull the trigger.

Something cold jammed hard against the back of his neck. A voice rasped in his ear.

"Drop that rifle, cock, like the sar'nt said, or you'll be wearin' a great bleedin' 'ole for an Adam's apple."

Lone Man slowly turned his head. Shock clouded his face. Standing behind him, holding a revolver against his neck, was another redcoat. Lone Man let his rifle drop to the ground as though it was a piece of hot steel.

"Now start walkin' straight ahead." Freddie gave him a helping jab with the gun barrel. Lone Man stumbled forward through the gap made by the watching braves, continuing on across the clearing toward Sergeant MacGregor. Marching right behind him, Freddie let out a shrill whistle. A moment later his horse came trotting from among the tepees and followed him.

"What the hell are you doing here, Freddie?" MacGregor said. "Nae that I'm n' damn glad to see you, but I gave you orders to escort that preacher and his daughter to Fort Walsh."

Freddie grinned. "Not long after you left, 'Frenchy'

118

LeBlanc passed through, carryin' dispatches from Wood Mountain to Fort Walsh. I couldn't see any point in two of us goin' to the same place, so I asked 'im to escort them. I reckoned you'd need 'elp with Walkin' Thunder, so I came ridin' north as fast as I could. Looks like I was right. I 'ope I'm not too late for the excitement."

Grinning back, MacGregor shook his head in disbelief. "There's nae any doubt about you, Freddie. Anyway, clap a pair of handcuffs around his wrists," he said, tilting his head at Lone Man. "Maybe he can tell us where Edson is."

Before Lone Man could open his mouth, two braves emerged from a tepee with a tall, black-mustached man between them. He stood rubbing his wrists where they had been tied.

MacGregor eyed him coldly as he approached. Apart from a black whisker growth and a haggard expression on his face, he seemed little the worse for his experience.

"You shouldna been so impatient, Mister Edson," MacGregor admonished. "You could hae saved yourself a wee bit of bother if you had waited at Pine Butte until I got back, as we agreed."

Edson nodded sheepishly.

MacGregor turned and looked sternly down at Walking Thunder. The Minnetaree chief still lay sprawled on the grass where MacGregor had knocked him, but he had raised his head and shoulders, propping himself up on an elbow. His face bruised and bloodied, he peered up at the redcoat through half-closed eyelids.

Placing his hands on his hips, MacGregor spoke to him.

"Listen to my words, Walking Thunder, and listen closely. I've heard all about you. My *metis* scout here, who rode with the redcoat with the steel-blue eyes, has told me all about you. You're a thug and the next thing to an outlaw. You're damned lucky I'm nae taking you to Fort Walsh and locking you up with Lone Man. You

119

better hae learned a lesson today. But I am warning you . . . if you break the White Mother's laws one more time, I will be back. If I hae to do that, I might hang you the next time."

Walking Thunder lifted a hand to his neck. He swallowed hard.

From Walking Thunder, MacGregor directed his attention back to Lone Man. "Where are your two friends?"

Lone Man shook his head. "I don' know."

MacGregor locked eyes with him for a moment, then looked over to Jules, still sitting on his saddle. "Ask the Minnetarees whether two white men came to their camp with Lone Man."

Jules spoke to the Minnetarees. They answered him immediately. Jules looked at MacGregor. "T'ey say Lone Man come alone."

"Are they telling the truth?"

Jules nodded. "I t'ink so."

"All right," MacGregor said. "Let's get out of here."

As soon as Deputy U.S. Marshal Edson recovered his guns and saddled his horse, they rode out of the Minnetaree camp. The Indians watched them ride away. There was no jeering.

MacGregor leaned over in his saddle and spoke to Jules, riding alongside. "I dinna think Walking Thunder will be leading that band astray again, Jules. For one thing, I dinna think he'll want to try it, and for another I dinna think they'll listen to him. Now that they've seen him defeated, they've lost their respect for him — *if* it was ever respect. Likely it was fear. Anyway, his power is broken, and all for the better."

CHAPTER 10

Swinging around the east side of Pine Butte, Sergeant MacGregor and his small party sighted the log buildings of the outpost half a mile ahead. It was late afternoon. They had been gone four days.

"We'll spend the night here and ride out for Fort Walsh first thing tomorrow morning," MacGregor said, glancing up at the sky, blue but heavily banked with great white cloud formations. "I'd like to stay here a full day to rest the horses, but I'm nae confident the weather will hold much longer. I've seen no more geese. They've probably all flown south by now. That's a sure sign winter is close. I want to get the prisoner locked up in Fort Walsh before snow falls. All we need is one good blizzard and the trails can be bluidy hell."

"How far is Fort Walsh?" Edson asked.

"A hundred miles."

"You making that trip just to lock up Lone Man here?"

"Aye."

Edson lolled in his saddle. "Seems like a mighty shame you have to be put to all that bother, especially when you've got a lot of other things to do. It'd sure be a lot simpler if you were to just hand him over to me, then I could take him back across the line into Montana and save you all that trouble."

121

"I dinna make the rules, Mister Edson. I just follow them. Lone Man has to be held at Fort Walsh pending proper legal proceedings. Of course, you're quite at liberty to ride to Fort Walsh with me and talk to Major Walsh about it. But I doubt it'll do any good. The major has to follow the rules too."

They reined to in front of the outpost. Edson scratched himself. MacGregor cast an eye at him. "You got the itches?"

"Yeah."

"You probably picked up something lying tied in that Indian camp. Lice or something. A hot bath will fix you. We'll haul some water frae the river and heat it. We've a bathtub in the barracks. Freddie and the laddies made it last winter. We hae some stuff in the medical stores that'll kill the little bastards. In fact, I think I'll hae a bath m'self."

They led their horses over to the stables, where they unsaddled them and gave them a rubdown. MacGregor told Lone Man to do the same.

"Why?" the Minnetaree prisoner grunted belligerently.

"Because I bluidy well said so, that's why," MacGregor growled back at him. "Horses need attention, and if you're nae prepared to give it to them, you should be bluidy well walking."

Later, in the barracks, MacGregor sat in a chair enjoying a pipe of tobacco following dinner and a bath, when Jules stepped into the large room the detachment used as sleeping and living quarters. MacGregor looked up from an old newspaper he was reading. He knew Jules wanted to ask him something. He could tell by the way the *metis* scout stood before him, nervously curling the brim of his hat held in both hands in front of him.

"Yes, Jules?" MacGregor asked, raising his eyebrows questioningly.

"You ride to Fort Walsh wit' prisoner tomorrow, *mon* Sergeant? Me, I lak ride wit' you. Mebbe I could have a little bit time off, just two, t'ree days to see my cousin, Pierre, at Fort Walsh."

MacGregor stared up at the scout. "Time off! Hell! I'm a sergeant and I canna get leave, yet you, a civilian member, want it!"

Jules looked thoroughly miserable. He had always stood a little in awe of the big Scottish sergeant. He felt much more at ease with his friend, Sergeant Cavannagh.

Then MacGregor laughed. Standing up, he clapped a hand on Jules's shoulder. "That's all right, Jules. We hae to take care of our civilian members. Aye, I think a few days leave would be in order. I dinna recall y' having any for quite a while. In fact, I think I could put you to good use on the ride to Fort Walsh. You and I can spell each other off guarding the prisoner when we camp at night. He'll be handcuffed and his feet will be tied, even when he sleeps. All the same, he's a bad one and I'm nae going to take any chances with him."

Bill Edson had been reclining in another chair, dozing after his warm bath, but now he opened his eyes.

"Seeing as how I'll be riding along with you, I'd be glad to take turns watching him at night, Sergeant."

MacGregor glanced at the American. "I appreciate your offer, Mister Edson, but the prisoner is a Mounted Police responsibility. We'll manage."

The next morning they saddled up. Edson glanced at the brass-buttoned blue greatcoat and cloak MacGregor had folded and tied with his bedroll onto the back of his saddle. MacGregor had also replaced his pillbox, wearing instead a regulation Hussar-pattern fur cap with yellow bag on the right side.

"You really expecting cold weather, Sergeant?"

Standing beside his horse, MacGregor looked at the American across the top of his saddle. Edson had put on a leather jacket in place of his gray coat. MacGregor nodded. "Aye, and you'd be advised to get yourself some warm clothing when we reach Fort Walsh."

MacGregor glanced around at Jules. "Ready, Jules?"

"*Oui, mon* Sergeant."

"Prisoner's horse saddled properly? Girth band tight?"

"*Oui.*"

"Guid. Let's get mounted and on our way."

They were halfway to Fort Walsh when they saw a bright scarlet tunic and a high-topped wagon coming along the trail toward them.

MacGregor recognized the wagon immediately. It took him an instant longer to identify the scarlet rider.

"I'll be damned!"

Constable Jean LeBlanc, of the Wood Mountain detachment, rode alongside the wagon that carried the Reverend Theodore Hatcher and his daughter Sarah on the front seat.

Constable LeBlanc, a pleasant-looking, dark-haired young man, smiled. "Hello, Sergeant MacGregor, Jules." He nodded politely to Edson, then glanced briefly at the handcuffed Lone Man. He looked back at MacGregor. "Your patrol to Walking Thunder's camp was successful, I see." Constable LeBlanc hailed from the largely French-speaking province of Quebec, in Eastern Canada, but he spoke without any trace of a French accent.

MacGregor nodded soberly. "Aye. I hae Freddie to thank for that. His arrival was timely." He looked up questioningly at the Reverend Hatcher.

A smug expression on his face, the preacher stared back at him, but said nothing. MacGregor looked at Constable LeBlanc. When Constable LeBlanc said nothing, Sergeant MacGregor couldn't resist the temptation to ask the question that had sprung into his mind.

"What are they doing here? Why aren't they on the way back to Fort Benton?"

The question was asked of Constable LeBlanc, but it was Reverend Hatcher who answered. "Your Major Walsh was kind enough to allow us to remain in Canadian territory." Reverend Hatcher's tone carried a note of almost malicious triumph. It irritated the big Scot.

"Nae to go back visiting a Sioux camp, I trust?"

The smugness left the Reverend Hatcher's face. "Sarah and I intend spreading the Lord's word among the Crees and Assiniboines, and among the *metis* settlements of the Wood Mountain district."

MacGregor grunted. "I'm sure the Catholic priests will appreciate you horning in on their ground."

"God's message draws no barriers of race or denomination, Sergeant. The only barriers are those that are imposed by bigoted and ignorant minds."

MacGregor moved his eyes from the Reverend Hatcher to Sarah, sitting primly, head and chin held high, beside him. She surveyed MacGregor coldly. She didn't look like her father, MacGregor thought, but she had the same damned irritating manner. He turned his attention back to the preacher.

"If you're implying that I'm a bigoted mon, Reverend, you're entirely mistaken," MacGregor snapped, trying to contain his rising anger. His mood seemed to convey itself to his horse, for the animal stamped a hoof and tossed its head impatiently. "I dinna care what y' do, as long as y' dinna poke your nose into places where you nae no business doing so."

Constable LeBlanc said, "These people have given their word to Major Walsh that they will not go near any of the Sioux camps, Sergeant."

MacGregor looked hard at the serious-faced younger man. "I'm glad Major Walsh is so sure that the reverend gentleman will keep his word, Constable. I'm sorry to nae to say that I dinna share the major's confidence in his word."

Sarah Thatcher sprang to her father's defense. "That's

a most unkind and ungentlemanly thing to say, Sergeant!"

MacGregor looked back at her. There was fire in her eyes. She was attractive in an aloof way when she was angry, and she really didn't look like her father at all. She had a directness about her that MacGregor reluctantly admired, a directness that her father did not have.

MacGregor said to Constable LeBlanc, "Are you their keeper, Constable?"

Constable LeBlanc's face reddened. "Major Walsh ordered me to guide them to Wood Mountain, Sergeant. I presume he did so because I was returning to Wood Mountain in any event. At least I can show them the way and be of whatever assistance I can."

MacGregor simmered down. "Hmmm." It wasn't Constable LeBlanc's fault. But MacGregor couldn't resist a parting shot. "Then I'll give you a wee piece of advice, Constable. I'd keep a close watch on them to make sure they dinna wander off to Sitting Bull's camp. The next time they mightn't be as lucky as they were the last time. And Major Walsh, as you well know, is a fine officer, but he has the temper of his Irish ancestors. He'll hold you accountable."

With that, MacGregor flicked his reins and cantered his horse along the trail to Fort Walsh. Jules glanced quickly at Constable Leblanc and shrugged. Then he legged his cayuse into a canter after his sergeant, towing the prisoner alongside him. Deputy United States Marshal Edson tipped his hat to Miss Hatcher, smiled, and followed the others.

Shortly after noon of their third day out of Pine Butte, they paused on top of a rolling hill and looked down onto the valley of Battle Creek.

"That's Fort Walsh," MacGregor said, swinging down from his saddle. "Hold my horse a wee moment, if y'

126

will." He passed the reins to Edson.

While MacGregor pulled a brush from one of his saddle wallets, Edson leaned a hand on the pommel of his California and gazed down at the fort on the valley floor. Jules and the handcuffed Lone Man sat their saddles alongside.

"Log stockade and the lot," Edson said. "Looks just like one of those old Kentucky frontier forts I used to read about when I was a kid. I've seen a lot of places that use the tag *fort* in their name, but none that really looked like one, not like the one down there. What's that place just beyond?"

Bending over a booted foot resting on a rock, MacGregor paused from his boot-brushing long enough to glance below. "Some call it Fort Walsh *Village*. I suppose that's as guid a name to give it as any."

"What's down there?"

"Saloons, billiard parlor, trading stores, a hotel, even a dance hall—except there's no women. At least, there weren't the last time I was there. Besides that, there's all the flotsam and drifters of the frontier hanging around the place at one time or another."

MacGregor resumed brushing. Edson continued to gaze down at the log fort and adjacent settlement.

When he had finished brushing his boots, MacGregor replaced the brush, then took from his breeches pocket a woman's stocking.

Edson grinned. "Is that a souvenir of some amorous conquest?"

MacGregor took the ends of the stocking, one in each hand, put a booted foot back on the rock, and began rubbing the stocking quickly backwards and forwards across the toe of the boot.

"A woman's stocking is unexcelled for putting a shine on a pair of boots."

"You didn't answer my question."

MacGregor laughed. "Aye, and I'll nae be answering

127

it."

Edson watched a moment longer, admiring the glossy appearance of MacGregor's boots.

"I was wondering how it is you boys always manage to look so smart in those uniforms. You do that with your buttons too?"

"In the dry air in this part of the country some idle constables try to get away wi' burnishing their buttons every second day. But I burnish mine daily."

"Even when you're busy?"

"I've been a professional soldier all my life. Brushing and burnishing is like eating and breathing. I'm never too busy to keep my kit in shape."

"How come you missed today?"

"I dinna miss. I burnished 'em back in camp early this morning when I was taking my turn guarding the prisoner. You were still sleeping."

"I offered to take turns with you and your scout watching Lone Man."

MacGregor nodded as he pulled the stocking backwards and forwards across the boot leather. "Aye, and I appreciate your offer, but as I told you, the prisoner is a Mounted Police responsibility."

Having said that, MacGregor glanced over at Jules. "Are you keeping an eye on the prisoner, Jules? I dinna want him getting any reckless ideas about making a sudden dash for freedom, especially not now that we're so close to the fort."

Jules nodded, his floppy hat brim flapping with the movement of his head. *"Oui.* I watch 'im."

"It still seems a shame," Edson said, "to have put you to all this trouble, seeing as how busy and shorthanded your force is, when I could just as easily have taken him off your hands and hauled him back across the line."

MacGregor didn't interrupt his polishing. "As I told you, Mister Edson, I dinna make the rules. I just follow them. And as I said, you're quite at liberty to accom-

128

pany us to Fort Walsh and put your case to the major, which, I expect, is the reason you've ridden along with us. But I doubt the major will change things. He has to follow the rules, too."

Edson sat his saddle looking down at MacGregor, watching until there was not a fleck of dust to mar the gloss on his riding boots. The boots finished, MacGregor unbuckled his gun belt and gave belt and holster a vigorous rubbing. Then he held the belt up to catch the afternoon sunlight. Belt and holster gleamed magnificently. Satisfied, he buckled the belt back around his tunic.

"I'm surprised you boys, being as how you're so busy, find time to do all that," Edson said. "Especially out here in the middle of nowhere."

MacGregor said, "I'm bucking for promotion to sergeant major."

Edson said nothing.

Grinning, MacGregor looked up at him. "Seriously, though, it's a matter of discipline. It's important to look smart and soldierly, *especially* out in the middle of nowhere. It impresses the Indians, and it helps unnerve the outlaws we chase. It's worked particularly well with the Blackfoot and Sioux. And it surprises the hell out of a camp of outlaws or whiskey-runners when we ride into them looking all polished up. It would hae less an effect if we looked dirty and scruffy and unshaven. It's all part of discipline, and discipline is verra much a part of the Mounted Police."

"But you're not riding down into any Indian camp now. You're about to ride down into a Mounted Police fort full of your own men. You don't need to impress them."

MacGregor wasn't sure whether the American was serious. Deciding he was serious, MacGregor said, "That's a verra strange way of looking at things. I'm a senior noncommissioned officer. It's up to NCOs to set

129

the example for the men to follow. If the constables see me looking polished and regimental all the time, and especially when I come in off patrol, they'll try to follow that example. Besides, I hae m' oon pride as a member of the Force."

MacGregor took his reins from Edson and swung himself back up onto the saddle.

They rode down the trail to the valley below. As they approached the fort, a trumpet call sounded, ringing stirringly across the valley.

"They're mounting the regimental guard," MacGregor said, legging his horse into a trot to reach the fort sooner.

"That sound reminds me of my army days," Edson said.

MacGregor looked at the American with renewed interest. "You were a soldier?"

Edson nodded. "For four years. Union cavalry, back during the War Between the States. Reached lieutenant before I got out."

"Did y' nae like the army well enough to stay in it after the war?"

Edson shook his head. "It was a bad time. The only job for the army was fighting Indians. I'd seen enough killing and destruction, seeing farms and homes burned to the ground. It was a hell of a mess, that war."

"Frae what I hear about gunfights and lawlessness and all that sort of thing down in your country, I'd reckon that wearing a deputy marshal's badge, you'd still be seeing a lot of death and destruction."

Edson nodded. "But on a smaller scale, a much smaller scale. This time it's vermin . . . vermin like Oates and his gang. They shoot down people in cold blood, innocent people mostly, people that ought'n to be shot down. Wearing a deputy marshal's badge, I feel like I'm doing something to clean up the mess, something to help reconstruct the country."

MacGregor was keen to reach the fort before the daily regimental mounting of the guard ceremony was over, to witness at least part of it, even though he had seen it and taken part in it countless times before. But he was curious about the tall, blue-eyed American law officer riding beside him.

"How did you become a deputy marshal?"

"After the war I drifted a bit. I was twenty-one when the war started, twenty-five when it ended. I'd done some cattle-punchin' before the war, so I drifted back into it after I got out of the army. Then I took a job as a sheriff's deputy in Colorado. In '69 I was offered an appointment as a deputy United States marshal. I took it for a spell, liked it, and I've been doing it ever since."

They reached the east gates, wheeled their horses, and rode into Fort Walsh. Scarlet tunics ablaze, afternoon sunlight dancing on the brass spikes on top of their white helmets, the regimental guard was marching off the parade ground.

"Agh! We just missed it! Pity. It's a verra impressive ceremony, as good as regular British troops changing the guard at St. James's Palace. The different barrack rooms compete with one another to see which can turn out the smartest-looking guard. They even carry their respective candidates frae their barrack rooms to the parade ground so they won't get dust on their boots on the way."

MacGregor led them past the flagpole toward the guardroom. Edson looked around as he rode by, taking in everything. His eyes lingered on the six field guns and the two polished brass mortars lined up along the square, not the type of equipment normally associated with a police force.

He said, "I see what Constable Jenkins meant when he said if there's soldiering to be done, you Mounted Police do it."

MacGregor nodded. "Aye, we're trained to act as sol-

131

diers or police, whichever happens to be necessary."

Upon reaching the guardroom they dismounted and handed Lone Man over to the provost sergeant. Taking Edson's warrant, the NCO wrote in a prisoners' book, then locked the Indian in a cell. MacGregor, Edson, and Jules stepped back outside.

Glancing at Jules, MacGregor said, "Look after the horses while Mister Edson and I go to Major Walsh's office. I'll get the major's authorization for your leave, then you can go."

MacGregor took Edson along a pathway neatly bordered with whitewashed rocks toward the headquarters offices. The fort was alive with military-like activity. A sergeant drilled a squad of men on the parade ground. Red-coated men marched smartly backwards and forwards between log buildings. Sergeant Major Francis and the orderly officer sauntered around the barrack square on their way toward the west palisade to inspect the stables. A sentry with shouldered carbine paced his beat beside the main gates. A sub-inspector led a four-man patrol that trotted out through the gates, swung south, and broke into a canter.

Outside Major Walsh's office, Sergeant MacGregor informed the orderly corporal that he wished to report to the commanding officer. A moment later the corporal held open the major's door. MacGregor and Edson walked through. MacGregor slammed to a drill-book halt in front of the major's desk and saluted.

"At ease, Sergeant," Major Walsh said, sitting back in his chair. From MacGregor, his eyes moved to Edson.

"This is Mister Edson, sir. He's a deputy United States marshal. Mister Edson, Major Walsh, commanding the post."

Major Walsh stood up, reached across his desk, and shook hands with the American. "Mister Edson."

"Major," Edson replied, touching the brim of his gray hat with two fingers.

"Mister Edson has warrants for the arrests of three criminals who crossed the border frae Montana, sir. We arrested one of them, a Minnetaree named Lone Man, in Walking Thunder's camp north of Pine Butte. We've brought him in and handed him over to the provost sergeant."

"May I see the warrants?" Major Walsh asked.

Reaching into an inside pocket of his leather jacket, Edson withdrew the warrants, together with a folded parchment, and handed them across the desk to the officer.

Waving the two men to chairs beside his desk, Major Walsh sat down as he unfolded the documents.

Edson said, "Those warrants are for the arrests of Ceston Parker Oates and Henri Foucade. They're somewhere this side of the border. Your guardroom sergeant has the warrant for the arrest of Lone Man. That other piece of paper, the one you're unfolding now, is my appointment as a deputy United States marshal, just so's you know I am who I say I am."

Major Walsh read the warrants and Edson's appointment document. He handed them back.

Edson slipped them back inside his jacket. "Thanks, Major. I appreciate the help your force is giving my government by rounding up Lone Man. I had sort of hoped I could have taken him straight back across the line into Montana, likewise with the other two. That would save a whole heap of trouble and effort by your men. Seems a shame to put your force, being busy like you are, to all the bother of escorting them long distances and then having to feed and guard 'em when I could just as easy take 'em back down into Montana. That's where they're going to wind up in the long run, anyways."

MacGregor said, "I've already explained to Mister Edson that what he asked for was impossible, sir, that we hae to hold the prisoner until formal extradition is applied for."

Major Walsh nodded. "That's correct, Sergeant." He turned his intense brown eyes onto the American law officer. "Your office will have to make formal application for extradition, Mister Edson. We can hold the prisoner on the strength of your warrant, but we can't turn him over to you without the proper extradition proceedings as provided for by the treaty between our two countries."

"The way Sergeant MacGregor explained it to me, that could take some time, Major."

Sunlight, shafting into the office through a window that looked out onto the parade ground, hit Major Walsh's left shoulder and sleeve, highlighting the brightness of his scarlet tunic and its gold cord trimming. He nodded again. "I'm afraid that's true. However, rest assured that we will hold him until extradition proceedings are completed. Now, you say two of the criminals are still at large in Canadian territory?"

"That's so."

"Naturally, we'll extend every cooperation to your government in apprehending them," Major Walsh said. "Do you have any idea where they might be?"

"Oates used to brag about how he peddled whiskey to Indians in the Cypress Hills back in the early seventies. That was before your force was organized, as I understand. He talked about a strong log cabin he and a pal of his built near where there was some sort of Indian battle in '71. He told someone he figgered on eventually going back to it to hole up. That was six months ago. Now he's crossed the border into Canadian territory somewheres close to where that cabin ought to be."

Major Walsh and Sergeant MacGregor exchanged glances. "We should be able to track that down, Sergeant. There's an old-timer in the village who would probably know where such a cabin might be. Dick Hardstone. He's a reformed, one-time whiskey peddler. If

134

anyone would know, he would."

"Aye, sir."

Major Walsh looked back at Edson. "As I said, Mister Edson, we'll extend your government every cooperation. In fact, I'll assign Sergeant MacGregor to assist you, seeing that he's already familiar with the matter."

Sergeant MacGregor stared questioningly at the major.

Major Walsh answered the sergeant's unspoken question. "Orders just arrived in the latest mail from Ottawa, Sergeant. Pine Butte is to be closed. I'm not happy with the order. I think it's a mistake. Personally, I think Ottawa is becoming unduly alarmed over the continued presence of the Sioux and the fact that Sitting Bull and the other Sioux chiefs turned down Washington's offer of an amnesty. I'm to concentrate most of my strength here and at Wood Mountain. In my opinion it's an alarmist view, but unfortunately I'm not in any position to make my views sufficiently well known to do any good. I'll send a couple of men and a wagon to Pine Butte to help Jenkins close the outpost and load up all the equipment and stores. They can bring your kit back with them."

MacGregor pushed his chair back and stood up. "Verra guid, sir. I'll give Mister Edson whatever assistance I can to apprehend those two criminals. They're to be locked up in the guardroom the same way as Lone Man, sir?"

"Certainly."

MacGregor was about to salute and march out until he remembered his scout. "Oh . . . Scout Prefontaine, sir . . . he rode in with me. He's asked for a few days' leave, sir. He wants to visit his cousin in the village. He has nae had any leave for quite a wee while, and he's been working well. In fact, he saved my life in Walking Thunder's camp by covering a brave who was pointing a rifle at me. He's a guid scout."

"Very well, Sergeant. Submit a leave form for my

signature. At the expiration of his leave, he will report to Sergeant Major Francis for duty as a scout at the fort."

"Verra guid, sir."

Major Walsh said to the American, "You're welcome to stay on the post as long as you require, Mister Edson. We'll put you up in the NCOs' quarters."

Edson stood up. "Thanks, Major. Much obliged."

Major Walsh rose from behind his desk. "Nice meeting you, Mister Edson." He extended his hand and he and the deputy United States marshal shook. "Good luck to you both."

MacGregor saluted, about-faced, and marched out of the major's office. Edson raised his fingers to his hat brim in some sort of imitation of MacGregor's stiff, British-style salute, turned around, and followed the sergeant out of the office.

Outside the building, MacGregor looked up at the sky. Although the sun was shining and the sky was blue overhead, masses of heavy gray clouds were building up in the west. He frowned. "There's some weather coming in frae the west. I knew this warm spell could nae last much longer." He gave Edson a nod. "You better go into the village and get yourself some warm clothes like I told you."

The village of Fort Walsh hadn't looked impressive from up on top of the hills surrounding the valley. From close up it didn't look any better. In contrast to the well-maintained neatness and orderliness of the Mounted Police fort, the village was ramshackle, haphazard, and untidy. Though overall it had a sprawled-out appearance, the odd assortment of log cabins, clapboard shacks, canvas tents, and shanties that comprised the village were at the same time huddled together for protection, either from the severe winters that held sway from November to March, or from a possible threat from the

136

savage Indian tribes that used to wage war upon one another around the Cypress Hills. However, the village stood within the shadow of the Mounted Police fort, drawing upon the protection and security the small force of one hundred redcoats provided.

Bill Edson rode his light bay along what passed as the village's main street. It looked as though it had been pegged out on the wanderings of some drunk who had staggered out of the local saloon.

He reined his horse aside to let pass a string of sixteen oxen hauling three covered wagons hitched together tandem-fashion. A squat, bearded bull-whacker walked alongside them, cracking his bullwhip over their backs as he drove them along, filling the air with colorful epithets. Edson sat his saddle watching them go, following a trail from the village that wound along around the fort and on south down the valley floor. A sign had been hammered into the ground, with the words *Fort Benton Trail* painted crudely on it.

The bull wagon had pulled out from a large frame building, with its fresh coat of white paint an oddity compared to most of the other structures. It bore a sign: *I.G. Baker Company. Trading Store.* Edson sat his saddle a moment longer, staring at it. He had heard of the Baker Company. They hailed from Montana, from Fort Benton. Edson recalled that the Fort Benton manager, Charles Conrad, came from an old Virginia family and had served in Stuart's cavalry during the war. Edson had fought against them once. Damn good cavalry, commanded by a damn fine general.

Edson suddenly shivered involuntarily. He glanced up at the sky. Those clouds MacGregor had been looking at were coming closer. And they looked heavier. There was a cool tang to the air. Edson figured the Baker store was a good place to buy the warm clothes MacGregor had suggested.

But first he had to find a man.

Where would be the most likely place to find an old one-time whiskey peddler? The local saloon, Edson reckoned. He legged the light bay farther along the crooked street.

Piles of garbage spilled out of narrow alleyways between the ramshackle buildings. A few doors beyond the Baker store, Edson saw a log building with the word *Saloon* painted above a door. Farther on stood a building that a sign indicated to be a hotel and restaurant. Next to it was a dance hall with the name *Four Jack Bob's*.

Edson reined to in front of the log saloon and swung down from his saddle. He tethered the horse to a hitching rail. There was a lot of noise coming from the saloon, and for a moment he could have sworn the building was actually bouncing from the activity inside, but he knew that couldn't be. It had been either an optical illusion or else his imagination. Honky-tonk music from a tinny, off-key piano was coming from a building along the street, possibly Four Jack Bob's.

Pushing open the saloon door, Edson lowered his head and stepped inside. The place was dimly lit by a few coal oil lamps hanging here and there from a low ceiling. He had to work his way around them rather than try to walk under them as he made his way among packed tables to a long bar. The bar was nothing more than a rough, unpainted length of board about twenty feet long supported by several upturned barrels. Behind the bar were a couple of shelves. There were half a dozen stools in front of the bar. One was vacant and Edson took it. A bartender came up to him, winked, and spoke.

"What'll be yore pleasure, mister?"

At least, Edson took him to be a bartender. He wore a dirty white apron and stood behind the bar, but otherwise any resemblance to a bartender was missing. He wore a bright orange beard, a purple vest, and a pink striped shirt with vivid red arm bands holding up the sleeves. His feet made no noise as he padded along behind the bar because he wore colorfully beaded Indian moccasins instead of boots or shoes. Not that he could have been heard anyway because of the shouting and cussing and raucous laughter coming from the patrons. To complete his outlandish garb he wore a bright green top hat. He stood behind the bar, big fists planted on his hips as he leered at Edson.

It took Edson a moment before he could decide whether this man was real or some sort of apparition. As if to help him make up his mind, the bartender spoke in an unusually high, squeaky sort of voice.

"Name's Peppermint Candy Jack, mister. I own this here place." He grinned, revealing a couple of missing teeth, but those that he still had were sparkling white. His grin was friendly, and he thrust out a beefy paw. Well, at least Edson knew he was no apparition.

Edson took the beefy paw and shook. "Bill Edson," he said.

Peppermint Candy Jack looked him up and down a second time. He'd already given Edson a cursory inspection as he'd made his way to the bar. He noted the stranger's trousers tucked into tall, high-heeled boots with big spurs, the wide-brimmed, low-crowned gray hat, the gun belt under the leather jacket. "You must be from below the line."

Edson grinned. "I didn't know it was that obvious."

"Hell!" squeaked Peppermint Candy Jack. "Three quarters of this place is from below the line. Me, I hail from Illinois originally, but I've been in all the cattle towns and half the mining camps between there and California since. Dodge City, Virginia City, Sheep Camp, Santa Fe, Witchita, Benton . . . jus' to name a few of the most recent."

Edson took it as an invitation to say where he was from. It could do no harm. "I've been hanging around Helena for a bit, but I've been moseyin' around Kansas

139

and Missouri a bit too."

"Cattleman?"

Edson nodded. "Have been."

Peppermint Candy Jack's eyes dropped to the gun belt beneath the open front of Edson's leather jacket. "But not right now, huh?" Without waiting for an answer, he said, "That gun you're wearin' . . . you won't find much need of it up on this side o' the line. Them Mounted Police up in the fort jus' younder, they keep the lid on real tight."

Edson nodded. "Thanks for the information. But you aren't doing yourself much of a service. You could've sold me a couple of drinks in the time we been talkin'. If you do that with all your customers, you aren't goin' to get rich too quick."

Peppermint Candy Jack tipped back his head and laughed. Like his voice, his laugh was high, almost shrill. "I ain't goin' to get rich anyhow . . . but that's all right. All I want is to make a reasonable livin'. But you're right. What'll be yore pleasure?"

"Depends on what you've got."

"Real liquor's prohibited in the Canadian territories, 'cept on special permit for medicinal purposes signed by the lieutenant governor. But I've got Perry Davis Painkiller, apple cider, or Jamaica Ginger. I recommend the Jamaica Ginger." He gave Edson another wink. "It's real good stuff."

Edson nodded. "Sounds fair." He slapped down an American silver dollar on the bar. "American silver dollars accepted up here in Canadian territory?"

"Good ol' American silver's acceptable anywheres, as far as I'm concerned."

He turned his back to Edson for a moment, selected an unlabeled bottle from several on the shelf, and poured into a none-too-clean glass. Turning back, he passed it across the bartop.

"Get that into y', Mister Edson, and I'll pour you a

second . . . on the house."

"That's right kind of you, Jack," Edson replied, lifting the glass to his lips. He took a mouthful, closed his eyes, and shook his head. Grinning, Peppermint Candy Jack stood behind his bar. He held the open bottle over Edson's glass and refilled it.

"Did you say real liquor's prohibited in these Canadian territories? Sure tasted to me like there was real liquor in that."

Peppermint Candy Jack laughed. "That's why I recommended it. We can always dig up a good drink for a appreciative friend." He winked a third time. Edson got the message. Although liquor was prohibited in Canada's North West Territories, some of it obviously found its way in. Which wasn't surprising, he reflected, considering that there had been a booming, if illicit, liquor trade in the Territories years before, until the Mounted Police arrived and put an end to most of it.

Edson looked around. It was only mid-afternoon, yet the place was packed. Cigarette, cigar, and pipe tobacco smoke hung blue and heavy over the room. There were card games going at some of the tables. At others men were gathered around talking. They were all sorts . . . bearded, long-haired plainsmen wearing buckskin, black-bearded half-breeds, flashily dressed cardsharks, young and old, in the kinds of clothing that didn't make Peppermint Candy Jack's outfit all that outrageous.

"What do all these men do for a living?" Edson asked. "Don't any of them work?"

Peppermint Candy Jack laughed again. "Sometimes. They're buffalo hunters, trappers, wolfers, squawmen, teamsters, gamblers . . . you name 'em, they're here. If they ain't here, they'll pass through here some time or another in the next six months."

"You get many strangers passing through here?"

"Hell! Everyone in here was a stranger at one time or another."

141

"You see a mean-looking cuss wearing a black hat in the last couple of weeks? He wears a black beard and has a white scar down the left side of his face. He tries to hide the scar, but his beard don't cover it. About forty-three, close to six foot. *Real* mean-looking cuss."

Looking thoughtful, Peppermint Candy Jack slowly shook his head. "Nope, no one that answers that description, not in the last two, three weeks, anyhow. Before that, I don't know. My memory ain't always that good."

"How about a feller name of . . . what was it Major Walsh said . . . Hardstone? Dick Hardstone?"

"Major Walsh?" Peppermint Candy Jack's eyes regarded Edson keenly. "You been talkin' to Major Walsh, huh?"

Edson nodded. "Sort of briefly. He mentioned in passing this Dick Hardstone might be able to help me with some local information."

Peppermint Candy Jack grinned. "Yeah? Well, the major's right about that. Dick's been around the Cypress Hills awhile. He's an old Fort Whoop-Up man. Anything you want to know 'bout this part of the country, Dick'd be able to tell you."

"Any idea where I might find him?"

Peppermint Candy Jack poured Edson another drink. Edson put another silver dollar on the bartop. "You ain't got far to travel to find Dick, as it happens." Jack turned his head and looked toward a corner. "That's him . . . over in the corner on that tipped-back chair . . . the old feller with the white hair under the Davey Crockett hat. You cain't hardly see him through all the smoke, but that's him, sure'n ratshit."

"Thanks, Jack." Edson nodded, tossed his drink down his throat, and made his way across the crowded floor to the corner Jack had indicated.

Patrons looked up at him with curiosity as he passed, but none stared too hard, then returned to whatever they had been doing.

The white-haired man wearing the fur cap—it was beaver, not coonskin—looked to be in his fifties, but he could have been older. He wore buckskins, and the fur cap was pushed back off his head, revealing a thatch of wiry, white hair spilling down over his eyes. An old corncob pipe was stuck between his teeth.

He peered up as the tall, black-mustached man in the wide-brimmed hat stopped beside his chair and stood looking down at him.

"You Dick Hardstone?"

The white-haired man swallowed as he looked up into the blue eyes staring down at him through the smoke. He took the corncob pipe from his mouth. "Reckon so," he said hesitatingly.

"You might be able to help me."

"Help you? How?"

"Mind if I sit down?"

"If you kin find yourself a chair, you're welcome to set."

Edson found a chair, lifted it across a couple of tables, and planted it down against the log wall beside Hardstone. "Name's Bill Edson. They tell me you know the Cypress Hills pretty good."

Dick Hardstone nodded. "I reckon that's right."

Edson lowered his voice so the others wouldn't hear. One or two, curious about what business the stranger might have with one of their own, looked and strained their ears to listen, but one look from Edson's steady blue eyes was enough to make them turn their heads back to their own business.

"I'm interested in finding a man who might be hanging around the Cypress Hills."

"The Cypress Hills is a big place."

"This feller used to brag about the time he peddled whiskey out of a cabin him and an other feller built in the Cypress Hills somewhere near the site of an Indian

143

battle."

Dick Hardstone's eyes squinted. "What's his name?"

"Oates. Ceston Parker Oates. They call him Cess, Cess Oates. He rode with the Red Legs down on the Kansas-Missouri border during the war. Has a white scar down the left side of his face. Tries to hide it with a beard, but it still shows. He mightn't have had the scar then, though. Feller about forty-three now."

Dick Hardstone shook his head. "Don't know him."

"How about the cabin?"

The older man regarded Edson shrewdly. "Maybe. What d' you want to know for? You some sort of bounty hunter? Or you got some personal score to settle agin' him?"

Edson slipped his hand into his jacket pocket and came out with the gold badge in his palm, which he showed to Hardstone in such a way that no one else could see. "He's wanted down in Montana, Missouri, and half a dozen states and territories for murder and bank robbery."

Hardstone's eyes went cold. "Yeah . . . I know the cabin. But there's someone else livin' in it . . . not that Oates feller. A trapper, headed out there last spring. Fat, bald-headed feller with a red beard, name of Casper Harper, from down Iwoway. I knowed that two fellers built that cabin to trade whiskey from back in the early seventies, but I never knowed 'em personally, only knowed that they stayed there one or two years. Built a damn good cabin, though. Built it real solid, so's to defend it agin' Indians if they had to."

"Reckon you could take me to it?"

"Why don't you get the Mounted Police to round him up?"

"They seem to have their hands full keeping the Sioux at peace. I don't want to bother them."

Dick Hardstone nodded slowly. "Yeah, I guess they would be pretty busy keepin' the Sioux quiet at that.

144

And a damn good thing for the rest of us too."

"Reckon you could take me to that cabin?" Edson asked a second time.

The older man looked insulted. "Sure I could. I know my way around these hills blindfolded."

"I want to start out right away, before nightfall. I'll make it worth your while. Dollar-fifty a day, paid in American greenbacks, all expenses. Fifty-dollar bonus, half now and the other half when we reach the cabin."

Dick Hardstone sat up in his chair. "Hmmm. That's not bad money. I ain't doin' too much right now. Twenty-five dollars paid now, you said?"

Edson reached into his pocket and produced a roll of bills. He peeled off twenty-five dollars and handed them to the older man. "On the understanding that we start right away."

Dick Hardstone got to his feet. "It's a deal. You just hired yourself a guide, Mister Edson."

CHAPTER 11

Conversation was lively among Fort Walsh's noncoms as they sat eating breakfast at their tables in the NCO quarters. It mixed with the smell of fried ham and coffee.

"The Dominion telegraph line should have almost reached Fort Saskatchewan by now."

"Pity it wasn't about to reach here. Then we'd at least have some idea of what's happening in the outside world instead of reading about it in old newspapers six months later."

"Personally, I think they're concentrating too much time and expense on the north. There's nothing up there other than Indians and half-breeds and a few trading posts. The government's pandering to the Hudson's Bay Company. They should be pushing the telegraph line more to the south, along where the railroad is supposed to be built."

A sergeant laughed. "Hah! I don't think Ottawa knows where to build the railroad."

"They'll build it straight across the prairies. It'll be easier that way."

"That will put it right through Blackfoot country. The Blackfoot won't view that kindly. Look at all the trouble the Americans had building railroads across Indian

146

land."

"Can't hold back the march of civilization just because of a few thousand redskins, old man."

On the other side of Colin MacGregor, another noncom was talking about a rumor that the Mounted Police band was being transferred from Fort Macleod to Fort Walsh.

"Can't see that happening, old chap. Colonel Macleod would never allow it. What do we want the band here for, anyway? To entertain the residents of the village with concerts on Sunday afternoons?"

"It would do wonders for the mounting of the guard."

"What would they do for martial music at Fort Macleod? They mount the guard there too, you know."

MacGregor only half listened to the talk. He wondered where Edson was. Major Walsh had offered him the hospitality of the NCO quarters, yet the American wasn't sitting at the tables eating breakfast and he hadn't spent the night in quarters. During most of the previous evening MacGregor had been visiting Sergeant Cavannagh at the post hospital and hadn't given Edson much thought. MacGregor had been preoccupied consoling his friend over Major Walsh's announcement that Ottawa had ordered the outpost at Pine Butte closed. Cavannagh had been chomping at the bit to get back there and was greatly disappointed.

A sergeant sitting next to MacGregor broke into the big Scot's thoughts. "So, you're back with us now that Pine Butte had been closed, Mac."

MacGregor turned his head to the sergeant beside him. "It has nae been closed yet, Bob. I dinna hear aboot it until the major told me yesterday afternoon. I escorted a prisoner into the guardroom, that's why I'm here."

"Then you'll be going back to close it? Too bad you didn't know it was being closed before you left. You could've closed the place then and saved yourself another

147

trip."

"The major's sending a couple of men with a team of horses and a wagon down there. They'll carry orders to Constable Jenkins and he'll close the place. Then he can bring back my kit together with the rest of the stores and whatever hay and feed there is for the horses."

"What will you be doing, Mac? General troop duties?"

"Major Walsh detailed me to round up a couple of American criminals for a deputy United States marshal. They crossed over to our side of the line ten days or so ago. In fact, I was just sitting here wondering where the marshal has got to. The major told him he could stay here in the NCO quarters, so I'm surprised he's nae somewhere around. You haven't seen him, hae you, Bob? Looks like an American—tall, keen-eyed, weathered face, wide-brimmed hat. Looks like a cattle rancher. Hell! He'd be the only civilian on the post. You could nae miss him."

The sergeant shook his head. "No, Mac . . . can't say that I have."

"Agh! He probably decided to take a bed at Red Fitzpatrick's hotel. I told him to go into the village and get himself some warm clothing. He likely went into the saloon after that and they poured too much Montana Redeye into him, and he couldn't make it back here to the post."

The sergeant laughed. The buzz of conversation continued, mingling with the sounds of knives and forks on tin plates. MacGregor drained his tin cup of coffee, got up from the table, and went over to his bunk, where he picked up his pipe and filled the bowl with tobacco.

Not having any post duties to perform—as a detached NCO he was not listed on the post's establishment—MacGregor sat on his bunk and smoked his pipe as he waited for the American to turn up.

When the trumpeter sounded *Morning Parade* and Edson still hadn't appeared, MacGregor decided to go looking for him.

To MacGregor's surprise, no snow had fallen overnight, but it was bitterly cold outside and he pulled on his greatcoat and cloak before leaving the fort. The wind whipping his cloak around his shoulders, he strode out the main gates and turned north beyond the log palisade toward the village. He went first to Red Fitzpatrick's hotel, expecting to find the deputy United States marshal there. When he didn't, he went to the T. C. Power store, then the Baker store, where he found out that a man answering Edson's description had bought a buffalo coat, lined mitts, fur cap, heavy wool socks, and moccasins the previous afternoon.

"That's a pretty complete list of winter clothing," MacGregor remarked to the store clerk. "I told him to get himself some warm clothes, but I dinna go into the matter in detail. Perhaps I shouldn've, but it sounds as though he got some good advice frae someone."

"He wasn't alone," the store clerk said.

MacGregor raised his eyebrows. "Oh? Who was wi' him?"

The clerk shook his head. "I don't know his name. Seen him around a lot, though . . . usually around the saloon. Old white-haired gent wearing buckskins and a beaver pelt cap. Smokes a corncob pipe."

MacGregor looked thoughtful. "Any idea where they went when they left here?"

The clerk shrugged. "I don't really know, Sergeant. They were talking some. I think they were talking about some trail, and seems to me they said something about a cabin. I wasn't with them all the time. I was busy hustling up their supplies. The old fella seemed to be giving all the advice, telling what to get. They bought some bacon, coffee, jerky, box of Winchester ammunition, and a few other odds and ends."

From the Baker store, MacGregor walked along the crooked street to the log saloon. Pushing his way inside, he glanced around the dimly lit interior. Peppermint Candy Jack stood behind his bar. Otherwise the place was empty. It was too early in the day.

"Morning, Sergeant," Peppermint Candy Jack said in his high-pitched voice. "Something I can do for you?"

MacGregor nodded a return greeting. His mood was darkening. "Any idea where I might find Dick Hardstone?"

Peppermint Candy Jack shrugged. "Maybe in his cabin . . . along near the end of the street. Little one-room shanty. Got a bearskin for a door. Hard t' tell with old Dick."

MacGregor looked at him. "He spends a lot of time around here, so I've been told. When was the last time you saw him?"

Jack glanced up at the low ceiling. "Yesterday afternoon, I'd say. Left with some stranger wearin' a gray hat, long brown boots, and big spurs."

MacGregor scowled. "This Dick Hardstone—does he smoke a corncob pipe?"

Jack nodded. "That's Dick. Always got the corncob pipe in his mouth. Ain't always smokin' it, mind you, but he's always got it in his mouth."

"Thanks," MacGregor muttered. He spun around on heel and toe. Spurs clinking, he strode across the room to the front door, his shoulder knocking one of the low hanging lamps as he passed, sending it spinning wildly around on its short chain.

Outside, MacGregor stormed along the crooked street until he almost reached the end, where he saw the sod-roofed log cabin with the bearskin covering. He whipped the bearskin aside, lowered his head, and peered in. There was no light other than from what entered over his shoulder, but it was enough for him to see that there was nobody inside.

MacGregor flung the bearskin covering back in place. *"God damn it!"*

Taking long, angry strides, he made his way quickly back along the street, out of the village, and back to the fort. He sought out Louis Leveille, Major Walsh's chief scout.

"A couple of Americans built a log cabin somewhere in these hills back in the early seventies, before the Force marched west. They built it near the site of some big Indian battle that took place about 1871. They traded whiskey frae it. Would y' hae any idea where it might be, Louis?"

A sad expression pulled the *metis*'s long, dark face, making it appear even longer. "I am sorry, *mon* Sergeant," he said, shaking his head. "I have heard t'ere were some Americans, two, t'ree mebbe, trading whiskey for buffalo robes in t'e hills about t'at time, but I do not know where. But Jules Prefontaine, he should know. He hunted t'e buffalo wit' t'e brigades about t'at time. Have you asked him?"

"No. Jules is on leave, visiting his cousin in the village. Would y' know where his cousin is? Pierre?"

"Pierre Prefontaine? *Oui*. He worked for one of t'e trading companies baling pels, but he is finished now. He is living in a tepee up on t'e side of t'e hills." The chief scout pointed to the northwest.

"Thanks, Louis."

Ten minutes later MacGregor rode out through the gates and headed across the valley toward the northwest. He spotted the solitary tepee up on the slope of the rolling hills, half-hidden among spruce and jack pine. He was glad to see Jules's unmistakable cayuse grazing on the slope with two other wiry mustangs.

MacGregor reined to beside the tepee and shouted. "Jules! Jules!"

Someone answered from inside the tepee but the big Scot couldn't understand what was said. It was spoken in French.

"Jules!" he shouted again. "It's Sergeant MacGregor. I

151

need you. Something important."

MacGregor didn't need to identify himself. Jules recognized his voice well enough, and the urgency in his tone. He poked a black-bearded face through the opening and stared bleary-eyed up at MacGregor.

MacGregor didn't give him time to open his mouth. "Do you know of a cabin somewhere in these hills where two Americans peddled whiskey to the Indians back in the early seventies? It was near where some big Indian battle took place. I asked Louis. He said you would know. I need to find that cabin, Jules."

A cold wind whistled down the slope, blowing MacGregor's blue cloak back over his shoulders. His horse turned its back to the wind, tail and mane flying as it stood stamping its hoofs, anxious to be off.

Jules's head remained sticking out through the tepee opening, the wind blowing his long black curls down over his face. He frowned his brow in thought, then slowly he nodded. *"Oui . . . oui.* I t'ink I know it."

"Then get yourself mounted and show me where it is, mon," MacGregor urged impatiently.

"But, *mon* Sergeant, I am on t'e leave."

"Damn it all, Jules! This is bluidy important. I'll see you get your leave back after you show me where that bluidy cabin is."

As they cantered their horses along the valley a few minutes later, MacGregor told Jules what had happened.

"It's that bluidy American. He was supposed to report to me and together we were to go looking for those two criminals he's been chasing. Major Walsh assigned me to find them for him. But Edson dinna like the idea of them being locked up in our guardroom while he has to apply for extradition. He wants to take 'em straight back to Montana with him. That's why he wouldna wait for me when he went off alone to Walking Thunder's camp. I thought he was just damn foolish and impatient when he rode there alone. Now I know better. He was hoping to find all three of those wanted men in Walking Thunder's camp, hoping he could sweet-talk Walking Thunder into letting him take them. Then he would hae slipped back down to Montana and taken the three wi' him as his prisoners, without any further contact wi' us at all. He would hae taken a different trail back, or maybe he would hae avoided trails altogether so as nae to bump into us. But he dinna figure on Walking Thunder being such a troublesome bastard, and he dinna figure on those three criminals splitting up."

Jules pointed toward the slopes to their left front, and they veered their horses southeast. MacGregor became angrier the more he talked.

"Now he's trying the same thing, damn him. He's going to try and take those other two, then yard them straight back across the border into United States territory wi' him. I suppose he thinks that two out of three is better than none at all. Of all the bluidy ingratitude! After all the help we've given him." MacGregor shook his head as he rode. "Christ! I dinna know what the world's coming to. People dinna seem to hae any sense of decency any more."

"Mebbe t'at American marshal, 'e bite off more t'an 'e can chew picking on t'em bad mans. Mebbe t'ey shoot 'im."

MacGregor grunted. "It would bluidy well serve him right. He's talked Dick Hardstone into helping him, or to at least guide him to where he wants to go. But I dinna think old Hardstone will be much good to him in a shooting showdown."

A bitterly cold wind howled across the Cypress Hills, but it carried no snow. Bill Edson huddled slumped in his saddle, shaggy buffalo coat with its upturned collar insulating him against the cold. Ahead, old Dick Hardstone bent himself over his saddle.

Edson wore his wide-brimmed hat jammed forward over his head so that the wind wouldn't whip it flying from his head. He refused to wear the fur cap he had bought—not yet, anyway. Not until the weather got colder. He also still wore his high-heeled boots and spurs. It wasn't cold enough yet to wear the heavy stockings and moccasins he'd bought. He'd wait for snow, or until the weather got too cold for comfort. At least if it did get that cold—and he well believed it probably would—he was prepared for it. Hopefully, though, he would have Oates and the Frenchman hand-cuffed together and back across the line into Montana by then.

Another thing Bill Edson wouldn't do, and that was button the buffalo coat down the front. He would have felt naked not having his .44 Smith & Wesson where he could get at it readily and get at it damn fast. He had to wear his gun belt underneath the coat; the coat was too bulky to wear the gun belt around it.

As he rode half a horse length behind his guide, Edson thought about how he would take Oates and the Frenchman. His only chance lay in getting the drop on them. He wondered how far he could rely on old Dick Hardstone. Would the old man be any good with a gun? Edson regretted in a way that Sergeant MacGregor wasn't riding alongside him.

They rode a little farther, and old Dick Hardstone, corncob pipe clenched between his teeth, twisted in his saddle. "Thet cabin, it ain't far now . . . another four, five mile . . . jes' over them next hills ahead."

"How close can we get to it without being seen?"

The old man, also wearing a shaggy buffalo coat, together with his beaver pelt cap, regarded Edson with a jaundiced eye. "You mean how close can *you* get to it without bein' seen. I don't fancy gettin' caught up in what I reckon you've got in mind. You want some help, mister, you shoulda got the Mounted Police to give you

154

a hand, like I told you."

Dick looked to his front again. His horse walked twenty yards more when he turned in his saddle again. "Near's I rec'lect, you kin get to within fifty yards of thet cabin from the west, the direction we're approachin' it from. Less from the east, none from the south 'cause it's up on a slope, and from the north you'd be comin' down onto it. They built it real strong, them two fellers did . . . like a small fort, 'cept they didn't throw no stockade 'round it. But I reck'n it'll all depend on jes' how watchful thet feller you're lookin' for is."

They rode the next three miles in silence, apart from the howling of the wind. When they reached the top of the next range of hills, Dick Hardstone pulled his horse to a stop.

"You see thet flat-bottomed valley down there, along between them second hills?" Hardstone said, pointing. "Thet's where thet Indian battle took place back in '71. Big war party of Sioux jumped some Cree buff'lo hunters an' wiped 'em out. Wal, jes' up thet slope is a stand o' jack pine. The cabin you're lookin' for is up among 'em. Should be able to see smoke comin' from the chimney. He'd be burnin' a fire on a day like this, thet's f'r sure."

Edson looked long and hard but couldn't see smoke., "Let's ride a little closer," he said.

Old Dick Hardstone shook his head. "Uh-uh. You ride closer, not me. I hired on to guide you to thet cabin. Wal, there it is, over in them jack pine. I've done guided you to it, or close enough, anyways. But I ain't gettin' caught up in no shootin', an' shootin' it's likely to be, judgin' from what thet jasper you're lookin' for is."

Edson nodded. "You're right. I only hired you to guide me."

He legged the light bay ahead in the direction Hardstone had pointed. He had gone two horse lengths when the older man's voice, shouted above the wind, stopped

155

him.

"How's about my pay? Dollar-fifty a day, you said. We bin ridin' two days. It'll take me another two days t' get back. Thet's six dollars, and with the other half of thet twenty-five dollar bonus you promised, thet makes thirty-one dollars."

Edson reined his horse around to face Dick Hardstone. The cold wind hit him in the face. The wind blew open the front of his buffalo coat. He grabbed it and pulled it together in front of him. He looked Hardstone right in the eye. "How do I know that cabin is over where you say it is?"

Old Dick Hardstone worked the corncob pipe around his mouth. His weathered face looked lined and pale, as though age had suddenly drained the color from it. He held the younger man's eyes. "I ain't 'xactly a coward," he called out, "and I ain't 'xactly a brave man either. Nor an unduly foolish one. But I ain't no liar. If'n I tell you thet cabin you're lookin' for is over yonder where I said, it's there."

Edson pulled off a leather glove and reached under his buffalo coat, pulling out a wad of greenbacks. Counting off thirty-one dollars, he kneed his horse forward and handed the money to the older man. "Obliged, Mister Hardstone."

With that, Edson reined the light bay around and walked it down along the trail toward the flat-bottomed valley Hardstone had pointed to.

As he rode, his eyes searched the jack pine-covered slopes up on his left front, looking for smoke from the still-hidden cabin. It worried him that he didn't see any. Oates and the Frenchman would surer than hell have a fire burning on a day like this.

It worried him that he might have misjudged their intentions. It worried him that they might not have headed for this cabin at all. But, on the other hand, Hardstone had said there was some Casper Harper fellow who had taken up residence in the cabin last spring. Someone should be living in it. There should have been someone's smoke coming from the cabin up among those jack pines.

CHAPTER 12

Edson rode up into the cover of the jack pines lining the valley slopes and approached the cabin through the trees. He still could not see the cabin nor any smoke.

He walked his horse slowly, guiding it around tree trunks as he rode through the stand of jack pine. The light bay's hoofs plodded softly across the needle-covered ground.

When he reckoned he was close enough, Edson reined in, pulled his Winchester from the scabbard in front of his right knee, and swung down from his saddle. He ground-picketed the horse where it could crop what little grass there was, but not so tight that the light bay couldn't eventually pull itself free if it was left too long. Not that he didn't expect to return for it, but just in case he didn't come out of this as well as he intended.

Levering a bullet into the breech, he gripped the Winchester in both hands, holding it ready for instant use as he moved stealthily through the jack pines toward the cabin.

At last he saw the cabin, about seventy-five yards away, half-hidden among trees on the far side of a clearing. There was no smoke coming from the stone chimney.

He could see a window. There was no light and no movement from within, at least none that he could see.

A chill convulsed through him as he watched, and it wasn't caused by the cold wind. He could see no movement, but he had the damnedest feeling that someone was looking at him. If he could see the cabin, it stood to reason—at least to his reasoning—that someone in the cabin could see him just as easily. Cautiously he drew back into the trees.

Still the feeling of being watched persisted. He looked around warily, but saw nothing other than trees, grass, valley, hills, and gray sky. Once again he wished he had Sergeant MacGregor with him.

Hell! he thought. *I can't stay here. Got to make a move.*

He decided it was the howling wind that gave him that eerie feeling. But, howling wind or not, he had to find Cess Oates and the Frenchman, and the obvious place to look was the cabin.

Edson moved back through the trees and climbed higher up the slope. There seemed to be more cover and he reckoned he could get closer to the cabin without being seen—he reckoned that if they had seen him already they probably would have opened fire on him.

It took the best part of half an hour to get higher up the slope, move across until he was above the cabin, and then creep down through the trees until it was no more than thirty yards below him. He was on the cabin's blind side, at the back of it. There was no window through which to see him. The door faced the east, off to his left. There was a corral at the back, and a stable lean-to built onto the back of the cabin. He could not see whether there were horses inside. The cabin appeared to be in good condition, but it didn't look as though anyone was around, and the thought struck him that Oates and the Frenchman might have been there but subsequently left for some reason. Oates had almost undoubtedly been there, thought Edson. Otherwise the fellow Dick Hardstone had talked about, Harper, should have been down there himself. Oates had probably killed him.

Holding the Winchester ready, Edson crouched and ran cautiously down the slope toward the corral fence. Twenty yards . . . ten . . . five. He reached the railings and looked around warily. Still there was no sign of movement, and no sound other than the howling wind. Tiny sandlike granules of snow pelted against his face, hurtled stingingly by the driving wind.

Stooping, he stepped through the fence and crossed the corral. His heart beat faster . . . fresh horse manure lay on the ground. Someone had been around, and not long ago.

He reached the stable door. It had been pulled to. He pushed it open with his rifle barrel. Daylight flooded into the stable's gloomy interior . . . there were no horses.

Disappointment washed over him. If Oates had left . . .

He moved along the cabin's back wall toward the corner. It was then that he noticed the holes in the log wall. *Son of a bitch!* The holes had been made to poke gun barrels through. They weren't new . . . they must have been put there when the cabin was built. Likely there were holes in the other three walls as well. The place was certainly a small fort.

He reached the corner. First he peered carefully around the log ends. Seeing nothing moving other than pine boughs in the wind, he stepped around the corner. The door was no more than an arm's length away. Still acting cautiously, even though he was sure there was no one inside—if there had been, they would surely have blown him away by now—he reached out with his rifle barrel and gave the door a nudge. It swung open, creaking as it moved. The creaking sound was like an agonized squeal that even the wind failed to drown. The unexpected noise startled him, grating on his already taut nerves. He steeled himself, half expecting the rattle of gunfire. But there was nothing except the damned wind. He jumped quickly inside, swinging the rifle barrel around the cabin's single room. Empty!

Edson relaxed, letting the air out of him with a rush. Disappointment stayed with him, but as he glanced around the cabin his spirits rose. There was gear about . . . a pair of trousers, a shirt, saddle, bridle, a few boxes of Winchester ammunition, a few other odds and ends, none of which he could identify with Oates or the Frenchman—until he spotted something lying on the dirt floor in a corner. He stepped over to it, leaned down and picked it up. A canvas sack, the sort used to carry money. Stenciled in black lettering was the name of an American bank, and below it, in smaller letters, *Fort Turner Branch Montana Terr.* He turned it inside out. It was empty. It had held the proceeds of the gang's last robbery. Oates must have taken the money from it before tossing it carelessly into the corner.

Edson looked around some more. There were two bunks against the back wall. There were blankets on one of them. On the other rested a sack of flour, some coffee, rice, tins of beans, jerky, tobacco. It looked as though only one man was living in the cabin. It had to be Oates. He had known where the cabin was. He must have turned up, discovered Harper living in his place, and killed him. But where was the Frenchman, Henri Foucade?

One thing was sure. Oates would be back. He had a stove, plenty of food, ammunition, a sturdy log cabin away from any traveled trail. He was about as safe and secure as he could be—or he thought he was. He would be back.

A slab of salted pork hung from a roof rafter in another corner, away from where the heat from the stove would reach it. But there was no other meat except jerky. Could be that Oates was out hunting some fresh meat.

Nosing around outside, Edson found a small mound of earth a short distance from the cabin where the pine needles on the ground had been dug up, something buried, and the earth replaced. Edson reckoned that if he dug down into that mound he would find the body of Casper Harper. Immediately Edson thought of Sergeant MacGregor. The Mounted Police would now want Oates for murder in Canadian territory. If he had teamed up with MacGregor, as Major Walsh had intended, MacGregor would arrest Oates for that crime. The Canadian courts would then deal with Oates. The Mounted Police wouldn't hold him for extradition proceedings. Oates would dance from a Canadian scaffold instead.

Edson was about to return to the cabin to wait for Oates to appear. He hadn't taken as much as a step when he heard, over the noise of the wind, the snorting of a horse from somewhere behind him. He whipped his head around and found himself staring into the small black hole of a rifle barrel.

Ceston Parker Oates sat his saddle twenty yards farther up the slope, Winchester held steady, pointed at him. Behind Oates was a pack horse, the carcass of a dead wapiti slung across its back. Oates's dark eyes bore into Edson. His face was hard, jaw clamped tight, the white scar vivid against the weathered brown of his cheek. His black hat was pulled down over his forehead, held in place by a leather thong drawn tight around his chin. The wind blew one side of the brim in a shallow curl upwards.

Hunter and hunted were face to face for the first time. The face that Deputy United States Marshal William James Edson had seen only an illustration of was now a stark, dangerous reality.

Neither man spoke. There was little need. The message was conveyed by the Winchester in Oates's hands.

Edson's mind raced furiously, gauging his chances of reaching the cover of the closest tree. Jack pine dotted the slope. If he was going to make a move, he would have to do it right away. Oates intended to kill him no matter what. He had nothing to lose. But, like a damn

162

fool, he had left his rifle back in the cabin.

Suddenly he lunged, diving head-first for a tree trunk a few feet away. The Winchester cracked. Edson felt the bullet pluck at the back of his shaggy buffalo coat. He hit the needle-covered ground, rolled forward on his shoulder, and came back up on his feet, at the same time reaching for the Smith & Wesson holstered under his buffalo coat.

Oates's Winchester cracked a second time. A bullet plowed into the tree beside Edson as he darted from tree to tree. He couldn't get at his pistol. The unfamiliar bulk of the buffalo coat hindered his movements.

"God damn it!" he cursed, clawing for the elusive holster.

Oates swiveled in his saddle, levering and firing the Winchester as he tried to put a bullet through Edson. He fired two more shots. Edson felt the buffalo coat plucked again.

Ramming his Winchester into its saddle scabbard, Oates drew a Colt .44 and legged his dark gray horse into action, riding it straight at Edson, firing as he went.

Reaching desperately for his pistol, Edson scrambled from tree to tree, trying to keep the trees between himself and Oates. Jets of red stabbed from the muzzle of Oates's Colt as he reined his horse in and out of the pines to close in on Edson.

Oates closed the distance to six yards. One of his bullets smashed into the heel of Edson's riding boot. The jarring force of it tore the heel away and threw Edson to the ground.

Rolling over onto his back, Edson finally got his Smith & Wesson out of the holster. Pounding hoofbeats drummed in his ears. Hoofs kicked out at him, dark gray horsehair hurtled over him. Edson saw, looming above, Oates's white-scarred face, the black beard, toneless flat eyes staring down at him, the tied-down black hat above them. Movement seemed to almost stand still, suddenly suspended in a time frame of slow motion.

Edson saw the muzzle of Oates's revolver pointing straight down at him. He saw Oates's gloved gun hand tighten, he saw the revolver cylinder turn. At the same instant Edson brought up his Smith & Wesson. Aiming instinctively he pulled the trigger. The Smith & Wesson bucked in his hand. A bullet exploded from the barrel. The next instant Oates's face contorted as the .44 slug slammed into his body. He pitched from the saddle. Seconds later his body landed heavily on the ground beside a tree trunk.

The horse thundered on. Edson lay there a moment, his gun pointed at the outlaw. Oates didn't move. He was dead.

CHAPTER 13

MacGregor saw the smoke as soon as he and Jules reached the flat-bottomed valley. It rose straight up, a dark, thin column against the gray-white of the sky.

MacGregor urged his horse on as it ploughed through the heavy covering of snow that lay white and unbroken across the valley floor. Jules's shorter-legged cayuse struggled gamely to keep up. The howling wind that had blown for two days had dropped. As soon as it had, snow had fallen until the Cypress Hills were like the scene from a Christmas card.

"T'ere it is, *mon* Sergeant," Jules said, pointing up to the jack-pined slopes after they had ridden along the valley for awhile. "T'at's t'e cabin for sure. I remember it."

MacGregor reined his horse to a stop and sat looking up at it a quarter of a mile up the slope. It was half-hidden among the trees, and if it hadn't been for the smoke rising from the stone chimney, they might have ridden by without seeing it.

Wondering what sort of a reception he would get, MacGregor stared up at the cabin in silence. He and Jules had met old Dick Hardstone on the way. The old one-time whiskey peddler had confirmed that he had guided the American lawman close to the cabin, and he'd told MacGregor that there had` been a Casper

Harper living in the cabin since spring. As he sat staring up at the cabin, MacGregor wondered who was up there . . . Harper, the two outlaws, Edson . . . ?

There was only one way to find out. With a clucking noise made by pressing his tongue against the roof of his mouth, MacGregor legged his horse up the slope. If the two outlaws were up in the cabin, they might shoot him, MacGregor reasoned. But if they had heard of the reputation of the Mounted Police, they should realized that if they shot him, another would follow in his place, and if necessary yet another and another until the outlaws were taken — dead or alive.

His scarlet tunic showing brightly against the dark blue of his brass-buttoned greatcoat where it opened at the neck, MacGregor legged his horse kicking and heaving its way through the deep snow up toward the cabin. Jules's cayuse followed two or three horse lengths behind, high-stepping and short-jumping along in the broken trail.

They were halfway up the slope when the cabin door opened and Edson stepped through and stood waiting for them. Relief flooded over the big Scot at the sight of the American. But anger too. Damn his Yankee hide!

MacGregor reined to beside the cabin. He looked Edson over quickly, then gruffly said, "What happened? Where's Casper Harper?"

Edson pointed farther up the slope, beyond the corral fence. "Buried up there. Oates murdered him."

"And Oates and that other fellow, the Frenchman?"

Edson inclined his head up the slope. "I buried Oates up there close to Harper. I put markers on their graves so you can find them under the snow. You can dig the bodies up if you want to look at them. As for the Frenchman . . ." Edson shrugged his shoulders. "I don't know. No sign of him."

"And nae doubt you put Oates in the condition necessitating his burial?" MacGregor's dark eyes were hard and accusing.

"He didn't leave me much choice. He had me covered

166

nd was going to kill me."

"But it didna matter much to you that you had to kill im. You wanted him dead or alive."

Edson held MacGregor's accusing eyes. "I would have aken him alive if he had let me. He started shooting irst."

"Aye, and if you had taken him alive, you would also nae tried to sneak him back across the border into your own country, the same as you would hae done with Lone Man if you could hae gotten away with it."

It was now Edson's turn to get angry. "Damn it all, Sergeant! That's where they belong. That's where they obbed and murdered. That's where they should answer or their crimes. This whole extradition business is a damn waste of time, a damn lot of trouble for no account. They're going to wind up back in the States, anyway. I'm just trying to make it happen a little sooner."

"The point is," MacGregor said, his voice getting ouder, booming in the stillness of snow-covered slope and white-mantled pines, "there are rules that hae to be observed. Damn it all, mon! Do you realize that you, an American law officer, hae killed a mon in Canadian erritory? You provoked the situation for your own self-sh purposes, when you should hae joined up wi' me at he fort, like Major Walsh wanted. I could arrest you for murder, you know."

Edson's blue eyes went stone cold. His face was dead sober. He stood just outside the cabin door, his feet spread apart, hands by his sides. He wore no coat. His pistol rested in its open holster. His eyes locked with MacGregor's. "Try it, Sergeant."

MacGregor sat stock-still on his saddle, staring down at the American. MacGregor's breath blew out of his nostrils in thin white frost clouds. HIs mustache bristled, his eyes were steady.

Neither man moved. Both were as immobile as statues. They stared unblinkingly back at each other.

It was Jules who broke the trancelike silence. Looking

167

bewildered, he sat astride his wiry cayuse a horse length away from the two men, his brown eyes darting from one to the other. He said, " 'Ey, *mon* Sergeant, *M'sieur* American . . . come on, t'is is crazee. You no acting like growed men."

Without moving his eyes, MacGregor said to Edson, "Your answer to everything seems to be that six-gun on your hip. But you're wrong—it isn't."

"Sometimes it's the only way."

"It might be where you come frae, but nae on this side of the line. Nae in the Mounted Police."

"Tell me, Sergeant, what would you have done if a known killer had you in his sights and was going to kill you?"

Several seconds passed before MacGregor dropped his eyes and answered in a rough growl. "Well . . . I'd nae hae let him shoot me—nae if I could hae stopped him."

Standing out in the cold, only a jumper over his shirt, Edson shuddered.

MacGregor nodded his head at the cabin door. "You better get yourself back inside the warmth of that cabin. It's winter noo, y'know. A mon can freeze to death verra quickly in this country."

An hour later, Edson, MacGregor and Jules sat around the table in the warm cabin eating a meal of fresh wapiti steaks from the animal Oates had shot, flavored with baked beans, which they washed down with cups of hot, black coffee.

"The three of them must have split up after they crossed the line," Edson was saying, "near as I can figure."

"Any idea where the Frenchman, Foucade, might hae headed?"

Edson shook his head. "I would have reckoned the logical thing for the three of them would have been to stick together after they crossed the line. There's not much up in your country in the way of people except

168

Indians and half-breeds, from what I've heard. So Walking Thunder's camp seemed like a good bet for them to have stayed the winter. I had heard about this cabin. Oates had made the mistake of bragging about it down south about six months or more back. I got to hear about it when I was following him and his gang. I didn't pay much heed to it then. If I had thought about it, I would've reckoned the place had probably fallen apart since it had been built, like they often do, or that Indians had burned it down or something. It wasn't until I found that Oates wasn't in Walking Thunder's camp that I thought about his cabin. Naturally, I reckoned the Frenchman would have been with him."

"Would Oates and this Frenchman hae had a falling oot?"

Edson had just forked a piece of steak into his mouth. He didn't answer MacGregor until he had chewed it down. He shook his head. "I don't rightly reckon so. They'd been together a long time. I reckon the most likely reason is they wanted to lay low for the winter, maybe longer, and figured the best way to do that was to be as inconspicuous as possible. Three men separate in different places would draw less notice than three together, even in lonely country like you've got up here."

"Any chance he might hae slipped back across the line into Montana?"

Edson shook his head again. "His face is too well known in Montana, and just about everywheres else, for that matter. Him and Oates both. That's why they left. The gang had been robbing and killing their way north for a long time with that in mind. There are wanted posters in every town and settlement, and just about every place people are likely to be. There's a three-thousand-dollar price on the Frenchman's head. That could've been increased by now. There are sheriffs, marshals, bounty hunters all on the lookout for him. He'd know that." Edson shook his head a third time, as though to emphasize his point. "No, he'll stay up on this side of the line."

"Hmmm," MacGregor said, laying his knife and fork on his tin plate and pushing the empty plate aside. "So, the big question is, where has he gone?"

Jules had wolfed down great portions of steak and beans, and particularly steak, displaying the gargantuan appetite for meat his mother's people were said to possess. He had been far too busy eating to display any apparent interest in the conversation the two men were having. But now he had finished eating. Wiping the back of a hairy black hand across his mouth, his brown eyes dancing, he grinned. "Hey, t'at fellow you talk about, 'e is Frenchman, *non?* Why don' 'e go east to Wood Mountain. Plenty *metis* villages t'ere. He speak French good. He mix in good aroun' t'ere."

MacGregor and Edson looked at each other across the table. MacGregor nodded agreement. "Aye. Jules is right. That would be a perfect place, one of the French half-breed settlements."

Edson furrowed his brow. "Wood Mountain? Seems I've heard of it."

"Aye. You probably saw it on the map at Pine Butte when you were looking for the way to Walking Thunder's camp. It's east of Pine Butte, a day's ride. There are several French *metis* settlements scattered around Wood Mountain in a seventy-five-mile radius."

"So we ride that way and start looking," Edson stated.

MacGregor nodded. "Aye . . . if you still want him."

Edson caught a questioning look in MacGregor's eyes. "Why wouldn't I still want him?"

MacGregor kept his eyes on the American's eyes. "I had rather gained the impression it was Oates you were mainly after, that this Frenchman is nae quite so important noo that Oates is dead."

Edson's reply was direct and his voice carried an intensity of feeling. "Oates and his gang were about the most active in Montana and the other territories. I've been chasing them for close to eight months. Every one of 'em is wanted—dead or alive. Oates and Zacks are now dead. Lone Man is locked up in your guardroom back at Fort Walsh. But the Frenchman is still on the loose. The gang isn't broken until all four of them are accounted for. Them and their likes are vermin, a curse on the country. If we don't get the Frenchman, he'll return eventually, join up with someone else, and go back to robbing and killing."

Holding MacGregor's steady gaze, Edson continued. "My country is said to be violent and lawless, at least out west in the territories. But that's not the way Americans like it or want it, Sergeant. Americans are mostly peaceable and hospitable folk. They want to go about their lives without danger of being robbed or shot, or otherwise interfered with. That's their right, and it's my job to see they enjoy that right. Yes . . . I want the Frenchman, just as bad as I wanted Oates and Lone Man."

"Then we'll find him," MacGregor said. "But I want one thing clearly understood. We'll bring him in the Mounted Police way—without shooting. We'll take him alive."

Edson nodded. "It's your territory. We'll do it your way."

MacGregor raised his tin cup to his lips and drank a mouthful of coffee. Setting the cup back down on the table, he said, "We'll ride over to Pine Butte. The order to close the outpost canna hae arrived yet. The wagon Major Walsh was sending to pick up kit and stores will nae hae made it yet. They'll hae to put runners on it to get through the snow. We'll take patrol rations and whatever else we need frae the outpost's supplies. Then we'll ride on to Wood Mountain. Sergeant Macdonell is in charge of the detachment there. He's a fellow Scot. I'll ask him for the loan of Constable LeBlanc to make inquiries in the *metis* settlements. LeBlanc speaks French."

Jules's black-bearded face took on a hurt expression. "Hey, Sergeant! What about me? I am *metis*," he said, jabbing a pointed forefinger into his chest. "I know t'ose places like the back of my 'and. Why you no trust me to do t'at?"

MacGregor looked at him. "You're on leave—or you will be as soon as you get back to Fort Walsh."

Jules screwed up his face. "Ah! I drink too much when I wit' my cousin Pierre. He damn bad influence. Me, I feel damn 'ealthier when I work. I ride to Wood Mountain wit' you."

"Major Walsh said you're to report to the sergeant major for assignment to scout's duties at the post when your leave's up."

The expression on the scout's face showed his disappointment.

Drinking coffee from the tin cup, MacGregor stared absently toward the window. After a moment, he said, "On the other hand, Fort Walsh has nae any pressing need for another scout right noo, nae that I can see. I could fix it up with the sergeant major. He's a friend of mine. I could send him a note with Freddie when he reports back to Fort Walsh on transfer."

Jules let out a sudden whoop for joy that almost split MacGregor's eardrum.

"*Christ,* mon!" MacGregor said, slapping a hand over his ear as he shied away from Jules. "Take it easy. Are y' trying to deafen me?"

The next day they left the cabin and rode toward Pine Butte.

CHAPTER 14

The Bonaventure Hotel in Ville Ste. Marie was pretentious in name only. After that all pretense ended. The only reason for a hotel at all in Ville Ste. Marie was that the little settlement of log buildings lay astride a trail that wound from Wood Mountain and the main Winnipeg trail in the north to Fort Buford, some eighty miles to the south at the junction of the Missouri and Yellowstone Rivers.

The hotel was no more than a low-roofed building of logs, much the same as the other log buildings in the settlement, except that it was longer and a lot noisier. During long winter nights it was the gathering place for the *metis* community, where all the men and some of the women assembled in what otherwise served as the dining room and played their fiddles and danced the Red River jig on a door they carried with them for just such a purpose. As for the unfortunate guests who occupied the half-dozen cubiclelike rooms, sleep was impossible until well into the following morning. The Bonaventure was the only hotel in the settlement, and in the entire district for that matter, so complaint was out of the question. There was no competition. It was a case of like it or lump it.

The uproarious festivities of the hot-blooded half-French, half-Cree *metis* of the night before had not found favor with the Reverend Theodore Hatcher or his daughter as they sat at the long, rough wooden table in the dining room eating an unappetizing breakfast of bacon, beans, bread, and coffee. The room smelled strongly of stale sweat and tobacco smoke, and it made Sarah feel sick to her stomach. The other table had been broken the night before, so they were forced to sit near two men when they would clearly have preferred to sit alone. One of the two was portly and talkative, and insisted on addressing himself to the Reverend Hatcher and Sarah. Reverend Hatcher's eyes were red-rimmed from lack of sleep and he was in anything but a congenial frame of mind.

"Yes, siree," the portly gentleman was saying as he forked baked beans into his mouth and talked with his mouth full, "it was quite a shindig last night. I couldn't sleep through it, so I thought, 'If you can't beat 'em, join 'em.' So I came out here and joined in the fun." He turned to the man sitting beside him. "Saw you out here too. You obviously found it entertaining, as I did. Or else you couldn't sleep either."

The other man had said nothing during breakfast. He was younger, with hollow cheeks, thinning black hair, and a sallow complexion. But the portly gentleman's remark invited some sort of reply.

"These people derive much pleasure from their music and dancing. Yes, it is an entertaining experience to watch them."

His voice caused Sarah to look up from her breakfast. Even though feeling off-color, she couldn't help studying him briefly during the few seconds that followed before the portly gentleman spoke again. There was something compelling about his voice. He spoke with an accent, but he was not a *metis*. His voice was soft and low, with a quality of refinement she found strangely out of place in the rough environment of the western frontier. And his face . . . he was good-looking in a gaunt sort of way. He had the brownest of eyes, deeply set under sensitive brows; they were eyes of feeling. She sensed something gentlemanly about him, something that didn't seem quite right in a small half-breed settlement.

"Yes," the portly gentleman agreed, nodding his head. "I'll grant you that. They were sure having a rip-snorting time. Part Indian, I understand. Part Indian and part French, what folks out here in the North West call the *mee-tees*. I've encountered them all over. I'll have quite a few stories to tell back home in St. Louis about the Canadian North West. I've been out here for the past six months. Made a circuit from Fargo, North Dakota, up the Red to Winnipeg, then west to Fort Ellice, then northwest to Fort Carlton. Liked to have gone on to Prince Albert, then west to Fort Edmonton, but I thought that if I did that I'd get caught in the North West for the winter, and I certainly didn't fancy that. I've heard about these North West winters. So I turned around and headed back south with a freighting outfit that was on its way east to Winnipeg hauling furs for the Hudson's Bay Company trading posts. But instead of going back to Winnipeg, where I'd already been, I headed down to Wood Mountain, then here. I'm on my way to Fort Buford, and from there back home. Been away longer than I expected." He laughed. "My wife and family will think I've been scalped. Business has been good. I'm in the cigar-selling business." He reached into his coat pocket and produced two wrapped cigars, handing one to Reverend Hatcher and the other to the black-haired younger man sitting beside him. "My compliments, gentlemen."

"Thank you," said the younger man, taking the cigar and slipping into his shirt pocket.

But the Reverend Hatcher put up his hand in refusal. "I don't smoke," he said bluntly.

The portly gentleman replaced the refused cigar back inside his coat pocket. Turning to the younger man beside him, he said, "And what sort of business are you in, Mister . . . I don't believe I caught your name."

The hollow-cheeked younger man glanced quickly at him. "Belanger," he said.

175

The portly gentleman laughed. "Belanger? Belanger? That's French, is it not?" He frowned. "But you're not one of these people . . . ?"

The younger man shook his head. "No. I am French, but I am from France."

The portly gentleman's eyes widened. "From France, eh? Lot of your people up here in Canada, I hear. And what's your line of business, Mister Belanger?"

The Frenchman hesitated, and Sarah found herself curious as to what indeed was the younger man's line of business. Although he didn't look as though he belonged in a half-breed settlement, neither did he look like a businessman, at least not any sort of businessman she could imagine. He wore clothing typical of the frontier she and her father had spent the past two years traveling through.

When the Frenchman replied, his eyes avoided Sarah's and those of the portly gentleman. "I am . . . what you would say in English, a gunsmith."

Sarah was surprised, and perhaps a little disappointed. An artificer. He didn't look like an artificer. There was something more to him than that. He had the look of an adventurer, or something like that, she thought. She could imagine him with a sword in hand as he pranced backwards and forwards across the tiled floor of an elaborate old French castle pitting his skill against a ruthless enemy. But not making and repairing guns. That seemed a little dull.

The portly gentleman smiled. "Well, I understand these *mee-tees* make their living hunting buffalo, so there would be a lot of guns around, but they don't look too prosperous. I wouldn't think there would be much money in repairing guns around here."

The Frenchman smiled. Sarah liked his smile. "One can make quite a lot of money with firearms if one is so inclined."

His curiosity about the younger man satisfied, the portly gentleman looked across the table at the Reverend Hatcher, who had finished eating and was drinking his

176

coffee. "And you, sir. What sort of business are you in?"

Reverend Hatcher regarded him coldly. "I am a minister of the Gospel."

The portly gentleman's eyes bugged with surprise. "You don't look like a minister. No white collar."

Reverend Hatcher pulled a handkerchief from his coat pocket and dabbed coffee from the corners of his mouth. "And, I might say, you don't look like a cigar salesman."

The portly gentleman leaned back on his chair and laughed heartily. "Well said, sir. Well said. But I hasten to disagree. I've been told that a cigar salesman is exactly what I look like."

Sarah was inclined to agree with him. He did indeed look like a cigar salesman, but then, she supposed, that depended upon what one's perception of a cigar salesman happened to be.

"Are you traveling on to Fort Buford?"

Reverend Hatcher shook his head. "No. My daughter and I are remaining. We are going to build a church and minister to these underprivileged people."

"But these *mee-tees* are French . . . they're Catholic. You won't be able to convert them."

The Reverend Hatcher's expression was bland. "They seem to have been abandoned by their own priests." There was a touch of sarcasm in his voice as he said, "Have you seen a church in this settlement?"

The portly gentleman pulled at the end of his mustache. "Now that you mention it, no, I haven't. Which is odd, because every other *mee-tees* settlement I've passed through, the church has always been the biggest building in the place."

The younger man looked as though he had been about to say something, but he apparently thought better of it.

The portly gentleman fixed an eye on the Reverend Hatcher. "If you'll pardon me saying so, Reverend, you don't look exactly like the type to be building a church. And with winter here, you'll sure need a church, or some sort of building, or you won't be having any congregation at all."

Sarah broke her silence. "The Lord will help us," she said resolutely.

The Reverend Hatcher dabbed the corners of his mouth with his handkerchief again, then stood up. "If you will excuse us," he said to the two men before glancing at his daughter and saying, "Come Sarah."

Sarah got quickly to her feet. She and her father had walked halfway across the rough board floor to the narrow hallway that led to their rooms at the end of the log building when the portly gentleman's voice stopped them, "Say, I know someone who just might be able to help you."

Slowly Reverend Hatcher turned around as his eyes sought those of the portly gentleman. "Oh? In what way?"

"There's a man who opened up a trading store here last spring. He's pulling up stakes and returning to Winnipeg. He has a good-size log place he built for his store. He'd be willing to let you have it very reasonably, I'm sure. I tried to sell him some cigars. That's how I met him. He said he would gladly have bought some if it weren't for the fact that he's pulling out."

The Reverend Hatcher listened with interest.

"I'd be glad to introduce you to him," the portly gentleman said.

"Came here from Winnipeg eight months ago," the trader, Mister Campbell, said as he stood behind the counter of his trading store talking to the Reverend Hatcher, Sarah, and the portly cigar salesman.

"Thought this little settlement would grow into a thriving town some day. I still think it will. It's buffalo range at the moment, but that will change. The buffalo are all being hunted out. It's a matter of common knowledge that they'll last only another four, five years at the most, particularly now that there's six thousand American Sioux up on this side of the international boundary helping to kill them off. Until that happens, there's a small fortune to be made buying up buffalo skins and shipping 'em down east to St. Louis. There's a boom market for buffalo hides at the moment. When the buffalo are all gone, homesteaders will start appearing, especially now that the Mounted Police have brought law and order. The soil is good and the country's easily reached from Winnipeg and other points east. Soon the railroad will be built, with branch lines running down into Dakota and Montana. That'll bring more and more people to open up the country. There's already a substantial *metis* and Indian population. There's only one other trading post here. Naturally, I assumed the prospects for trading would be excellent. I did what any competitive trader worth his salt would have done in the same circumstances. I hired someone to build a bigger and better trading post, as you can see by comparing this building"—he waved his arm around the room—"with anything else in Ville Ste. Marie. I offered better prices for buffalo skins and trade goods in the belief that whatever I lost that way I'd make up with the volume of trade I believed I could look forward to.

"The trouble was, I overlooked one thing. These are *metis*. The other trader is a *metis*. They're incredibly clannish, these people, so I found out. On top of that they don't like English Canadians. They've resented us ever since the Dominion took over what was once called Rupert's Land from the Hudson Bay's Company. They don't trust us. Look what happened when Louis Riel led the Red River *metis* in rebellion against the government back in '69. Ottawa sent an English-speaking army from Ontario to put them down. Many of the *metis* fled west and built up little settlements like Ville Ste. Marie. They want nothing to do with English Canada."

Mister Campbell sighed. "I'm afraid I couldn't break through their clannishness. I was going to stick it out and hope for better results next year, but I'd just be fooling myself. So I decided to cut my losses and get out now, before the winter really sets in." He swept his arm

179

around the store again. The shelves behind him were practically bare. "As you can see, there's hardly anything here. I've packed everything up and am freighting it out within the next two days."

The Reverend Hatcher was busy looking around, only half paying attention to what the trader had been saying. The room they were standing in, which served as the business part of the store, was comparatively roomy, with two windows looking out onto the street. Frost was building around the edges of the window panes, but the glass was clean, in contrast to the grubby windows of the Bonaventure Hotel. Snow was falling, large white flakes floating down from leaden skies. Although it was not unduly cold outside, winter looked as though it was already settling in. Inside, they were comfortably warm, heat radiating from a pot-bellied stove in the centre of the room.

The room would be big enough for an assembly room, Reverend Hatcher thought, at least for a start, until he built up his congregation. He could have the counter and shelves pulled out, and the stove moved to another part of the room. He would need someone to build seats, and an altar. He would require a tower, of course, and church bells, but they would come later.

There were two rooms and a kitchen at the back, which the trader used as living quarters and a store room. They would do nicely for himself and Sarah. The sooner they could get out of that hole of a so-called hotel the better.

Mister Campbell stopped speaking and looked the Reverend Hatcher up and down, then did the same to Sarah, although politeness and deference to a lady caused him to do so less obviously in her case. His eyes settled again on Reverend Hatcher.

"I understand you're looking for a place to set up a church. Well, I suppose you know what you're doing," he said with a shrug. "Why the fathers from the local diocese haven't built a church here, I don't know. I'm sure they will one day. So, whatever converts you might

180

make here, you're likely to lose when that time comes."

The expression on Reverend Hatcher's face remained unchanged, as though he had heard those same arguments, or at least had already considered them. As for Sarah, she smiled serenely, perhaps envisioning a shining future for the ministry in which she so loyally and diligently assisted her father.

Trader Campbell shrugged his shoulders again. He looked around the large room. "I paid good money to have this place built." He stamped a booted foot on the floor. "Even got a board floor, which is more than I'll say for most of the cabins around here. Most of 'em have got dirt floors. Frankly, the building's not my idea of one suitable for a church, but it's better than no building at all. Come to think of it, Jesus preached out in the open, didn't he? If you can use it, you're welcome to it. I can't sell it to any of the *metis*. Even if any of them had the money, I doubt they'd buy it from me. They'd rather wait until I leave, then they'd simply move in." His mouth tightened for an instant before he resumed talking. "Well, rather than let them do that, seeing as how they forced me out, I'll donate the place to you for your church."

Reverend Hatcher's face beamed with delight. "That is most charitable of you, Mister Campbell."

The trader shook his head. "Not at all. It's in a good cause. I'm a respectable, churchgoing man. Glad to do whatever I can to help. I'll be gone day after tomorrow. Got a freighting outfit coming in from Wood Mountain. It'll take me and my stock back to Winnipeg." He glanced at the cigar salesman. "Seeing as how you're going back east, you're welcome to ride with me."

The cigar salesman shook his head. "Thank you all the same, but I'm getting a ride south to Fort Buford tomorrow. A mail runner has agreed to carry me on his sleigh for the price of a box of cigars." He grinned. "I intend making a killing selling cigars to the army at Fort Buford. There's a sizeable garrison down there at the moment."

181

Hands clasped behind his back, Reverend Hatcher strutted stiff-legged around the room, like a king surveying his realm. His eyes shone with pleasure. What a tremendous stroke of good . . . fortune. He declined to call it luck. It was not luck. It was the Lord's will.

CHAPTER 15

When the Reverend Hatcher and Sarah sat down for dinner at the crudely built table in the Bonaventure Hotel's so-called dining room, Reverend Hatcher was in a more agreeable frame of mind than he had been at breakfast, although he dreaded the noise of the forthcoming night's revelry, with its squeaky fiddles, wild shouting, excited laughter, and dozens of pairs of dancing moccasined feet. He was buoyed by the knowledge that he would have a building for his church services much sooner than he had otherwise anticipated.

They were alone at the solitary table. The other table had not been repaired. There was no sign of either the cigar salesman or the gaunt-faced Frenchman.

The *metis* proprietor padded over to their table in his moccasined feet, put their plates down in front of them, and padded silently back to join his *metis* wife in the adjoining kitchen. Dinner was *rechaud*—pemmican stew with preserved potatoes, followed by bread pudding for dessert and hot black tea.

Reverend Hatcher wrinkled his nose in distaste. "I can hardly wait to move into the manse, away from this squalid hovel." He waved his arm around the room, to the tiny, flimsily partitioned cubiclelike rooms down the short, narrow hallway, with their dirt floors and unlockable doors. "It will be a delight to enjoy your cooking again, daughter."

Sarah looked across the table at her father and smiled. She noted his use of the term *manse,* and she was pleased. She had already seen a change in him, a lifting of his spirits as he mentally prepared himself to once again assume the role of a minister with a congregation. She was aware of the amount of work that lay ahead of him before he realized his goal. She was perhaps more aware of it than he, but she was equally confident that he would succeed. Whatever else he was, he was utterly dedicated to his calling and determined to succeed at it. He would show the bishop, Doctor Tanner, back in Chicago.

"Only two days, Sarah, and we will move into the manse. Then we will prepare to conduct services. We should be able to get fifty or sixty souls in the church with little trouble."

"But Father, are there that many people here?"

"There must be, Sarah. I would say there are well over a hundred people in this community. And there are others in the surrounding areas. And we mustn't overlook the Indians. There might even be an occasional white, perhaps a settler or two and his family."

Sarah said, "Do you think that what Mister Campbell said is true, Father, that the converts we make we will lose when the Catholics build a church?"

Reverend Hatcher dismissed the question with a wave of his fork. *"If* the Catholics build a church."

"But they will, Father. You know they will."

Sighing, Reverend Hatcher nodded slowly. "Yes, Sarah . . . I'm afraid you're right. The Catholics will. But I will deliver better sermons than the priests." Fork in hand, he squared his shoulders and looked steadily across the table at his daughter, his eyes shining brightly. "It will be a challenge. It will be up to me to present the word of the Lord in such a way that it will not only draw the half-breeds and Indians to us, but will keep them, that it will spread far and wide, and draw more and more of the peoples of the North West flocking to our banner. Then Doctor Tanner will have to sit up and take notice.

Sarah smiled back at him. "Oh, I do hope so, Father."

"Doctor Tanner should be most pleased. We got that building at no cost to the church, at least no capital cost. There will, of course, be some expense incurred for necessary renovations and furniture, but that should be relatively small. The finance committee will be most pleased. I hope they will appreciate it."

Sarah reached her hand across the table and rested it on her father's hand. "I hope they will appreciate *you*, Father."

There was a movement in the shadows along the short hallway leading from the rooms at the end of the building, and the Frenchman stepped into the light of the dining room and sat down at the table, on the same side as Sarah.

"Good evening," he said.

"Good evening," Sarah and her father chorused together.

The Frenchman's cheeks were red. He had just come in from the cold outside.

"Where is your friend?" the Reverend Hatcher asked by way of conversation.

The Frenchman frowned. "My *friend?*"

"Yes . . . the cigar salesman."

"Oh," the Frenchman replied, smiling upon understanding. "He is not really my friend. I only know 'im through sitting at the table 'ere. I do not think he will be joining us this evening. I saw 'im going into the English-speaking trader's store. I think they 'ad managed to get their 'ands on a bottle of illegal whiskey that 'ad been smuggled across the border from Montana. They will spend the evening drinking it."

A scowl covered Reverend Hatcher's face. "The temptation of drink is the ruination of man."

"Yes," Sarah added, disapproval evident on her face. "And that ruination is compounded when man breaks the laws to obtain liquor."

The hotel proprietor brought the Frenchman a plate of *rechaud*. They spoke briefly to each other in French, and the proprietor cackled before he padded noiselessly back to the kitchen. The *metis* proprietor, Sarah had noticed, although uncommunicative when serving her and her father, almost to the point of surliness, was totally different when serving the dark, gaunt-faced Frenchman. She supposed that was because they spoke the same language. She remembered what Mister Campbell had said about the *metis*'s distrust of English-speaking people, and her bright confidence for the future of her father's projected ministry took a quick beating.

They ate in silence for several minutes, and after the proprietor had brought bread pudding dessert and cups of steaming black tea, Reverend Hatcher said, "Have you lived in Ville Ste. Marie long, Mister Belanger?"

Shaking his head, the Frenchman replied, "No. I arrived three weeks ago."

"From Winnipeg?"

The Frenchman hesitated. Sitting alongside him, her eyes down on the bread pudding she was finishing, Sarah noticed that his hand had stopped moving the food on his plate. His left hand, holding his fork—the hand closest to her—had tightened, as though he had tensed. He had stopped eating. Then she noticed that his hands were strong hands, but they were not the hands of an artificer.

"No," he finally answered. "I came from the west."

"Did you, by any chance, pass close to any of the Sioux camps?"

"No."

"No, I suppose you wouldn't have," the Reverend Hatcher replied, pushing aside his dessert dish. "That could be dangerous, I have been told. The Sioux are restless."

The Frenchman's hand started moving pemmican stew around his plate again as he resumed eating, and Sarah noticed that the tenseness had left him. But it posed a question in her mind, and her curiosity about the gaunt-

186

faced man beside her sharpened.

"What is it about these people," the Reverend Hatcher asked as he looked across the table at the Frenchman, "that makes them so wary of outsiders?"

The Frenchman shrugged. "Perhaps it is an insularity common to those who live amongst themselves, cut off from others."

"But they don't treat you as an outsider," Sarah commented, glancing sideways at him. "At least the proprietor of this lodging place speaks to you. That is more than he does to Father and me."

"Perhaps that is because I speak French," he replied, giving her a quick but warm smile.

"He also speaks English. Not particularly well, but passably. Yet he is not at all friendly with us, even though we have been here four days."

The Frenchman finished eating his stew. "Perhaps you should consider that to be, what you say . . . an omen?"

Sarah frowned, "An *omen?*"

The Frenchman nodded. "Yes, I think that is the word . . . that this place, Ville Ste. Marie, is not the place for you to start your church."

Sarah saw the disappointment flicker across her father's eyes, but it was only momentary, and was almost instantly replaced by his characteristic stubbornness. "That is nonsense!" he said sharply.

The Frenchman looked hard at him across the table for an instant, before shrugging and dropping his eyes back to the food in front of him, the bread pudding and cup of tea.

Turning her head sideways again, Sarah looked at the Frenchman. Hope ringing in her voice, she suddenly asked, "Will you help us?"

He looked at her, his eyes brown and intense. "How can I 'elp?"

"Yes, Sarah," the Reverend Hatcher said, staring at his daughter. "How can he help us?"

Sarah spread her hands in front of her as she looked from the Frenchman to her father and back to the

Frenchman. "You could tell these people that we are here to help them, to minister to them, to teach them about the ways of the Lord, to show them the light."

The Frenchman idly chased his spoon around his dish after a solitary raisin, the last of his bread pudding. He said, "The people in this village are Catholics. They know about Jesus Christ."

Reverend Hatcher leaned across the table. "But there is no Catholic church in Ville Ste. Marie. Their Church has abandoned them, it seems."

"A priest comes 'ere from one of the other settlements sometimes, I think."

"But that is not enough," Sarah said. "We will live here among them. We will build our church. We will be here for them whenever they need us. I am a teacher. I can teach them and their children. There is no school in Ville Ste. Marie. And no doctor. Father has medical knowledge."

The Frenchman looked at the Reverend Hatcher. "You are not a doctor of medicine, of course."

The Reverend Hatcher shook his head. "I took two years of medicine before I decided I wanted to heal people's spirits and save their souls, not their bodies."

"We have much to offer," Sarah said eagerly. "We ask nothing in return. We simply want to be of service."

The Frenchman was silent for a long moment. Finally he said, "It is rare that someone wishes only to give but not receive."

"We are of the Faith," the Reverend Hatcher said.

"Priests are of the Faith," the Frenchman said.

"You are a Catholic?" the Reverend Hatcher asked.

"I was raised a Catholic."

"Are you still a Catholic?"

The Frenchman seemed reluctant to answer. Reluctantly he said, "Once a Catholic, always a Catholic."

"Do you go to church regularly?"

The Frenchman hesitated. "No," he answered finally.

There was more silence before Sarah asked, "Will you help us?"

188

The Frenchman looked into her eyes. "Yes."

Snow fell in large, wet flakes, until drifts piled up alongside log cabins, on wood piles, on roofs, and on the dark boughs of the spruce and pine trees that crowded around Ville Ste. Marie. Smoke rose lazily toward the gray sky from chimneys protruding out of the white-blanketed roofs of the little settlement.

A *metis* bended over a team of six dogs as he harnessed them in tandem to a long low sled made of buffalo skins stretched tightly over a wooden frame.

Approaching footsteps crunched across the snow. The *metis* paid them no attention until they suddenly stopped a few feet from him.

"Bon jour, m'sieur," a voice greeted.

The *metis* looked up. A stranger in buffalo coat stood looking down at him. He recognized the stranger. He had seen him around the hotel at night, but had never spoken to him.

"Bon jour," he replied, then went back to hitching up the dogs.

"Fine-looking animals," the stranger said, speaking in French. It was a different French from the *patois* spoken by the *metis*. All the same, it was understandable.

"Oui," the *metis* replied, without displaying any indication of being inclined to converse.

The stranger stood watching for a moment, then said, "What is that you are tying them to?"

"A sled."

"And the dogs, they pull it?"

"Oui,"

"Why? What is the purpose of that?"

The *metis* straightened up and faced the stranger, staring at him for a long moment. The *metis* was swarthy-faced, with glittering black eyes, and looked more like an Indian than a part-white man. "Hey, you ask the lot of questions, Johnny. Who are you, and where do you come from? You speak the French, but it is different from the French I speak. You are not *metis*. Your French, she is hard to understand. You come from Quebec, *non?*"

The stranger suppressed a grin. It was not *his* French that was hard to understand. His was the true French; it was the *patois* spoken by the *metis* that was hard to understand. He shook his head. *"Non.* I am from across the sea, from the mother country."

The *metis* regarded him with sudden interest. "From France?"

The Frenchman nodded. *"Oui."*

The *metis* made a noise that was a cross between a grunt and a laugh. "I have heard my papa talk about that place. He was never there, he was born in Canada, but he used to listen to his papa talk about it."

The Frenchman pointed to the dogs, sitting on their haunches in the snow, their eyes round and bright as they watched the two men. They looked something like wolves to the Frenchman, except that they were not as large, yet they were larger than the coyote.

"You put things in the sled, and the dogs pull it?"

The *metis* nodded. *"Oui.* I come from the Saskatchewan. There we use the dogs all the time when the winter come. They are better than the horse then. They run across the snow and they pull the sled behind them, in places where the horse cannot go because the snow is too deep."

"How do they know when you want them to go? How do they know when you want them to go in one direction, or when you want them to turn, or to stop? They are dogs."

"You ride the horse, *m'sieur?"*

The Frenchman nodded. "Of course. That is how I got here."

"Well, then . . . the horse, he no understands the French, but he knows what you want. You teach him. The dogs are the same. You teach them."

"How fast will they go?"

"In condition, on a cold day, with the snow firm, they

will pull the sled forty or fifty or sixty miles, depending on the sort of country you drive them through."

The Frenchman pointed again, this time to the sled. "Do you sit in that?"

The *metis* laughed. "*Non.* I run alongside. I hold on to the rope. If I don't, the dogs might run away from me and take the sled with them."

The Frenchman stood looking down at the dogs and the sled. The expression on his face was one of skepticism. "Will they outdistance a horse?"

Again the *metis* laughed. "Hah! In cold weather, in deep snow, they leave the horse stuck in the drifts. The horseman, he freeze. His legs get cold from him sitting in the saddle, pressed against the cold leather. But me, I run alongside the sled, I wear the snowshoes, and I skim across the snow because the webbing on the snowshoes stop me from sinking. And while the horseman freezes his legs, I run and the blood flows warmly through my body and keeps me fit and alive. That is why I bring the dogs with me from the Saskatchewan when I come here."

The Frenchman listened intently. It wasn't idle curiosity that had prompted him to ask about the dogs. An idea was forming in his mind.

"What do you put in the sled?"

"You put whatever you want to carry, *m'sieur.*"

"Do the dogs pull a good weight?"

The *metis* nodded emphatically. "Each dog will pull one hundred pounds. Not only that, but he pull it farther and faster than will a horse."

"What do you feed them?"

"In Saskatchewan country, frozen fish. But here, where there are not the fish, frozen meat. But not too much. Just enough. You keep them a little bit hungry, so they keep lean and fit. That way they work better and they run faster."

"Interesting," mused the Frenchman, his mind racing. "Very interesting."

"Hey," the *metis* said, pointing a forefinger at him.

"Tomorrow I take them on a practice run, to get them fit. I get them ready for work now that the snow has come. You want to join me, I show you how the dogs work, how to drive the sled, and I show you how to use the snowshoe. *Non?*"

"*Oui,*" the Frenchman nodded enthusiastically. "*Bon! Bon!*"

The *metis* frowned, his black eyes taking in the shaggy buffalo coat the Frenchman was wearing. "But you better get rid of that. It smells. It frighten the dogs if you get too close to them. You look too much like the English in it. I get you the capote, eh?" He laughed, slapping the Frenchman's arm with the back of his mitted hand. "I make you look like *metis. Non?* I remember . . . I see you last night at the hotel. You watch the dancing. How do you like the Red River jig, eh? You want to be one of us? Then you will be! Maybe we will find you the Cree woman and you can make many little *metis*. Then there will be more of us than there are the English from Ontario. That way the West will always belong to the *metis*."

The *metis* broke out in hearty laughter. The Frenchman joined him. But Henri Foucade had other things on his mind.

Amid the gently falling snow, Reverend Hatcher and Sarah strolled around the little *metis* village. Their faces, cheeks tinged red from the cold, peeked out from black Persian lamb fur hats and the upturned collars of their long black overcoats. Wrapped around their necks were pale blue scarves, long ends hanging down over their shoulders. Heavy woolen mitts protected their hands. Rugged up the way they were, they barely felt the nip of the cold.

They were enjoying their exercise. Anything was better than sitting in the cramped, dingy cubicles of rooms they had back at the hotel.

There was a certain charm about Ville St. Marie,

Sarah thought. The log cabins, snow white upon their roofs and piling up around the walls, frost caking the window panes, had a picture-book quaintness about them.

Occasionally a dog barked at the crunching noise their boots made in the snow as they walked by the log cabins, but there was little other noise. It was mid-morning. All the noise had been made the night before at the usual gathering and dancing of the Red River jig in the Bonaventure Hotel's misnamed dining room.

When they reached the large log building that the Winnipeg trader had donated to them and their church, they stopped. They didn't go in. The trader wouldn't be moving out until the following day. They simply stood and looked at it. The Reverend Hatcher smiled content-edly. He could already see its spire, could already hear its pealing church bells. Sarah stood alongside him, her arm through his.

"We will have to find someone who can build an altar, and seats for the congregation," Reverend Hatcher said. "Someone who can do some simple carpentry. There must be someone in the village. If they can build these log cabins, with their own furniture, they can surely build what we need. They might be glad of the money. We can't pay them much, but it will be better than nothing."

Her eyes shining brightly, Sarah looked up quickly at her father. "We could ask Mister Belanger. Perhaps he can help."

Reverend Hatcher glanced sideways at his daughter. "But he's a gunsmith. He wouldn't know anything about carpentry."

"Often, Father, tradesmen have knowledge of more than one trade."

Reverend Hatcher frowned. His breath frosted in front of him as he talked. "I've had second thoughts about having that man help us."

Sarah frowned as she stood looking up at her father. "Why, Father?"

Shaking his head, Reverend Hatcher said, "I'm not quite sure. I'm not sure I know what to make of him. He seems an unusual sort of man to find in an out of the way place like this. Besides, as a Catholic, and these people being Catholics, he could turn them against us."

"But why would he do that, Father? He could just as simply have declined to help us. Besides, he said he doesn't go to church regularly. He might have fallen by the wayside. If he has, we may be able to save him."

When the Reverend Hatcher didn't reply, simply turning his head from her and staring up at the large log building that he envisioned as his cathedral of the plains, Sarah said, "Anyway, I'm sure it can't do any harm."

CHAPTER 16

Sergeant MacGregor reined to in front of the log barracks of the Mounted Police detachment at Wood Mountain. Deputy U.S. Marshal Edson and Scout Prefontaine reined to alongside him. All three swung down from their saddles.

The barracks were similar to those at Pine Butte. They were log cabins, but they were larger and had been standing considerably longer than the barracks at Pine Butte. Like everything else in the country since winter had started, they were covered with snow.

MacGregor stepped inside the main building, stamping his feet to rid his regulation-issue moccasins of loose snow. Sergeant Macdonell, in charge of the detachment, stood up behind his desk.

"Well, well . . . Sergeant MacGregor," he greeted him. "What brings you over frae Pine Butte?"

Sergeant Macdonell's eyes alighted on the other two as they followed MacGregor inside. He nodded. He knew the scout, but the stranger he did not.

"I'll detail a mon to look after your horses. Noo doubt you'll be staying long enough that you'll want to rest them."

MacGregor shook snow from his brass-buttoned buffalo coat and pulled off his mitts. "Aye, Alex. Long enough to get the blood flowing again, and if you're going to invite us to dinner, we'll stay for that too."

Sergeant Macdonell grinned. MacGregor introduced Deputy U.S. Marshal Edson. MacGregor's fellow Scot and the American lawman shook hands.

After the three men had taken off their heavy buffalo coats and fur caps and were seated around Sergeant Macdonell's desk smoking their pipes, or—in Edson's case—a hand-rolled cigarette, Sergeant MacGregor explained the American's presence.

"Deputy Marshal Edson is chasing an American outlaw. Actually, he's a Frenchman named Henry Foucade, but he's robbed banks and committed other crimes in United States territory and crossed to our side of the line. We hae reason to believe he might be laying low in one of the *metis* settlements in your area."

Bill Edson reached into a pocket, withdrew a *Wanted* poster bearing the Frenchman's likeness, and passed it to Sergeant Macdonell. Sergeant Macdonell glanced at the picture, then read the printing.

"Dinna look too much like a *metis,* except maybe his coloring," Sergeant Macdonell said, "but if he's a Frenchman, he could probably merge among them without too much difficulty. There's been a few strangers moving around the country lately. Some of Louis Riel's *metis* sympathizers frae across the line in Montana and Dakota agitating among the Indians, particularly among the Sioux, who seem to be vulnerable to a little stirring. And, I suspect, the odd Fenian has been involved in that too, using the *metis* for their own nefarious ends."

Sergeant MacGregor said, "You've nae seen anyone like that around here, Alex?"

Still looking at the poster, Sergeant Macdonell shook his head. "Noo, I ha' nae, Colin. But that dinna mean he couldna be around. I've had m' hands full just keeping an eye on Sitting Bull. I'll show this poster to LeBlanc and the other men. They might hae seen him. Failing that, I suppose you'll be visiting the *metis* settlements?"

MacGregor nodded. "Aye."

Sergeant Macdonell inclined his head at Jules. "Well, you know where they are, Jules. They hae nae moved around much. They're still where they used to be."

He stood up and stepped over to a map hanging on the log wall. Using the stem of his pipe, he pointed at the map. "There's Willow Bunch. Seeing as how this mon is on the dodge, I dinna think he's likely to hide oot there. We patrol that way all the time." He moved the pipe stem across the map. "There's Bonneau's, Gabriel's, then farther east and a wee bit south is Ambroise's . . . then doon here, closer to the international boundary, Ville Ste. Marie. It's larger than the others."

From the map he turned back, glancing at the black-bearded scout. "You know all that, Jules. I dinna hae to tell you. You can guide Sergeant MacGregor and Mister Edson to those settlements. But the trails will be a wee bit heavy noo that all this snow is falling. Travel might be slow. Perhaps you should stay here until the snow stops."

MacGregor shook his head. "Nae, Alex. We'll push on, unless it blows into a blizzard. Major Walsh has given me orders to work with the marshal here until we find that Frenchman. And find him we will. It's just a matter of time."

Reverend Hatcher and Sarah moved into Trader Campbell's former trading store. With the help of Henri Foucade—Mister Belanger to them—they hired a *metis* carpenter, who ripped out the corner and shelves and built seats for the congregation that Reverend Hatcher expected to draw to his church, and an altar and platform from which he could preach to an assembly.

"We'll wait a little while for a tower," Reverend Hatcher said to Sarah. "We don't need it until I can order the bells."

The Frenchman had helped the Hatchers unload books, bibles, and personal belongings from the high-topped wagon and carry them into the makeshift church.

He spent much of his time supervising the *metis* carpenter and interpreting the Reverend Hatcher's wishes. He also spent much time talking with Sarah. While in the building working, the men ate a meal a day with the Hatchers, enjoying Sarah's cooking. The Frenchman was ecstatic.

"I 'ave traveled much," he said with a smile one day as the four of them sat at the table the *metis* carpenter had built in what the Reverend Hatcher constantly referred to as 'the manse,' "but I 'ave never tasted such cooking. Yet the choice of food you can get here is so limited at this time of the year." He waved his arm around the kitchen. "You 'ave 'ad so little opportunity to acquire those things the housewife usually 'as in her kitchen. I can hardly believe you can cook so well."

Sarah blushed at the praise. Apart from her father, no one had praised her cooking before. Seldom had anyone had the occasion to do so.

The Frenchman glanced at the Reverend Hatcher, sitting at the head of the table. "You must be very strong-willed, *m'sieur,* that you manage to look so fit when you 'ave a daughter who cooks so well. Hah, if it were me, I would be big and fat. You should hope that no dashing, 'andsome young man one day comes along and asks for her 'and in marriage. Then you would lose your wonderful cook, no?"

The Reverend Hatcher simply looked across the table at him. He neither smiled nor replied, then continued eating.

The Frenchman and his newfound *metis* friend, Baptiste, mushed across the plain. Baptiste held the sled rope in one hand, dog whip in the other. Both men wore snowshoes on their feet, and long capotes with hoods to protect their faces from the cold wind. The capotes were tied around the waist by brightly colored sashes, crimson for Baptiste, yellow for the Frenchman. The capotes were warm but loose enough to allow freedom of body movement. The snowshoes—long, narrow frames of light wood with skin or gut crisscross lacing—were strapped to the moccasins they wore. They reminded the Frenchman of tennis rackets.

The dogs pulled the sled at a fast clip. The two men ran along behind. If the dogs got too far ahead, Baptiste slowed them down or stopped them by pulling back on the rope as though he was an anchor. Baptiste had no trouble keeping up with the sled, but the Frenchman, puffing hard, was falling behind.

Baptiste turned his swarthy face, glanced back over his shoulder at the Frenchman, and grinned. "Hey, Johnny, you not in ver' good shape." Baptiste, when he spoke to outsiders at all, always addressed them as Johnny.

The Frenchman grinned gamely back at him. "That is why . . . I ride horses," he called out between puffing, "so I do not . . . have to run."

"Hah! You better get in shape to run with the dog team, Johnny."

"These snowshoes . . . they slow . . . me down."

Baptiste glanced back over his shoulder again. "That is because you not doing it right, Johnny. You lift your 'shoes too high. You do not need to do that. Shuffle your feet, slide them. Lift your 'shoes just high enough to clear the snow. Watch me. Do the same as me."

"If you . . . get tired . . . can you . . . jump on the . . . sled and ride? Can . . . the dogs . . . still pull it?"

Baptiste laughed. "Sure they pull it. I told you before, they pull heavy load."

It had stopped snowing, but the sky was overcast and they were out on the open prairie, with no trees in sight except behind them, where they had come from. Everywhere else the Frenchman looked was a sea of white and gray, and it was difficult to see where land ended and sky began. A cold wind cut down from the north, and they wore their hoods over their heads to protect their faces.

Baptiste pulled the dog team into the overhang of a cutback, and they sat on the sled and rested, the cutback protecting them from the wind.

"I think you need more lessons, Johnny," Baptiste said laughingly. "But we make *metis* out of you yet. I take you with me again tomorrow. You learn."

The Frenchman shook his head. "Tomorrow I cannot come, but I would like to. I have promised to help the missionary tomorrow."

Baptiste shrugged a shoulder. "The day after, then." He paused, then said, "That fellow and his daughter, what do they want in Ville Ste. Marie?"

"To build a church and have a following, like a parish priest."

"And the woman?"

"She helps him in his work."

Baptiste made a face. "That is no good, a woman helping a priest in his work. But then, he is not really a priest."

"Maybe it is not so bad. She is a teacher, and she can teach the children. There is no school in Ville Ste. Marie. The missionary once studied to be a doctor. There is no doctor in Ville Ste. Marie either. I think they will be good for your village. You should go to their church when they hold their first service next Sunday. You can see for yourself. If you like what he preaches, you could go again the Sunday after. If you do not like it, then you do not go again."

Baptiste shook his head. "It will be time enough for me to go to church when the priest comes from Willow Bunch. Then I have to go, but until then I do not have to go."

"Do you think some of the others in the village will go? They are Catholic. This missionary is not Catholic, of course. He is a Protestant."

Baptiste shrugged his shoulders again. "I do not know, but I do know that when the priests find out there is this missionary in Ville Ste. Marie, they pretty quick build the church in Ville Ste. Marie, I bet."

They fell silent for a few moments. The dogs lay in the snow, tails curled up over their noses. Baptiste sat on

200

the sled looking at them. Finally he said, "The dogs, they look like they enjoy the rest. They are getting lazy. I think we better go before they think to themselves that they like this lying around better than working."

"How far is Ville St. Marie from the border?" the Frenchman asked before Baptiste moved from the sled.

"Twelve miles."

"How far is the nearest town across the border?"

Baptiste looked thoughtful for a moment. "Another fifteen miles, maybe."

"Is there a bank there?"

Again Baptiste looked thoughtful before replying. "Yes, I think so. I don't have any money, so I do not need the bank, but yes, I think there is a bank there. You have some banking business to do?"

The Frenchman nodded.

"Then that would be the closest place."

The Frenchman pointed to the dogs. "These dogs, if they are carrying a load, would they outdistance men on horses?"

Baptiste glanced from the Frenchman to the dogs, then back to the Frenchman. He nodded. *"Oui.* With all the snow that has fallen, there are heavy drifts. Dogs travel much faster than horses when there is heavy snow on the ground. Especially when it is cold. Why?"

The Frenchman looked him square in the eye. "Do you want to help me rob the bank in that place?"

Baptiste looked back at him, black eyes wide with incredulity. *"Rob the bank!"* Then he threw back his head and broke out in laughter. "Ha ha ha ha. Rob the bank. That is ver' funny. You make the good joke, Johnny."

"It is no joke, Baptiste. We split the money. You drive the dogs, I rob the bank. I give you half the money."

Baptiste looked scared. "Rob the bank?" he said, half to himself. "That sounds dangerous. "Me, I no mind breaking the law a little bit sometime. Sometime I smuggle the American whiskey across the border, but . . . *rob the bank?* Slowly he shook his head. *"Non,* Johnny . . .

I don't think I could do that."

"Will you lend me your dogs so I can do it?"

Baptiste frowned. "What happen to my dogs if you get caught?"

The Frenchman shoook his head. "I will not get caught, *mon ami*. Believe me, I will not get caught."

The frown remained on Baptiste's face. "I have to think about that, Johnny . . . I have to think about that."

Using a small printing press he and the Frenchman had carried from the back of the high-topped wagon into his manse, Reverend Hatcher printed a hundred notices in French which Henri Foucade had translated from Hatcher's English. The notices outlined teaching and medical services Reverend Hatcher's church would provide, as well as announcing the forthcoming Sunday's opening church service. Then Sarah, accompanied by the Frenchman as interpreter, delivered them around the village. Reverend Hatcher did not go with them. He remained in his manse preparing for his inaugural service.

Sarah and the Frenchman met a mixed reception, but overall not a very encouraging one. Sarah worried.

"They don't seem very enthusiastic," she said as she and the Frenchman crunched through the snow from door to door.

The Frenchman shrugged. "It might take time. You must be patient. These people may be suspicious or wary of you, but as they come to know you, they will hopefully change."

"They do not seem to be wary of you."

"That is because I speak their language."

"Some of them speak some English."

"Ah, yes," the Frenchman replied, glancing down at her and smiling as she walked alongside him, "but they think in French, or perhaps they think in Cree. I do not know. But they are also warm people inside." He touched a mittened hand to his chest. "I think when they get to know you, they will gradually change."

"Oh, I hope so, for Father's sake."

"And your own?"

"I suppose so. My wishes, my hopes, are for Father. More than anything I want him to be successful. I want him to be able to show the bishop of our church what a good man he is, what a good minister he is, how dedicated he is to the Lord's service."

They paused outside the next cabin as Sarah continued what she had been saying.

"Father and Doctor Tanner—he's the bishop—have never seen eye to eye. I suppose they are so different, and they clash. They are both stubborn men, and Doctor Tanner banished Father to the western territories. That was when I gave up teaching, to accompany him and help him.

"Father has been bitter and resentful ever since, but he is a proud man and would never ask permission to return to the East. He wants to do something really big, to attract attention back home. He wants his name to become known and respected across the country. He wanted to go into the camps of the Sioux Indians, who fled across the border into this country after slaughtering General Custer and his regiment. Father hoped to convert them to Christianity, to turn them from warlike savages into peaceful people. But the Mounted Police stopped him. They thought he was trying to persuade Sitting Bull to return to the United States. That wasn't really what father intended, although he would have been more than pleased if the Sioux had decided to go back as a result of his influence—provided of course that they did so with peaceful intentions. Most of all, though, he wanted to save their souls. Father is utterly dedicated to the Lord's work. He is not a humble man, and perhaps that is his greatest fault. However, he is a good man at heart."

The reception at the next three cabins was more positive, and by the time they had visited all the cabins in Ville Ste. Marie, Sarah felt more encouraged.

She had also enjoyed the company of the Frenchman as her interpreter. It had increased her confidence. A new light began to shine in her eyes. A light-hearted gayness came to her, and her father was quick to notice it. He also knew its cause.

Wrapped in her long black overcoat and Persian lamb cap, Sarah crunched across the snow as she walked through the village from her father's manse toward the livery stable at the rear of the Bonaventure Hotel. The stable was owned by the hotel proprietor, and was intended for the benefit of hotel guests and travelers passing through, and occasionally for horses used to haul the infrequent and irregular stagecoach that traveled between Wood Mountain and Fort Buford. Because there was no other livery stable in Ville Ste. Marie, the Reverend Hatcher had arranged with the hotel proprietor to stable their team of horses until such time as the reverend could have a stable built at the rear of his manse.

Although the proprietor had agreed for adequate financial remuneration to stable the horses and to provide feed, straw, and water, he had drawn the line at performing any of the physical work involved in the actual care of the horses. This left little alternative but for Reverend Hatcher and Sarah to do the work themselves. Sometimes they did it together, sometime they took turns.

Reaching the stable door, Sarah swung it open and stepped inside. There were five horses in the log stables, the two team horses belonging to her and her father—or more precisely to the church—and a black gelding with a white blaze on its forehead, a nondescript brown, and a shaggy cayuse of the same type used by the *metis* buffalo hunters.

"Hello, Peter and Paul," Sarah said to the two team horses. "How are you today?"

At the sound of her voice, the two team horses turned their heads to look at her.

She stepped into Peter's stall first, pulled off her

glove, and ran her hand over the animal's long face, ruffled its ears, and slid her hand along its neck. Peter nuzzled her affectionately. Then she stepped into Paul's stall and repeated the process.

"I think we'll have to give you both a good grooming," she said, glancing down at the straw in the stalls. Some of it was soiled and needed changing. "But first I'll water and feed you, then I'll change your straw. After that I'll give you both a good brushing." She stepped out into the aisle, then turned around to look back at the two horses. She stood there for a moment, her elbow bent, her hand up to her chin, deep in thought. Presently she said, "I should give you some exercise too. Now, how can I do that? You'd never be able to pull the wagon through all the snow. I might just have to be content to walk you through the village."

"I believe I could find a sleigh for them to pull," said a voice from the door behind her.

Sarah jumped, her hand flew up to her throat, and she whirled around. The voice had startled her. She found herself looking up into the smiling face of Henri Foucade, standing in the doorway through which she had passed a moment before.

"Oh! Mister Belanger. You frightened me. I didn't hear you come in."

"I am sorry. I did not mean to frighten you. I was in my room in the hotel when I saw you come in 'ere. I decided I would come and 'elp you with your horses."

She smiled. "That's very kind of you, but I can manage."

"Please," he insisted, with a Gallic gesture, "let me 'elp. Cleaning out horses' stalls is not a woman's job."

"Oh," she replied, laughing lightly. "I grew up on a farm. I've been around horses and barns all my life. Even when I was teaching school I used to ride. Since I've been working with Father, I have looked after the horses more often than he has, because his work allows him so little time."

He helped her water and feed the horses, and as they

did so they continued talking.

"I don't ride anymore," Sarah said. "Father thinks it to be not very ladylike. He doesn't think it proper. Do you like horses?"

"Yes. I rode in France. I lived in the country and I also grew up around horses. I 'ave always liked them. It is different riding in North America, out 'ere in the West. It took me time to get used to the western saddle, but now that I am used to it, I like it."

"Are you going to continue living in the hotel?"

"Yes."

"It's not very nice, is it?"

The Frenchman smiled. "No, but when I arrived 'ere it was too late to build a log cabin. Besides, I am not a builder. If it were summer, I might perhaps pitch a tent and live in it. I 'ave been used to more of the comforts of life than there are in this village, but I can manage. I 'ave become used to 'ardship."

"Do you always find work as a gunsmith?"

He hesitated a moment before answering. For some reason, which he did not understand, he did not want to lie to her, yet he could hardly tell her the truth. "I always work with guns."

When they had finished watering and feeding, Sarah held the two horses in the narrow aisle, while Henri Foucade took a pitchfork and cleaned soiled straw out of the stalls. Then he broke apart a fresh bale and spread clean straw on the floor. After that he and Sarah put the two horses back in their stalls, and together they stood back to back as they each brushed a horse.

"Do you intend staying in Ville Ste. Marie, Mister Belanger?"

"My name is . . . Henri. Please call me that."

Sarah reddened and fell silent as she brushed.

"May I call you Sarah?" the Frenchman asked quietly.

After a moment's hesitation, Sarah said, "Yes . . . yes, I would like it if you would."

He turned around to look at her across the stall. They were so close, only a single horizontal rail three feet above the floor separated them. "You are a very surprising woman, Sarah. You 'ave taught school, you 'elp your father in his missionary work, you are an excellent cook, and you are an equestrienne. Those are so many skills in a woman."

Sarah blushed. She kept her back to him so that he couldn't see her face. "Not really," she said as she continued brushing. "When you grow up on a farm, you learn to do things that people in cities never have an opportunity to do."

"Ah, you are too modest, Sarah. Much too modest. Do you like working for your father?" He remained turned toward her, seeing the back of her long black overcoat. She had removed her black Persian lamb hat. Her hair shone reddish-brown, smelling clean and fresh. He raised his hand and touched it.

His touch sent electric tremors down her spine. He kept his hand there. Sarah froze, hardly even breathing.

"You are very pretty, Sarah," he said, moving nearer to her, his lips close to her ear.

"No . . . no, I'm not," she said, her voice barely a whisper.

From her hair, his hand moved to her cheek. His touch turned her cheek to instant flame. Then he pulled her to him, leaning his head down until his cheek was against hers.

Alarm bells tingled urgently within her. "Don't," she whispered. "Please . . . don't."

"Why not, Sarah?" he whispered back into her ear. "When was the last time a man touched you?"

Sarah didn't answer. Nor did she make any attempt to move away from him.

The Frenchman placed both hands on her shoulders. Gently he turned her around until she was facing him. He stepped across the wood rail and pressing himself against her. The next instant his arms encircled her, drawing her hard to him. With one hand he touched her chin, tilting it upwards, then he lowered his lips until they touched fully upon hers. Sarah's arms went up

207

around him, her hands reaching up to his shoulders, pulling him down on her. Hungrily, she began to devour him.

Suddenly the stable door was flung open and a shaft of light fell across the straw-colored floor.

"*Stop it! Stop it at once!* What is the meaning of this?"

Startled beyond belief, Sarah whipped her head around, to see her father standing just inside the door, his face a mask of indignation and disbelief.

The Reverend Hatcher's eyes darted from his daughter to the Frenchman. "Take your filthy hands off my daughter, you scoundrel!"

But the Frenchman did not. He held Sarah to him. Confused and frightened, she tried to pull away, but the Frenchman held her in defiance of her father.

The Reverend Hatcher's face went white with rage. Looking wildly around the stable, he saw a horsewhip leaning against a wall close to the door. He flung out his arm, his hand grasping the whip. The next instant he pulled it from the wall, raised his arm, and with amazing speed he brought the whip cracking sharply against the Frenchman's face.

The Frenchman released Sarah immediately. His face stinging horribly, Foucade slapped his left hand to his waist. It was an instinctive reaction, reaching for the Smith & Wesson .44 he had worn for so long. But he was wearing the capote, and he had stopped carrying the gun since he had met Sarah.

An ugly red welt rose darkly on the Frenchman's sallow cheek. The Reverend Hatcher raised the whip to strike Foucade again.

"*Father!*" cried Sarah. "*Don't!*"

Whip held high, Reverend Hatcher stood glaring at them both.

"Please, Father! Don't strike him again!"

"Don't you dare tell me what not to do, you . . . you . . . you . . ." he sputtered, spittle shooting out of his mouth as he shouted. "You've disgraced yourself! You've disgraced me and you've disgraced the church. Get home, get back to the manse immediately!"

"Do not go, Sarah," the Frenchman said. "You are too old to allow him to bully you."

Reverend Hatcher glared at the Frenchman. "How dare you! How dare you!" The next instant he swung his arm and brought the whip arcing down at the Frenchman. This time the Frenchman was ready. He threw up his arm and caught the whip before it struck him. With a sharp, snaplike flick of his left arm, he pulled the whip out of the Reverend Hatcher's hand and threw it on the floor.

Frothing at the mouth, Reverend Hatcher stooped to pick it up. He got his hand around it but before he could pick it up, the Frenchman slammed down a moccasined foot hard on it. In vain Reverend Hatcher tried to pull it free. The Frenchman grasped the preacher by his coat collar and pulled him upright.

The Frenchman's eyes stared hard into Reverend Hatcher's eyes as he held the preacher, their faces inches apart. The Frenchman's grip was almost choking the older man.

"I could kill you!" the Frenchman hissed.

Eyes wide with sudden fear, the preacher stared back at him, too frightened to speak.

Sarah darted forward and grasped the Frenchman's arm. "No, Henri! No! Please let him go!"

The Frenchman snapped his head sideways to look at her through eyes still smoldering with anger. Blood oozed from the whip welt on the side of his face.

He turned his head back to look into the Reverend Hatcher's face for a second or two longer. The next instant he tossed the preacher aside and stalked angrily out through the door and across the snow.

CHAPTER 17

Clanton's founders had built the town on a high bank overlooking Muddy Creek. The Muddy, more a small river than a creek, flowed across the Canadian border fifteen miles to the north and continued on to empty into the Missouri, fifty miles farther south. In summer Clanton could be described as a sleepy little town at best, serving a far-flung but growing horse-raising industry. In winter it was locked into the frozen white expanse of the northern plains.

Clanton had come alive a little of late, mainly because of the business passing army patrols brought to it. The patrols were large, sometimes troop strength or more, occasionally as much as half a regiment. The soldiers had been actively patrolling the border country on the lookout for Sioux hostiles trying to flee the nation's wrath at their victory over Custer's command down on the Little Big Horn the previous year. The army used Clanton as a staging point between Fort Buford, farther east along the Missouri, and Forts Belknap and Assiniboine, off to the west. The soldiers spent some of their hard-earned pay in the town.

In November and December there was little movement on the plains, apart from the army patrols, and even they tended to slow down when the weather got too cold, because it was hard both on men and horses, and particularly on horses.

The Frenchman took his time getting to Clanton. He rode out of Ville Ste. Marie at night, when most of the villagers were dancing in the Bonaventure Hotel's dining room. He rode through the night, following the bank of the Muddy. It was a hard ride, for the snow was deep. Sitting astride the saddle on Ben Zacks's horse, he burrowed his head down into the upturned collar of his buffalo coat as protection against the cold. In place of leather boots he wore a pair of Indian moccasins, under which he had pulled on two pairs of heavy socks. He would have frozen his feet in leather boots. It had been snowing, not heavily but steadily, but it had stopped. That was good. It was what he wanted.

He sighted Clanton early in the afternoon as he rode up out of a dip a mile away, perched above the left bank of the river, a collection of unpainted buildings thrown roughly together, stark against the gray whiteness of the horizonless distance. It was next to impossible to see where sky ended and land began. It was all the same color.

Pulling a piece of folded paper out of his pocket, he opened it up, holding it tight in his mittened hands to prevent the biting prairie wind from whipping it away. He stared down at a simple drawing, actually a crude map. Drawn across the paper was a crooked line, with the penciled words *Muddy Cr.*, and alongside it a shaded area marked *Clanton*. Just below the shaded area the crooked line jutted sharply, and beside it was marked a large *X*.

Lifting his eyes from the map, he peered ahead. The whiteness irritated his eyes and he squinted against the dull, flat light. He reined his horse closer to the river bank, taking care not to get too close for fear of the horse stepping into loose snow and toppling over and down onto the ice below.

He rode that way for a hundred yards or more, before he saw what he was looking for, barely visible down on the river ice because it was tucked in under the overhang of the bank. The bank presented about a fifteen-foot drop to the ice below. His face creased into a mirthless grin.

From the river he veered off sharply, reining the horse toward the town. Fifteen minutes later he was riding down the snow-covered main street.

He appeared casual the way he rode into town, but his practiced eyes took in every detail. He had seen dozens like it and he knew what to look for. The main street ran north-south, and on the west side, the riverbank side, stood the inevitable saloon, a clapboard building with a pair of horns nailed above the door. In a way the place reminded him of the log saloon in Fort Turner, except that the horns were not from an elk; they looked like they once belonged to a Texas longhorn. Next to the saloon was a general store, and next to that a mail station. On the opposite side of the street stood a livery stable and a blacksmith's shop, then a couple of other buildings.

He saw the bank farther down the street, on the same side as the saloon. Beside it was another building, then nothing else. That was Clanton, Montana. Nine buildings in all. Not one accommodated a sheriff's or town marshal's office.

It wasn't until then that he spotted, a hundred yards or more beyond the town, three rows of tents. His heart skipped a beat. He hadn't seen them before because their white silhouettes blended in with the snow-covered landscape. He saw them now because of smoke rising from chimneys poking through openings in their sides. The tents had portable stoves. Soldiers!

The first thought that went through Henri Foucade's mind was to abort what he had planned, to turn his horse around and ride right on out of town before someone recognized him. What a stroke of bad luck! He should have foreseen the possibility. Like almost everyone living or traveling on the northern plains, he had been well aware of the Sioux situation. For that matter, so was most of the nation, and much of the civilized world. The so-called Custer massacre had received widespread newspaper coverage. Damn the soldiers! They should have all been withdrawn to Fort Buford and the other military stations. Didn't the army know the weather was getting too cold even for Sioux hostiles?

Then Henri Foucade had second thoughts. He didn't see any soldiers, and no saddled horses. Indeed, he didn't see anyone around anywhere. The town could just as easily have been dead, a ghost town, except for smoke rising from chimneys along the street. The presence of the soldiers might even serve to his advantage—it would add to a false sense of security the town might have. No one would expect a bank robbery at this time of the year, in such weather, and with an army patrol camped just beyond town they would expect it even less. On top of that, soldiers spent money. There might be more money in the bank.

These thoughts flashed through the Frenchman's mind in a matter of seconds. He didn't break his horse's gait. Instantly he turned his mind back to the job at hand. He really needed two more men, one to assist him in the bank, the other to stand guard outside in the street. However, he had the element of surprise, and his getaway would be unique.

He reined to outside the bank. Before dismounting he glanced quickly back along the street. There was still no sign of movement anywhere. A final look in the direction of the army camp. There was no movement there either. He swung down from his saddle. Then he lifted a pair of saddlebags off his horse's back, slung them over his shoulder, and stepped through the bank's front door.

A teller stood behind the counter, a barred grill in front of him, and in a glass-enclosed office farther along the counter, the bank manager sat at his desk. Both men looked up at the sound of the door being opened. Neither were alarmed at the sight of the man in buffalo coat and fur cap. Most of the ranchers and ranch hands on the northern plains wore buffalo coats in winter, and a good many replaced their wide-brimmed hats with fur caps. The northern plains were unpredictable and the climate savage. You never could be sure when winter would lay its icy grip across the country, you never knew when a life-taking blizzard would sweep down out of the north, or across the prairie from the mountains far to the west.

The teller nodded from behind his grill. "Howdy. Bad day to be out."

Fur cap pulled down low over his head, the Frenchman drew off his mitts and unbuttoned his coat. He nodded in agreement. "Yes, but the snow 'as stopped."

The teller's eyes alighted on the leather saddlebags over the Frenchman's shoulder. Although the hollow-cheeked stranger looked vaguely familiar, the teller couldn't place him as a local rancher, and he didn't expect a hand would be depositing a saddlebag full of money into the bank. On the other hand there were new ranches popping up all over the territory, and this man could be a rancher from one of them. Most were raising horses for the army, taking advantage of the cavalry's need for horses as they maintained their patrols campaigning against the last of the Sioux hostiles.

"You putting money in?" the teller asked.

"No," said the Frenchman, pulling his pistol from its holster and pointing it at the teller. "I am taking money out." He slapped the saddlebags down onto the counter. "Fill these—*quickly!* Make one false move and I will kill you."

The teller's face went white.

The Frenchman held the gun pointed at the teller in his left hand. With his right he drew another gun and pointed it at the manager in the glass-enclosed office. "You in there, get out here immediately. *Quickly,* or I will shoot!"

The manager jumped to his feet as though he had been stung. He scurried from his office.

The Frenchman pointed his gun at an iron safe that stood against the wall. "Open it!"

Henri Foucade watched as the bank manager knelt

214

down beside the safe door and began twirling the combination dials. The manager's hands trembled. One look at the Frenchman's face behind the pointed guns had been enough. With the red welt vivid on his cheek, the Frenchman's appearance was frightening enough.

"Hurry!" he urged.

Foucade took his eyes from the manager to the teller, busily stuffing bank notes into the saddlebags. "Silver too," he said. "Everything."

The safe door swung open. From where he stood he could see lots of cash inside. He would do better here than he and the other members of the gang had done at Fort Turner. And this time it didn't have to be split three ways.

"Get over beside 'im and 'elp," he ordered the teller. "Take the saddlebags and put everything from the safe into them." He waved one of his guns around to emphasize his words.

The teller hurried to obey. He knelt down next to the manager and the two men swept bank notes and bags of silver from the safe into the saddlebags.

Standing at the counter watching, the Frenchman felt a quiver of exhilaration surge through him. He enjoyed the excitement of a bank holdup. It felt strange doing it alone, without Cess Oates beside him and Ben Zacks outside watching the street and the horses. He didn't miss Lone Man. Lone Man was a vicious killer, too ready to shoot when it wasn't necessary. Gunshots attracted attention, alarm. With that thought flashing through his mind, he realized that if he had to back up his threats to shoot either of the two men kneeling down in front of the safe, it would alert the town, and the soldiers in their camp as well. But he had already thought about that and had decided to take the chance. That was what added to the thrill of the holdup.

He turned his head and looked toward the front door for just an instant. Through the partly frosted window, he could see some of the street. But he saw no movement. The town still looked dead.

He turned his head back to the safe. *"Hurry!"* he snapped.

His voice, cracking out suddenly, startled the already frightened teller.

The two men finished filling the saddlebags.

"Bring them over here."

His eyes glued to the gun muzzle, the teller held one of the saddlebags as he and the manager carried them to the counter.

"You can't get away with this," the manager said, showing sudden bravado. "You'll hardly get out of town before you'll be caught. There's a troop of cavalry camped just beyond the street."

The Frenchman ignored him. He motioned with his pistol. "Get over in that corner."

"Wh—what are you going to do?"

"Get over there!"

They did as they were told. The teller was shaking like a leaf.

"Now keep your noses into the corner, or I'll kill you both."

He slipped one of his guns back into its holster, picked up the saddlebags, and went to swing them over his shoulder. The weight of the silver almost threw him off balance. He grinned. *Bon.* This job was worth the risk. He hefted the bags over his shoulder and backed quietly across the floor in his moccasined feet until he reached the front door. Turning, he opened it, and the next instant was outside in the frigid, arctic-like air.

Wasting not a second, he heaved the saddlebags up onto his horse's back and swung up into the saddle. He grabbed the reins and pulled the horse around. With a shout and a kick of his legs he sent it galloping along the street.

He didn't bother to look left or right. He simply stuck his head down and rode. He was out of the town, galloping north, in seconds. He heard shouting from behind and something whizzed through the air above him, followed by the crack of a rifle shot. Legging furiously, he rode the horse like the wind. He didn't glance back over his shoulder. He just rode for his life. Indeed, it was his life he was riding for. If he was caught, the rest of his life would be short.

There was more shouting from the town, more rifle shots. With the town falling behind, he veered to the left and rode wildly toward the river.

"Baptiste!" he shouted. *"Baptiste!"*

Down on the frozen river ice, hidden under a snow-covered overhang, Baptiste heard him. He had been waiting for hours, resting the dogs. He and the Frenchman had left Ville Ste. Marie the same time, but Baptiste had traveled down the river ice. With enough of a covering of packed snow, it was like a highway and he had easily outdistanced the Frenchman.

Hearing the name, Baptiste sprung into action. The waiting had made him jumpy and he was a bundle of nerves. He had spent the last two hours regretting that he had let himself be talked into this venture. He was scared and had been on the verge of pulling out when he heard the first rifle shot. That had scared him all the more, but at least it had told him that his friend was on the way and that the waiting was coming to an end.

At their master's urgent shouts, the dogs jumped quickly to their feet and stood poised, ready to throw their shoulders into their padded harness. Baptiste looked anxiously to the north as he impatiently waited the last minute or two.

Reaching the river bank, the Frenchman reined the horse to a snow-showering stop, slid down from the saddle, pulling the heavy saddlebags off with him. He turned the horse around, pointed it in the direction of Clanton, and slapped it on the rump. "Go, boy. Back into town. Someone there will claim you. You will find a warm shelter and a good feed tonight. You are a good fellow."

He stood in snow up to his thighs, watching the hindquarters of Ben Zacks's horse as it struggled through the snow back toward Clanton. At the same time he saw horsemen riding rapidly out of town in pursuit of him.

The heavy saddlebags over his arm, he turned around and waded through the snow until he reached the edge of the embankment. The next instant he slid down through the snow onto the river ice fifteen feet below.

He landed in a heap a few yards from Baptiste and the dogs.

"Hey, it's about time, Johnny. I was worried. I get damn scared. I thought you be here long time back."

"Don't waste time talking, Baptiste. Help me. We must get away from here quickly."

The Frenchman clambered to his feet. He picked up the heavy saddlebags and threw them onto the sled. Baptiste tossed him his capote and a pair of snowshoes. While the Frenchman peeled off his bulky buffalo coat and pulled on the capote, Baptiste lashed the saddlebags securely onto the sled.

Above, the shouts of the pursuing posse grew louder.

"Spread out, boys! He went down onto the river ice. He might try to get to the other side."

"Hell! He ain't got a chance. He's on foot. His hoss must've throwed him."

"If he does get across, we can pick him off with our rifles."

Baptiste looked anxiously at the Frenchman, bent over strapping the snowshoes onto his moccasined feet.

"Come on, Johnny!" His voice was raw and edgy.

The Frenchman nodded, stood up, and stamped his feet. "I am ready."

"Good! We go!"

Baptiste raised his whip above his head, cracked it over the dogs' backs, and shouted. Eager to be off after their period of inactivity, the dogs threw themselves into their harness. The sled jerked into movement, picked up speed, and went skimming quickly along the ice. Baptiste, gripping the guide rope, ran alongside. The Frenchman, benefitting from practice runs around Ville Ste. Marie, ran beside him.

There was shouting from up on the riverbank.

"The son of a bitch has got a dog team!"

"There's two of 'em, goddamn it!"

"Shoot! Don't let 'em get away!"

Shots rang out. Spurs of snow flew up on the river ice as bullets thudded into it.

"Keep in close to the bank, Baptiste!" shouted the Frenchman. "The bank is high here. Use it as cover. They have little chance of hitting us here."

"Ride, goddamn it!" shouted one of the men in the posse of seven. "Don't let 'em get away."

"Outflank 'em!"

"Can't," shouted a rider in reply. "Snow's too deep."

One of the riders dismounted and kneeled down above the bank with his rifle pointed down along the river. He pulled the weapon into his shoulder, took aim, and fired.

"Did you get one of 'em?"

"Naw, goddamn it. Cain't see 'em long enough to get a bead on either one of 'em."

"Two of you boys climb down the bank and get onto the ice. Try and pick 'em off with your rifles."

While two men clambered down through the snow onto the river ice, the other five urged their horses through the snow along the top of the bank in pursuit. But the snow was too deep. The horses heaved and floundered in the drifts.

"They're gettin' clear away," one of the riders shouted.

Back in Clanton a party of cavalry pounded up the street, blue cloaks flying back over their shoulders as they bent low over their horses. The horses' hoofs kicked up a cloud of snow as they burst out of the north end of the town. They had turned out quickly, considering the unexpectedness of the bank robbery, and had covered the distance from their camp at the south end of town in record time. They as yet did not know they were chasing a dog team. But it was too late anyway; the sled was too far away, with too great a headstart.

Shots rang out from the frozen river. Even for the two riflemen down on the ice, the sled was moving too fast and was already beyond effective range. Besides, snow was falling again, and the light fading. The two riflemen poured a fusilade of fire at the two distant figures running with the sled. But it was a fusilade of frustration.

An hour later the Frenchman and Baptiste were more than halfway back to the Canadian border. They looked behind them. There was no sign of pursuit. Then they looked at each other. The next instant they burst into laughter.

CHAPTER 18

Sarah pounded urgently on the Frenchman's door.

"Henri! It's me—Sarah. Are you there? Please answer."

There was no sound from within the small, cubiclelike room he occupied at the Benaventure Hotel.

"Oh! Where can he be?" she asked herself in desperation.

If her father knew she was at the hotel looking for Henri—

She had not seen Henri for four days, not since the time he'd stormed out of the stable after her father had struck him with the horsewhip. Her father had forbidden her to ever see him or talk to him again, and Henri had not been near the makeshift church since. But it wasn't simply that she hadn't seen him for four days that compelled her to find him now. It was something far more important.

Her heart hammering wildly, Sarah slipped out the back door of the hotel and hurried through the snow-covered village to one place where she thought she might find him. She had seen him there in the yard once, talking to the man with the dogs.

Sarah avoided the street. She took a back way, along an alley, the same back way she had taken to get from her father's manse to the hotel. She didn't want to be seen, not by *them,* for Henri's sake. If *they* saw her, they might guess Henri had been warned, and that might make it worse.

She reached Baptiste's cabin. What if Henri wasn't there, she thought, or if there was no one there? But smoke rose from the chimney, she noticed.

As Sarah approached the door, the dogs in their pen at the back of the cabin started barking. They startled her momentarily, and her hand flew up to her throat. She took a deep breath, walked the remaining two steps, and knocked sharply, urgently, on the door.

There was no answer.

But someone was in there. She knew. She could sense it. She knocked again, more urgently.

"Henri!" she called, almost in a whisper, as though stealth was important. "It's Sarah. I must talk to you. It's important, terribly important."

The door was flung open. Baptiste stood there, and behind him the Frenchman. His appearance took her back momentarily. She hadn't seen him look this way before. He was wild-eyed and his sallow-colored face was black with whiskers. He looked as though he hadn't shaved since she'd last seen him. The welt on the side of his face looked red and raw, even under the whiskers, and her heart went out to him.

At the same time relief flooded over her at having found him. She had been very much afraid she mightn't have found him in time. Yet even now could be too late.

The two men stared out at her as she stood before them, the ends of her long blue scarf hanging down the front of her long black overcoat. Her eyes were wide and blue, her high cheekbones prominent under her freckled face, her auburn hair shining lustrously under her black Persian lamb hat.

The Frenchman spoke first. "Come in." He placed a hand on Baptiste's arm. The swarthy-faced *metis* stood aside to allow her to enter.

Sarah stepped quickly inside. She wasted no time with

222

preliminaries.

"There are three men in the village looking for someone named Henri Foucade," she burst out breathlessly, staring up into the Frenchman's face. "They say he has robbed banks in the United States. They say he is a Frenchman. They have a picture of him. He looks like you, Henri. One of them is wearing a red coat."

"*Sacre bleu!*" Fear drained Baptiste's face.

"It isn't true, is it, Henri?" Sarah asked, still staring up into the Frenchman's face. "Bank robbery? There must be some mistake. It . . . it wasn't a very good picture."

"*Sacre bleu!*" Baptiste repeated, speaking French. "*Gendarmerie auchuval!* I knew I should not have changed my mind. I knew I should not have let you talk me into going with you while you rob the bank. Now they have come for us."

The Frenchman turned to Baptiste. Putting a hand on Baptiste's shoulder, he replied in French. "It is me they are after, *mon ami,* not you. They could not yet know about the bank robbery in Clanton. They need never know you were with me. I robbed the bank. I alone did it. No one saw your face. They cannot identify you. Have no fear. I will take the blame. I will tell no one that you had anything to do with it."

He turned back to Sarah. There was a fear in her eyes. Fear he had not seen in them before.

"Tell me it isn't true," she said again.

He swallowed and looked down at her. "Where are they?"

Sarah shook her head. "I . . . I'm not sure. They were talking with father. He . . . he told them . . ." She took a deep breath. "He sent them to the hotel. They must have gone there looking for you."

"You better run away, Johnny," Baptiste said suddenly, his black eyes shining with excitement.

"Run away?" The Frenchman shrugged his shoulders. "Where?"

"You can no hide in Ville Ste. Marie. They find you

223

sure."

Sarah's face was a mixture of conflicting emotions. "Then it *is* true!"

The Frenchman looked back at her. "It depends what they said. That I robbed banks?" He nodded. "Yes, it is true. But if they said I am a murderer, a killer like the other two, no, it is not true."

"Then give yourself up," she said, a pleading look in her eyes.

He shook his head. "I cannot do that. I was with others when they shot and killed. The courts, they will 'ang me too. Or else they will leave me in prison to rot. I would rather be dead."

Baptiste grabbed the Frenchman's arm and shook him. "Get dressed, Johnny. *Quickly!* You are one of us now. I give you my dogs. Here, I draw you map." He snatched up a piece of paper and a pen and sat down at a table and started to draw. "Drive northwest until you come to the Saskatchewan, then go straight north until you reach Batoche. It is long way, but you make it. My brother in Batoche, Jacques, he look after you. You tell him I sent you. He will know the dogs."

He finished drawing the map, stood up, and handed it to Henri. "Get dressed. I load the sled with what you need for the trail. Then I hitch the dogs. Then you go. You go for your life, Johnny. You follow the map, like I say. You understand, Johnny?"

Henri Foucade nodded. Without another word, Baptiste threw on his capote and stepped outside. Foucade started gathering together a few things that he had at Baptiste's cabin. His two pistols, rifle, trail clothes, proceeds from the bank robbery at Clanton. Whatever else he possessed, back at the hotel, he had to leave. Sarah watched him, conflicting emotions drawing her face.

"Take me with you!" she said suddenly, impulsively.

He stood bolt upright from what he had been doing, turned, and looked at her. "I cannot do that."

"Please!" she implored, a desperate, pleading look in her eyes.

"Why?" His voice was little more than a hoarse whisper.

"Because I love you! I can't live without you!" Then she looked quickly away, her eyes cast down onto the floor.

Henri Foucade stood staring at her for a long moment. He stepped over to her, placed a thumb and forefinger around her chin, and gently turned her face up so that her eyes were looking up into his.

"Do you realize what you say?"

"Yes."

"What about your father?"

"Please take me with you," she replied, ignoring the question.

He looked at her a moment longer, then said, "I cannot do that." He turned away from her and resolutely resumed his packing. But he moved about reluctantly, as though regretting his decision.

Baptiste appeared at the door. "Come on, Johnny. You have no time to spare."

The Frenchman picked up his bedroll and rifle, lifted a pair of snowshoes off the wall, and moved out through the door. Baptiste had the dogs harnessed, the sled packed and ready to go.

"Henri!" Sarah sobbed. "Don't leave me. *Please!*"

He turned and gazed at her. A tear rolled down her cheek. She lifted a glove hand to wipe it away. She looked a small, forlorn figure dressed in black as she stood in the doorway just inside the cabin.

"Come on, Johnny," Baptiste urged. "You better go."

The Frenchman held out a hand to her. "Come."

She ran to him, taking his hand.

"Sacre Dieu!" breathed Baptiste.

The Frenchman looked around at Baptiste. "I must take her, *mon ami.*"

Baptiste stared at her for fifteen or more seconds, then shrugged. He stepped inside the cabin, reappearing half a minute later carrying a rabbit-skin robe, holding it while she climbed onto the sled.

"Put this around you," he said to her. "It keep you warm." He glanced at the Frenchman. "When you get away on the trail, you can stop at a trading post and buy trail clothing for her."

The Frenchman nodded, shuffled his feet into his snowshoes, knelt down and fastened them.

Baptiste handed him the dog whip. *"Bon voyage,* Johnny."

Henri Foucade clapped an affectionate hand on Baptiste's shoulder. "Thank you, *mon ami."*

He lifted the whip, cracked it above the dogs as Baptiste had shown him, and shouted. The dogs jumped forward, pulling the sled behind them. They ran from Baptiste's yard and out along the snow-covered street. Henri Foucade ran alongside them, the guide rope in his hand.

Suddenly a shout carried along the street from behind. The Frenchman looked back over his shoulder. Three men on horses were riding around the corner. They wore shaggy buffalo coats; a flash of scarlet showed in the collar of one of them.

"Stop!" shouted Sergeant MacGregor. "In the name of the Queen!"

The Frenchman cracked his whip again. *"Marche!"* he shouted. *"Marche!"*

The dogs raced ahead, pulling the sled skimming along the snow behind them. Henri Foucade ran faster.

The three horseman legged their horses into a canter along the street. The horses' hoofs kicked up clods of snow behind them.

"Stop!" shouted Sergeant MacGregor again.

But Henri Foucade steered the sled out of the village and across the snow-covered open country. The dogs' padded feet carried them fleetly over the snow, the sled's runners gliding smoothly along behind. Foucade, supported by the frame and webbing of his snowshoes, ran lightly alongside them.

Sergeant MacGregor and Deputy U.S. Marshal Edson rode their horses at a gallop, Jules following on his shorter-legged cayuse. The horses carried them along the street, then they were out of the village riding north. Almost immediately the horses were floundering in deep snow. They plunged through the drifts up to their bellies, heaving, fighting their way. Snow built up under their hoofs, weighing them down.

The Frenchman drove the dogs farther across open country. Ville Ste. Marie dropped behind. The three horsemen rode doggedly after him, but they fell farther and farther behind.

Henri Foucade ran relentlessly on beside the sled, guide rope in one hand, whip in the other. Sarah sat on the sled, staring fixedly ahead.

"Marche! Marche!"

"Stop in the name of the Queen," the voice sounded distantly behind.

Jules lifted his rifle from the saddle bucket, but MacGregor stopped him. "Noo, he's got a woman wi' him."

Soon the sled was far ahead, a speck on the distant white landscape. Henri Foucade glanced behind him again. The three horsemen were equally distant specks. he laughed. Then he looked to his front again. Trees stood on his left, and beyond them hills which continued west to Wood Mountain. To his right, the country flattened to open prairie. The same to the north. The horizon was invisible in the white distance.

Henri Foucade drove the dogs northward. He squinted his eyes against the dull, flat glare of the white countryside. It hurt his eyes, but he squinted harder and continued running.

The Frenchman pushed steadily on. Once he passed the lifting land of the western hills and leveled out onto flat prairie, he veered northwest, heading for the Saskatchewan, as Baptiste had told him. From time to time he consulted Baptiste's map, but map drawing was not one of Baptiste's finer accomplishments, and it was a very rudimentary sketch at best. The Saskatchewan was much farther away than the map indicated.

As the day wore on, the Frenchman alternated running with standing on the back of the sled runners while he rested. His additional weight slowed the dogs but he had far outdistanced his pursuers—they were nowhere in sight. Perhaps they had given up, he thought. Baptiste had told him there was no one else in Ville Ste. Marie who had dogs. Although common in the Saskatchewan country, dogs were not widely used on the prairies. Mail carriers sometimes used them, but a mail delivery had been made two days earlier and there wouldn't be another for a month, until well after Christmas.

Henri Foucade stood on the back of the runners and looked ahead as the six dogs, their tails curled up over their backs, ran tirelessly, breath forming thin white clouds in front of their mouths for only an instant until it was whipped away by the wind and the force of their movement. The sled, seemingly fragile, yet light and strong in its construction of wood and skin, loaded with provisions . . . Sarah, sitting just beneath and in front of him, her black Persian lamb hat and coat visible above the rabbin-skin robe Baptiste had given her. . .

Sarah had said little since they let, and but for the movement of her head from time to time as they traveled, might have been asleep. But sleep would have been difficult. The sled was designed to pack provisions and equipment, or perhaps light freight, and an injured person if necessary; it was not designed as a bed. Besides, the ride was bumpy as they crested humps and hillocks, or raced down into low spots. And there was noise . . . the occasional bark of one of the dogs having a disagreement with the dog ahead or behind, the constant low rasping whine of the wooden runners across the snow. Baptiste had iced them to give them greater glide, but they still made a noise.

They traveled until sundown, when the Frenchman pulled into a clump of poplar and camped. He tied the sled to a tree, as Baptiste had taught him, in case the dogs tried to run off and take the sled with them, or in case they sighted a rabbit or some other animal and succumbed to their canine instincts and chased it. Then, when he unhitched the dogs, he chained them to another tree. After that he got busy with an axe and cut down a tree for a fire. Baptiste had told him there would be little timber until he neared the Saskatchewan; he cut enough wood to carry for a campfire for the next two nights.

They sat huddled together around their fire, eating a meal Sarah had cooked.

"You are very quiet, Sarah. Is it that you are sorry you have come with me?"

She smiled as she stared into the fire. It was a sad smile. "I was thinking about Father."

"What about him?"

"How he will manage without me."

"He managed before you were born."

"He had Mother then. She died when I was seven. Father raised me from then on."

"Do you have any brothers or sisters?"

"A brother, four years older. He took over the farm. And a sister, three years older. She married."

They ate the remainder of their meal in silence. When she had finished, Sarah placed her tin plate on the snow beside her and leaned her head against his shoulder. The only noise was the crackling of the fire. There was barely any wind. The night was crystal clear. The clouds that had hung above the prairies for weeks had gone and the stars sparkled brightly against the velvet blackness of the sky.

"It's very lonely, isn't it?" Sarah said.

Henri let his head incline so that it rested on hers. "Yes."

They sat like that, quietly, for what seemed a long time. The fire burned brightly in front of them, giving off a comforting warmth.

"Why did you hold up banks?" Sarah asked suddenly.

The question, in its stark simplicity, startled him. Her head still on his shoulder, he shrugged, but only slightly, not enough to dislodge her. "I think it was some sort of adventure. A sense of excitement, of being in control."

She took her head from his shoulder and sat looking up at him. *"Control?"* she asked. "How do you mean?"

"When you 'ave a gun in your 'and and you are pointing it at someone, and you tell 'im to give you all the money, you are the . . . 'ow you say . . . the boss? For those few moments, anyway."

"What happened if they didn't give you the money?"

"They always did. They always did because I 'ad the gun pointed at them. I was . . . *boss.*"

"But it is wrong to rob."

He shrugged again. "Many things are wrong, but they are done, and many times there is an air of respectability, of righteousness, depending upon who is the doer. It is wrong to send armies into a neighbor's country and seize territory and kill and destroy. It is wrong for kings and queens, emperors, czars, rulers, sultans, to live in opulent splendor while hundreds of thousands of their peoples live in poverty or die of starvation and illness. It is wrong to make slaves of colored people, it is wrong to drive Indians from their hunting lands. It is wrong to oppress in the name of greed or religion. However, these things are all done and condoned. It is all right to do those things if you are big and wealthy. It is only wrong to do them if you are small and without power."

"But robbing banks is not justified by the things you just mentioned, Henri, because they are done. You're stealing money from people who put it there because they think it will be safe."

"People who put money in the bank can afford to lose it. I 'ave never robbed the poor or passengers on stage-coaches or trains."

"Is that why you did it? Because of some sense of social injustice?"

He shook his head. "No. It would perhaps sound noble if I were to say that was the reason, but I would be telling the lie. I did it because it was easier than working. And I could make very much more money. But

230

I think mostly it was because of the sense of excitement. Yet there were times when I thought holding up banks, being 'unted and chased, was perhaps more trouble than it was worth. But by then it was too late. I was already an outlaw."

"Didn't it ever occur to you that you might get caught?"

"I thought about that, but I did not believe I would get caught." He laughed, a brittle laugh; there was no mirth to it. "I was right."

The next day dawned bright and blue, without a cloud in the sky. They struck out shortly after daybreak, following breakfast. The Frenchman drove the dogs northwest across flat prairie covered with dazzling white snow.

Sarah sat on the sled, her hand held above her eyes shading them from the glaring reflection of the sun's bright light off the snow. Running alongside the sled, sometimes standing balanced on the back runners, sometimes sitting on the sled behind her for short periods, the Frenchman squinted his eyes against the glare. As the day wore on, his eyes became increasingly more sore.

Sarah offered to get off the sled and run, but the Frenchman would not hear of it. "Without snowshoes you would sink into the snow. No, ride. You are not 'eavy."

They traveled all day, without sighting a tree or anything to break the flatness of the endless prairie. They did not see another soul, nor even an animal. They might as well have been alone, the only creatures in a white wilderness. There was little wind and the temperature was low, but it was ideal for travel because the cold gave the dogs energy and incentive, and it had the same effect on Henri Foucade, snowshoeing along behind them.

But by the end of the day his eyes were painful from the constant glare of sun on snow.

They camped that night on open prairie, for there was nowhere else. The Frenchman was thankful Baptiste had warned him of the absence of trees on the prairie. He

231

was thankful he had cut enough wood to last two nights. From what Baptiste had told him, by the third day they should reach a settlement or an Indian camp where they could obtain shelter overnight and perhaps buy food.

The Frenchman built his fire in a hollow, where the snow was deeper. He dug out a shelter and banked it to provide insulation. Then he pounded a wooden stake into the frozen ground and chained the dogs to it. He built his fire and broke out the food for their night's meal, which Sarah cooked while he kept the fire blazing.

"Are you sorry you didn't stay behind?" he asked.

She shook her head. "No. Why do you ask?"

"Because I would not want to think that I 'ad you from somewhere you wanted to be and subjected you to the 'ardship of the trail."

After they had eaten, Sarah asked, "What will happen to us, Henri?"

"We will go north to the Saskatchewan country, like Baptiste said, to Batoche, and find his brother, Jacques. He will help us. We will remain there until the spring. Perhaps I will ask Jacques to teach me to trap. There is much trapping of the animals for fur in Saskatchewan country, and farther north, Baptiste told me. If we like it there, we can stay. Baptiste said it is very pretty in the summer. Full of lakes and rivers and lush green forests, and all sorts of animals and fish."

"What about the Mounted Police? There must be some there."

"We will avoid them. Besides, they will not know me. I do not think there are telegraph lines in the north."

Their third day dawned bright and cloudless again. They came across an Indian camp nestling at the foot of a low hill beside a frozen lake and a few willows. It was earlier than the Frenchman would have liked to camp. There were still two or three hours of daylight left, but he decided to spend the night with the Indians anyway. It was too good an opportunity to miss, a place where they could shelter and buy some food. The Indians were more interested in trade goods than money, so he gave them one of his pistols in exchange for a small quantity of frozen fish. The Indians told him where there was a trading post and a small settlement two days' travel to the northwest.

The fourth day was again clear and bright and they struck out once more. They mushed all day, but the bright sun shining down from the cloudless sky bounced glaringly off the white snow. Sitting on the sled, wrapped in her rabbit-skin robe, Sarah closed her eyes to it, as she had done for the past two days, but Henri Foucade squinted his aching eyes and pushed doggedly on. There were times when he longed to close them, and there were times when he did, sitting on the sled and riding, but when he closed them they were just as painful, feeling as though hundreds of grains of sand were embedded under his eyelids. Yet he couldn't ride with eyes closed for long. He had to constantly guide the dogs, keeping them headed northwest, to watch that they didn't sight a rabbit and go chasing it, or that they didn't race too wildly down a slope and upset the sled, or that they didn't start fighting among themselves.

By evening he was glad to pull into another depression—there were lots of them, buffalo wallows, ideal camping spots because if a traveler dug down far enough into the snow, he could find buffalo "chips"—dung—which made a perfect, slow-burning fuel that gave off an amazing warmth.

"What's wrong, Henri?" Sarah asked anxiously as she watched Henri sitting on the edge of the sled rubbing his eyes.

"My eyes ache. They are very sore. I think it is because of the glare of the sun on the snow. I will turn in early and rest them. I think they will be better in the morning if I do that."

When he woke up the next morning, he could not see. Panic gripped him and he floundered out of his blankets, thrashing around wildly.

Startled, Sarah sat up bolt upright. *"Henri!"* she cried. "What's wrong?"

233

"It is my eyes! I cannot see. They are like hot coals burning in my 'ead. I cannot see anything. I 'ave gone blind! I cannot see! I cannot see!"

Sarah jumped out from her blankets and rushed over to him, putting her arms around him protectively, trying to comfort him.

"I cannot see!" he gasped. "I 'ave gone blind!"

Sarah didn't know what to do. They were out in the middle of a white wasteland, alone. They were almost out of firewood. Henri was panicking. He was desperate. He could't see. He was blind. God had smitten him. They could not stay where they were. She had to do something. She could not drive the dogs. She did not know how. Oh, if only they had a team of horses and a sleigh, she could get Henri to help.

"Tell me how to harness the dogs, Henri. I will take you where someone can help us. The Indians said there is a settlement another day's travel. I will take you there."

He shook his head. "No. You could not drive the dogs. You do not know 'ow to hitch them. There is a trick to it. They could get vicious. If they sense you do not know 'ow to 'andle them, they could attack you. I know 'ow to do it because Baptiste taught me, and the dogs are used to me. But it took practice. You could not possibly do it. Oh! God 'elp me! I am blind!"

"Then I will go for help. I will go back to the Indian camp. I can find the way. I'll follow the tracks we made. I'll take your snowshoes. If I hurry, I can reach the Indian camp before nightfall."

"No, Sarah. It is too risky. It is too far. You are not dressed for travel on the trail. *Sacre Dieu!* I should never 'ave taken you with me. It was idiotic."

"I must go, Henri. I can wear some of your spare clothes. It is the only way. There is no wind. I will find the Indian camp. There was a full moon last night. It will be full again tonight. I will follow the tracks until I reach the camp. It will be easier walking along the trail that we have already made. Lie down and rest, dear, and keep warm. I will be back with help as quickly as possible.

They found her staggering alone across the frozen white prairie, a small black figure in the distance. She had walked all day and throughout the night and into the second day, and she was only a mile from the Indian camp, almost exhausted. It was a tremendous feat of strength, of determination, of faith and will power.

"My God!" exclaimed MacGregor when he recognized her staggering toward them.

She was about to faint from exhaustion. She was half-delirious. Edson was the first to reach her. He leaned over in his saddle and lifted her up as she was about to fall into the snow.

They turned around and rode as fast as they could back to the Indian camp.

Beside a fire in one of the buffalo-hide tepees, they wrapped her in buffalo robes and spooned hot broth and tea between her lips. But she remained delirious, ranting.

"Must get help . . . Henri, can't see . . . blind . . . Don't worry, Henri . . . I'll get help . . . I'm coming, my darling . . . I'm coming . . ."

MacGregor and Edson exchanged glances.

"Something must've happened to him," MacGregor said. "Sounds like he's gone snow-blind. This is the sort of weather that'll do it, lots of glare frae the sun shining on the snow. It dinna last once you're out of it for awhile, but it can be verra painful while you've got it. We'd better get back on the trail and find him."

They found him the next day. Their cheeks and noses smeared black from the charred remains of their last campfire to counter the glare of the sun off the snow, they sat their saddles and stared down at him. He was propped against the sled. The dogs, barking furiously, were chained nearby. What had been a campfire was nothing more than black ashes in the snow.

MacGregor and Edson swung down from their saddles. Handing their reins to Jules, they crunched across the snow in their moccasins.

MacGregor kneeled down beside the still figure. It was frozen, revolver in right hand. MacGregor reached out and pulled aside the hood from the face. A small black hole was in the Frenchman's head, with a trickle of frozen blood running partway down his temple. The back of his head was a frozen mess of blood, brain, and bone. The .44-caliber bullet had blown out the back of his head.

MacGregor looked up at Edson. "Well, Marshal. Here's your mon, but he'll nae be going back to the United States to stand trial."

Edson said, "Looks like he already stood trial."

Sarah was sitting up in the tepee when they got back to the Indian camp. Her face was pale and drawn, but the delirium was gone. Warmth from a fire, and shelter, together with hot broth and tea, had restored body heat, while rest had brought her out of the state of exhaustion. She had suffered from minor frostbite, but otherwise she was little the worse for her ordeal, at least physically. Emotionally she was drained. She had wanted to set out immediately back to where she had left Henri, but the Indian woman looking after her—acting on Sergeant MacGregor's instructions—had refused to let her go.

One look at Sergeant MacGregor's face told her what she dreaded finding out.

MacGregor shook his head slowly. "I'm sorry, Miss Hatcher. He's dead."

Sarah's hands flew up to her throat. *"Dead?"*

"Aye. He shot himself. It would hae been quick and painless."

"Oh . . . *no!"* she screamed. She threw both hands up and buried her face in them. She sat there sobbing.

236

MacGregor kneeled down beside her and put a comforting arm around her shoulder. "There, there, lassie," he said gently. "I know it's a terrible shock. But maybe it's all for the best. You must hae seen guid in the mon, otherwise I dinna believe you would hae taken up with him. So maybe it's the best thing. We would hae caught up with him in the end. He would hae had to go back to America to stand trial for the crimes he was involved in."

"But . . . he said," she sobbed, "that he never . . . killed anyone . . . except in self-defense."

"That's right, ma'am," Bill Edson said, standing in the tepee awkwardly, looking down at her. "That's true. Of the gang he rode with, he was the least bad, if I can put it like that. But the trouble, ma'am, is that he rode with outlaws who robbed and killed, and even if he didn't kill anyone in cold blood himself, he was with others when they did it, and in the eyes of the law he was equally guilty."

She broke out into uncontrollable sobbing.

MacGregor tightened his arm around her. "That's all right, lassie. Go ahead and cry. What you did was verra brave . . . traveling like you did across the snow in the depths of winter, trying to get help for him. I dinna know how you did it, walking all the way, without any food or proper clothes, but plainly God was on your side. He was looking down on you. Right noo you're going through a crisis in your life. Maybe you think you loved that mon. Maybe you did. Personally, I think love only comes aboot after y' get to know someone, and it generally takes time to know someone that well. It may hae been more a matter of infatuation you had for him. But whatever it was, you'll live through it. In a month or two, it'll be almost as though it never happened. You'll settle back into your life, helping your father in his work."

"I . . . I can never go back. Father would . . . never want me back."

"Agh! You're wrong there, lassie. I had a wee talk

with your father before we struck out frae Ville Ste. Marie. You might think he's angry with you, but the fact is he's angry with himself. He said he always turned a blind eye to the fact that you're a woman. He always thought of you as his young daughter, as a girl, nae as a woman. He said that if he'd recognized that fact a long time ago, you might hae settled down, got married, and borne children, the way God meant women to do. Your father, to put it in his own words, is truly repentent, and he's hoping you'll forgive him for having been blind and selfish.

"It seems your father has learned a lesson. Maybe Henri Foucade left a legacy of some guid behind him. He might hae been pleased if he'd known that. It's an ill wind that blows no guid, lassie.

"Noo, in a day or so you'll be well enough to travel. Then we'll take you home to your father. We brought the dogs and the sled back with us. We'll return them to their owner. He turned over some American money he found. Probably the proceeds from some bank holdup in Montana. We found some more American money on the sled. We'll find out where it came frae and return it. Some people will be glad to get their money back. As I said, lassie, it's an ill wind that blows no guid."